A NEON DARKNESS

ALSO BY LAUREN SHIPPEN

The Infinite Noise

THE BRIGHT SESSIONS

A NEON DARKNESS

Lauren Shippen

TOR
TEEN

A TOM DOHERTY ASSOCIATES BOOK
NEW YORK

A NEON DARKNESS

Copyright © 2020 by Lauren Shippen

A Tor Teen Book
Published by Tom Doherty Associates
120 Broadway
New York, NY 10271

www.tor-forge.com

Tor® is a registered trademark of Macmillan Publishing Group, LLC.

The Library of Congress Cataloging-in-Publication Data
is available upon request.

ISBN 978-1-250-29754-9 (hardcover)
ISBN 978-1-250-29755-6 (ebook)

Our books may be purchased in bulk for promotional, educational, or business use. Please contact your local bookseller or the Macmillan Corporate and Premium Sales Department at 1-800-221-7945, extension 5442, or by email at MacmillanSpecialMarkets@macmillan.com.

First Edition: September 2020

Printed in the United States of America

0 9 8 7 6 5 4 3 2 1

to Los Angeles

to your neon lights and inky darkness

to your sharp sounds and soft breezes

to all the places that I call home

and to all the extraordinary, unusual people I've met here

CONTENTS

Prologue: The Fire **11**

Part One: The Sunset **15**

Part Two: The Hills **73**

Part Three: The Loft **141**

Part Four: The West Side **213**

Epilogue: The Water **235**

PROLOGUE: THE FIRE

There are benefits to driving without a map.

This country is sprawling and full of detours. The "Best Specific Local Food Item" here and the "World's Largest Mundane Object" there. Usually the best places aren't on any map. If you hurtle toward your destination on the most direct route you can find, you miss the nooks and crannies, the strange offshoots and odd corners of the country. The warm, welcoming towns. The wonders of nature. The breathtaking vistas.

The road between Las Vegas and Los Angeles is barren. There's no detour to take, no paths splintering from the highway beneath your tires. One road, a vein connecting two bloodless hearts, and the vastness of dry desert surrounding it. There's no map to ignore, just a blank stretch of pavement in front of you. It's easy to keep your eyes on the road. A yellow line illuminated in staccato bursts while blackness stretches out on either side. It's impossible to say what happens out in that black, what things lurk in the desert. Darkness invites darkness; it folds in on itself, hides the things that seek hiding.

That unfaltering darkness was interrupted in spectacular fashion on the night of October 31, 2006. If you'd been driving along that road that night—that endless, unchanging path—you'd have seen a burst of light so bright you'd have wondered if the sun was coming back from its sleep prematurely. A star in the middle of the sand, a nuclear blast, an explosion—it was over as quickly as it began, the monotony of the desert returning so rapidly that it was unclear if there had ever been any light at all, or if it had been merely a mirage conjured by a brain desperate for change.

Alex really shouldn't have come here. He knew it was a risk—trusting the strange man who promised to help him with his unique problem, agreeing to meet him in an alley downtown in the middle of the night. But Alex met strange men every day in Los Angeles, had met them in alleys before. And now his problem had gotten so bad—just kept getting worse and worse—that Alex wasn't sure he had much of a choice.

He wasn't like the others—he didn't *want* this. It was tiring, being this full of fire all the time, worrying that you were going to destroy your favorite jacket, your furniture, the guy in your bed, your *life*. He could feel it now, burning under his skin, threatening to burst out and destroy the cool autumn night. His body itched with the need to explode and with a deeper hunger, a *new* hunger. His skin cried out in craving, wanting the only thing that seemed to soothe the burning, even as it slowly rotted the rest of him.

Alex tried to think of his friends. Things had gotten easier since he'd joined up with that merry band of weirdos, but picturing their faces just made him think about how much better they all were than him. They weren't perfect, but they were getting there. Alex was nowhere close to perfect. He was never going to get to perfect. And if it couldn't be perfect, if it couldn't be perfectly controlled, useful, and *safe*, he didn't want it. Which is why he was now pacing up and down an alley waiting for a tall figure to step out of the street and into the shadows and give him a magical solution.

What Alex didn't realize, what he didn't see in his pacing, was that the tall figure was already in the shadows. He loomed there, waiting. Waiting for Alex to pace past him. Waiting for his moment. Waiting to set off an explosion.

PART ONE

THE SUNSET

In retrospect, going on a power spree in Las Vegas was not my smartest move.

Typically, using my ability to get things—money, food, cars, you name it—isn't too much of a problem as long as I keep the mark in my sights or move on quickly. But I didn't think about the cameras. A security guy watching me take a table for all their chips with a pair of twos isn't going to be susceptible to what I do. Not from a surveillance room all the way across a crowded casino.

After a few hours on the empty, endless expanse of desert highway, I've traded the claustrophobia of Vegas for the traffic jams of Los Angeles. The sun is starting to set, making me squint as it beams through my windshield, but my wince turns into a smile as I think about the look on the head of security's face when he said he'd never met anyone like me. That glow of admiration, the slight tinge of confusion. It felt good, seeing that expression on someone like that. His job is to make sure that the house always wins, and I won.

I could have stayed, could have rubbed it in, hit up every casino on the strip, but after being taken to a back room with five guys twice my size, I figured it was time to cut my losses and get the hell out of dodge. Things turned out all right in the end, but I spare a thought for the fact that my face is still all over their security tapes. Still, I can't imagine they'll come after me for taking twelve grand. That amount of money means about as much to the Bellagio as it does to me. Which is to say, not much.

LA seemed as good a place as any to hit up next on my haphazard tour of the western United States. Anything's better than goddamned Nebraska. But, in another boneheaded move, I haven't looked at a calendar in weeks, which means I've somehow timed it so that I'm driving into Los Angeles on the night of Halloween.

So now I'm sitting in traffic on Santa Monica Boulevard, just trying to get to the ocean—I've never seen the Pacific Ocean before—while swarms of people in absurd costumes walk west. I can barely see the next intersection for all the bodies in the street. I expected Los Angeles to have a light, nice sea breeze, but I have to roll up my windows against the hot October air carrying the smell of body spray and sickly sweet party drinks.

"Screw this," I say to no one, pulling over. I grab a couple of stacks from the bag of cash flopped uselessly on the backseat and shove them in my pockets. I can get by without it but it's always nice to have the extra security. I leave the car unlocked, keys on the dash—it served me fine through the Nevada desert, but I'm going to want something slicker for LA.

The street is loud and a lot more Vegas-like than I would have thought, people shouting and stumbling through the streets in bright costumes. Vegas was fun, but I was hoping for a different scene. After two weeks there, I think I'm starting to discover that I like things a bit . . . quieter. Everything is easier to manage with fewer people. Less chance I'll slip up. Less chance something will go terribly wrong. I look at the flow of people headed down the block toward booming music—groups of friends smiling and laughing with each other. I feel a pang low in my gut and I'm taking a step toward the teeming crowd before I have a chance to think about it. Maybe things could be different this time—maybe I'll join the revelers and then it will be me laughing and smiling like I have no cares in the world and I'll *mean* it.

But before I can even make a plan of attack for how I would go about joining in the celebration, my feet stop in their tracks, the pang overwhelmed by roiling anxiety. There are too many people, moving too quickly, already too drunk. It would be impossible to hold any influence and without it, I highly doubt anyone is going to welcome the baby-faced kid in a hoodie and scuffed-up shoes with open arms.

I'm thinking about just calling it a night, starting the process of finding a place to crash, when I glance across the street to see a bright red neon sign proclaiming BAR LUBITSCH. There's a bored guy out front, smoking a cigarette, but otherwise the place looks a hell of a lot emptier than the street. Emptier and easier. Eventually I'll have to sleep, but right now I just want to sit in something other than the driver's seat. I take a deep breath and saunter across the street, plastering on my most innocuous "nothing to see here" face.

"ID?" the guy asks when I reach the gate. He squints at me through the smoke and I smile at him, the motion of my mouth curving feeling foreign and fake like always.

"That's okay," I say smoothly, heart beating in my chest. "I don't need one."

He exhales. More smoke. More squinting. I stand perfectly still and focus on what I want, and then:

"Right," he drawls, and then his eyes relax and his lips twitch around the cigarette he's put back in his mouth. "Right, yeah, sure thing. Go on in."

My shoulders relax and I nod in thanks as I move through the tiny front patio, filled with a few more solo smokers. Eyes swivel, following me as I open the door.

Inside it's significantly less smoky but equally dark and empty. The whole thing has a real "Leon Trotsky would have hung out here" kind of vibe—little café tables and dark wood booths, blocky Cyrillic painted onto large mirrors, everything in black and red. It feels like another world compared to the noisy, chaotic streets. I let out a breath I didn't even realize I was holding. God, I am sick of driving. Cramped and crowded with nothing but my own thoughts and the monotony of the constantly changing radio stations as I moved across state lines. I need a new sound—someone else's voice in my ears, in my head.

"What can I get ya?" I hear as I slink onto a bar stool at the long and empty wood bar. I swivel around to see a woman a few years older than me behind the bar, moving toward me. She's stunning—tall, tan, and slender, her cheekbones lifted with a warm smile, her whole face glowing. But as she approaches me, her smile sinks a bit. Like the bouncer, she squints.

"Whatever's good here." I shrug, going for nonchalant. "Which I'm assuming is . . . something with vodka?" I add, gazing pointedly at the Russian decor before throwing her my best rakish smile, ignoring the uncomfortable pinching in my cheeks.

"Can I see an ID?" She smiles, her eyebrows lifting.

"Nah, that's okay." I wave a hand. "Just the drink will be fine."

A beat. That familiar beat that sometimes happens in the blink of an eye—usually without my realizing what I'm doing—and that sometimes takes an eon. But no matter how long it takes, I almost always get where I'm trying to go.

"Sure thing." She nods, moving away, and I settle my arms onto the bar, leaning forward to watch her. She's got tattoos up and down her arms and pink in her brown hair, and I can't tell if that's how she always looks or if it's for a costume. If it is, I don't get what she's supposed to be. The black tank top she's wearing looks like it's seen better days, but if she works here, it's possible she lives in the area. Even if her apartment is as worn as her shirt, it's better than sleeping in a Subaru and easier than trying to find a hotel in the middle of the night when the street is packed with people. And there's something about her . . . something friendly and inviting, that makes me want to lean farther over the bar until I'm fully caught in her orbit.

But I can't rely on the bartender—if I've learned anything in the past few years, it's that it's important always to have a Plan B. So I swivel back to face the rest of the bar, looking for a potential patron. Glancing at the prices on the menu board tells me this place is probably only frequented by people with cash, and based on the amount of people in here versus out on the street, I'm going to assume I'm looking at a room of mostly regulars.

There's a couple cozying up in one of the booths—ugh, no, I hate dealing with couples. That kind of closeness is alien and impossible to navigate, my desire always swinging from wanting to be more than a third wheel to wanting to break the whole damn bicycle. But my gaze lingers on the pair, watching the guy's arm grasp his girlfriend's shoulder, watching her put her hand on his face, and I feel the same pang I felt out in the street. I'm in a much smaller space now though—much closer to them than I was to the crowd outside—so if I'm not careful, I might find myself dealing with a couple all the same. I tear my eyes away.

There's a group of guys around one of the café tables, vodka shots in each of their hands, egging each other on. I already got too much of the frat house vibe in Vegas. No thanks.

A much older woman is tucked into a corner booth, sipping on something that—based on her expression—is either very bad vodka or very *strong* vodka. She's wearing what looks like expensive jewelry and definitely seems like a regular. That looks promising. I might not even need to do anything. She looks lonely—just talking to her might drum up enough sympathy for her to offer me a place to crash.

I'm contemplating my next move when the bartender says, "Here you go," and I spin around again to see her placing a drink in front of me.

"This is on fire," I say pointlessly, looking at the flames rising out of the alcohol and licking the edge of the glass.

"A Molotov Cocktail." She smirks and I can feel the corner of my mouth lift involuntarily in response, the shadow of my first genuine smile in months.

"A Molotov . . . did you give me a bomb?" I ask patiently, nervous excitement building in me. Her grin grows wider.

"It's one of our unique creations," she explains. "Vodka and apple juice that we then, you know—"

"Light on fire," I finish.

"Yep." She smiles.

"How do I drink it?" I ask, refusing to feel stupid about being reluctant to put a flaming cocktail anywhere near my mouth.

"Like a Russian," she deadpans.

"Well"—I swallow around my suddenly very dry mouth—"*na zdorovie.*"

"—and then I went to, uh, Denver," I say. "And then . . . um, Salt Lake City, I think? I don't know, somewhere in Utah. Then I spent some time in Vegas, made some money, and now I'm here." I finish with a flourish, gesturing loosely around the bar.

Once she found out I was new in town, the bartender, Indah, asked me where I was from and I decided to give her my life story. Well, my *highly* edited life story. My life story for the past two years. I've had several drinks at this point—though not all flaming, thank god—and am feeling very amicable. She seems to be feeling amicable too, pouring me drink after drink, despite the fact that I don't think I want anything except her attention.

"My goodness." She smiles and shakes her head. "You're quite the nomad, aren't you?"

I shrug, maybe a little too big, because I catch Indah trying to stifle a laugh before she restarts her interrogation.

"Why go to so many places?" She leans forward on the bar, her duties as bartender largely over now that the only other person left in the place is the old woman in the corner booth. "Is it for work? What do you do?"

"I travel," I say loftily.

"Doing what?" she laughs. "How old are you anyway?"

"What about you, *Indah*?" I pivot, putting emphasis on her name. She should know that I know it. People like when you remember their names. At least, I think they do. *I* like when people remember *my* name. It means something when someone knows who you are. "What do you do?"

I may be drunker than I thought because she gives me a blank look at that idiotic question and stretches her arm to indicate the old wood bar wrapped around her.

"Well, yeah, that." I wave my hands in front of me and nearly knock over the several glasses that have stacked up in the past few hours. "But I mean, like, who are you? What's your deal?"

"Well . . . ," she begins, smiling. She smiles so easily. I'm so envious of that. The vodka turns in my stomach and suddenly the last thing I want is to watch her smile around another adorable quip. I wish she would stop smiling, rubbing her happiness in my face.

And then, after a beat—simultaneously in slow motion and instantaneously—she stops smiling. It's like the corners of her mouth are being pulled down by invisible strings. The frown has reached her eyes now and she's stopped talking. She's just staring at me with large, frightened eyes.

"Well, what?" I snap, and she flinches. Shit.

I close my eyes for a moment, focus on letting go of the envy, the bitterness. I don't want her to not smile. I want her face to do whatever it wants to do. I do my best to drop the strings.

"Sorry, I—" She shakes her head like she's clearing cobwebs from her hair. "I must have lost my train of thought."

She smiles at me again, this time with shades of sadness to it.

"Can I have another?" I ask, indicating the glass in front of me. She nods, turning for the bottle, but having her back to me doesn't break whatever strange tension I created. I knew I shouldn't have gotten drunk. I always get sloppy when I get drunk.

"You could probably pour yourself a drink if you wanted," I suggest, hoping maybe if she gets drunk too we can get back to the easy rapport I thought we might have been building. "This place is basically empty and I doubt anyone else is coming in tonight."

"I don't drink," Indah says as she pours me more vodka.

"What?" I blanch. "A bartender who doesn't drink? What kind of crappy punch line is that?"

She huffs a laugh as she puts down the vodka bottle and starts wiping down the bar, not meeting my eyes.

"Oh shit, is this an alcoholism thing?" I wince. "Like, is this part of your recovery or something?" I make a vague gesture at her general situation.

That brings her eyes up as she laughs heartily, the sound like a beautiful bell that clashes with the tinny sound of Fergie coming through the bar speakers.

"What kind of twelve-step program has an alcoholic working in a bar?" She giggles, and it helps me not feel stupid for suggesting it.

"Okay, then why not?" I press. "Alcohol is *great*." I smile wide at her but her giggles stop and her shoulders square off defensively.

"Yeah, well, the Qur'an feels a little differently," she mumbles.

"The Qur'an?" I ask, my fuzzy head not putting two and two together.

The movement of her arm stops for a second before she continues.

"I used to drink, but then I . . ." She trails off, her hesitancy making me more alert, more curious. I lean forward, my elbows sliding farther onto the bar top.

"Things change," she finishes anticlimactically.

She keeps moving her arm in circles, cleaning an already pristine bar, when my curiosity finally does the work for me and prompts her to say more.

"I'm Muslim," she spells out. "A lot of us don't drink alcohol. Working in a bar is questionable to begin with, but, well . . ."

She trails off again and I opt for nodding like I know exactly what she's talking about. I want her to say more but the desire is dulled by the feeling that I've said something stupid. The vodka running through my veins lets me admit to myself that I want Indah to think I'm cool.

"You've never met a Muslim person before, have you?" she asks, cocking her head as she peers at me and breaking me out of my reverie.

"I'm from Kansas." I shrug like I'm being clever and it makes her laugh that big laugh again.

"You know," she says, "they have Muslims in Kansas too."

"Figure of speech," I clarify. "I'm from more of a nowheresville than even Kansas has."

"Oh yeah?" She cocks her head. "Where you from then?"

"Wait," I say, deflecting, "aren't you supposed to be, you know, wearing one of those, you know . . ."

I circle my head sloppily with my hand and Indah clenches her jaw but smiles through it.

"There's lots of ways to practice Islam," she says simply, and I nod sagely like I understand the conversation we're having at all.

"You're sweet for asking though," she continues, her jaw relaxed, the smile easy again. I'm pretty sure it's *me* making her smile like that, brush off my ignorance, but I have a hard time feeling too bad about it with the vodka warming in my blood. Her smile is so beautiful, so welcoming—I can't be blamed for wanting to see it over and over.

"You're not a bad sort," she continues, looking at me sappily. Blankly. Her smile is turning generic and there's a familiar rush of delight and disgust coursing through me.

"Nice of you to say, darlin'," I say, pushing away the bad feeling, and she giggles again.

"You're a hoot." She snorts.

Encouraged, I say: "You wanna know how old I really am?"

She leans her elbows onto the bar, mirroring my posture.

"Sure." She wiggles her eyebrows like she's indulging me.

"*Eighteen*," I whisper, and her eyes widen.

"No, you're not," she gasps over-dramatically.

"No, I really am."

"You couldn't have gotten in here if you were eighteen." She looks at me dubiously.

"I have my ways," I purr, and she rolls her eyes.

"Why would you tell me that *now*?" She smiles. "I should report you." She crosses her arms, but she's still grinning playfully.

"To who?" I ask. "The alcohol police?"

She just lifts a single eyebrow and leans against the back counter.

"I really shouldn't have served you." She shakes her head, the grin collapsing. "I thought I checked your ID . . ."

"Don't worry about it, sweetheart," I croon, liking the way the

endearments flow off my vodka-soaked tongue. "Just pour me another drink and forget I said anything."

And she does exactly that. Almost as if she's asleep, Indah grabs
the nearly empty vodka bottle and pours me another double. I have
no intention of drinking it—any drunker and things will get very
bad—but I take pleasure in watching her hands do the work while
her mind is somewhere else.

She seems smart. Maybe she'll catch on. Some people do, like
the head of security at the Bellagio. They never understand what
it is they're catching on to, but I see a revelation dawn in their eyes
and make sure to leave them before they can examine it, or me, too
closely.

"Why . . . ," she starts, looking at the drink she just poured.

"Do you have a place I could crash at?" I interrupt.

I already know the answer. But my parents taught me to be polite.

"Robert?"

I spin around to try to find the source of my mother's voice. She
can't be here. She can't be in LA.

"Robert?" I hear again, and I spin and spin and suddenly I'm
not in LA either. I'm sitting at my kitchen table. The table I sat at
when I was small. The table where we had every meal together, as
a family.

"Robert, eat your peas," my mother tells me gently. She's smiling down at me, love in her eyes.

"I don't wanna." I pout, swinging my legs back and forth, my
toes inches from the ground.

"Robert, remember what we talked about," my father says, his
voice strong and warm and never stern. "Sometimes we have to do
things we don't want to do, but we do them because they're good
for us."

"But I don't wanna," I whine again, voice rising. They both sigh,
their breath a soft breeze over me. They tilt their heads in unison,
shaking them slightly.

"Oh, you sweet boy," they say, their hands brushing softly along my cheeks. "Remember: sometimes we have to do things we don't want to do, but we do them because—"

"I don't wanna!" I screech. The hands recoil from me, leaving my face cold. Their mouths snap shut. And then they have no mouths. Their skin grows over their lips, their eyes, their noses. They are blank and screaming and I wanted them to stop. I wanted them to stop telling me what to do and now they can't tell me anything. I've taken it all away and suddenly their faceless bodies are gone too and I'm left alone with two empty chairs and the echoes of their screams—

I gasp awake.

It's not so dramatic as it is in the movies. I don't shout out, don't jolt upright in bed. Just a quick inhale of breath, the opening of the eyes.

I am in a cold sweat though. That much translates from the screen. I soaked through my T-shirt. My jeans stick to my legs, suffocating my lower half.

Indah's couch is serviceably comfortable. It's not the MGM Grand, but tomorrow I'll find a more permanent crash pad. Some hotel suite or maybe a Malibu mansion. I should get a car first, but then the world is my oyster.

I make the short walk from Indah's couch to her kitchen and pour myself a glass of water. It might be worth it to try to fall back asleep but I don't like my chances. I'm never able to get back to sleep after a dream about Them. My watch reads 4:02. The worst goddamn hour of the night, four a.m. Too late to hit up a bar, too early to hit up a diner. Might be the perfect time to go lift a car, even though I'd prefer just to get the keys from someone. I still haven't really mastered the hot-wire—

"Robert?"

The glass falls from my hands as I spin around in panic. The shattering gives me an extra jolt of adrenaline, and in the few seconds it takes my eyes to adjust to the darkness and make out Indah's confused face, my heart has made a pretty decent bid to permanently exit my chest.

"Shit," I breathe out, stepping back from the pieces of glass scattered around my feet.

"Wait, Robert, the glass—" she warns as she steps forward, her arms reaching out to me instinctively. Something about the way she says it—the way her hands extend to me—places me back in my nightmare, waiting for Indah's face to close up the way my mom's did.

"I'm okay," I breathe, carefully stepping around the glass.

"Didn't mean to startle you," she murmurs. "Let me get the broom."

She walks into the hallway and I hear her rummaging through some cabinets in the dark before swearing quietly to herself.

"Hold on," she calls from the hall, "I don't know what my roommates did with the dustpan but I know there's one in the building's laundry room. I'll be back."

There's the sound of Indah slipping on her shoes and the door opening and closing and then I'm alone in the apartment. I don't know where the laundry room is or how long it will take her, so I tiptoe over to the door and look through the peephole. The hallway is empty.

I grab my jacket, throw on my shoes without lacing them up, and make a run for it.

I don't think a city has ever been as empty as Los Angeles is at four in the morning. There's barely any sound. No sirens, no honking, no bars throwing out the last of their patrons. It's so different from Vegas, from Chicago. It's closer to Denver, which I didn't expect. Like a warm, sea-level Denver. I could live with that for a while.

Okay, game plan, Robert. You've had an eventful first night in town—found a cool bar and immediately ensured you can never go back there. Telling the bartender she broke the law by serving you and then crashing at her place, breaking her stuff, and fleeing is maybe not the best way to make friends. But not the worst. I'm familiar with the worst way to make friends by this point.

"Hey, man, could you spare some change?"

I didn't even notice the man lurking under a building's over-hang. He's got no shoes and reeks to high heaven.

"Uh, yeah," I say, digging into my pockets. I pull out the stacks of cash I took from my casino winnings and take a cautious step toward the man. "Here you go."

His eyes widen comically in shock and I move down the street before I have to listen to him thank me. I feel suddenly stupid, handing a stranger a few thousand dollars when I should have left it at Indah's in apology. Money means so little to me that I always forget what a difference it can make to some people.

I turn a corner and stumble onto what looks like the remains of a massive block party. Right. Halloween. I nearly forgot, Indah tak-ing up all the available real estate in my head. The street is covered in paper and glitter, strings of pennants spreading from the fronts of bars onto the sidewalk like vines. There are a couple of drunken, costumed stragglers, stumbling their way down the middle of the road, leaning on each other and singing—well, no, *yelling*—a pop song. I give them a wide berth.

I walk. I walk and I walk. I think about taking a car. I'm back on Santa Monica Boulevard, now blissfully clear of traffic, and there are plenty parked along the road that would be serviceable. But the sweat is finally cooling off my clothes, the fresh(ish) air clearing my cluttered head. The idea of climbing into a confined space right now is less than appealing.

I should get a convertible. Once I've found a place to stay, I'll find a convertible. I'll find a great spot, a great car, and live the great LA life. After the past few months, lying low seems like a smart idea, and what better place to disappear than a city of a million people desperately trying to be noticed.

Eventually the road splits and I decide to walk uphill and get away from the stretch of party-ruined streets. My watch tells me it's now past five a.m., but the sun has yet to dawn over the city. I thought going farther south would mean near-permanent daylight, but I suppose I'll be forever chasing the sun.

Ironically, I soon come upon the famed Sunset Boulevard and a little more wandering brings me to the secluded entrance of the

Sunset Marquis. Something about the name registers in the back of my mind and that's enough for me to go in. The hour or so I've somewhat unintentionally spent walking has taken a toll and I'm ready to fall asleep again. Ideally, un-nightmare-ified sleep.

"Can I help you, young man?" the night clerk calls out to me the moment I walk through the front doors. The "young man" grates, but I'm not close enough to him to make him call me "sir" or something else. Sometimes I wish that proximity wasn't such a factor in what I can do. Other times, it's about the only thing in my life I'm grateful for.

"Yeah, I need a room," I say, walking toward the reception desk but looking around the lobby instead of at him. "For a while, I think. At least a month."

"I see." He stays neutral, typing on the computer in front of him. "We don't have many suites available at the moment . . ."

I sigh in annoyance. I really don't want to have to kick someone out of their room—the more people I use my powers on, the more potential for discovery there is. But the idea of being in a tiny room for a month is making me preemptively tired.

"I'd be fine with whatever for tonight," I say, cutting my losses, "but, you know, a suite would be preferable for a month obviously. Don't want to be cooped up for that whole time."

"Oh, I apologize, sir," he says. Hell yeah, I got the "sir." "Our suites are our standard rooms. If you'd like something more spacious, we have our villas."

What kind of joint is this? Suites are the *smaller* rooms?

"Oh." I try to cover up my surprise, acting like this is a problem I encounter regularly. "In that case, a villa would be fine."

"Very good, sir." He nods once, deferentially. "It looks like we have one of our Deluxe Villas available—that's twelve hundred a night."

I nod at the price like it means anything at all to me. I have no idea what a hotel room is supposed to cost, because I've barely paid for anything since I was fourteen.

"Sounds great." I smile.

The clerk looks at me in anticipation for a moment, expecting a credit card that's never going to come, before his face smooths over and he nods again, this time to himself more than to me.

"Very good," he says, matter-of-fact. "How many copies of your key will you require?"

"Just one should do it," I say, the sentence getting caught in my throat. A familiar daydream starts to come up in my head—one where I'm traveling with someone, where a "villa" in a fancy hotel is something I choose so that I can share it, not just because I can— but I quash it down before the fantasy can take root and keep me awake for the rest of the night.

He hands me the key and shows me to my room. The hotel property is huge—winding paths through gardens, past pools and bars. The villa is tucked into a corner of the garden, nicely isolated. I couldn't have picked a better place even if I'd bothered to look online before driving into the city. Looks like Lady Luck followed me from Vegas. Not that I ever need to rely on luck. I *am* luck.

The clerk leaves me with a, "Let me know if you need anything else, *sir*," and I start to explore the room. "Villa." It really is more than a room. It's several rooms, with a fireplace and a piano and everything. This will do very nicely indeed. I haven't gotten that good at spinning stays more than a month, but maybe this is the perfect time to practice.

The sun is just beginning to peek through the shades but I ignore it in favor of the plush bed in front of me. I sleep like the dead.

"Excuse me," a voice calls out as I walk through the lobby, "young man! Excuse me."

I turn to see a woman waving me over from reception. I barely suppress a sigh and eye roll as I saunter over to the desk.

"Yes?" I ask politely.

"You arrived earlier this morning, correct?" she asks, narrowing her eyes at me. "You're staying in one of our Deluxe Villas?"

"That's right." I nod.

"Peter mentioned you would be staying with us for a while," she continues. "But it seems he forgot to get your payment information."

I clench my jaw in annoyance, distantly hoping I didn't get this Peter guy in trouble and wondering how much I should spell this out for her.

"Yeah, look," I say after a moment, deciding on the blunt approach, "you're not going to get payment info from me. And you're going to let me stay in that room for as long as I want, and it's not going to be a problem. So write whatever little note in your system you have to to make sure that happens."

As I'm speaking, I'm thinking, *Believe me believe me believe me*, even though thinking it doesn't seem to make a difference. As long as I want it, even if it's subconscious, it happens. But it still feels good to try, to put effort and intention behind it, giving me the illusion of control. And sure enough, she nods, hits a few keys on her computer, and then looks back at me. Blank. They're always blank. I sometimes wonder if wanting people not to be blank is something I could make happen. Maybe I just don't want it enough.

As luck would have it, the Sunset Marquis is part of one of the most famous music scenes in the entire world, the name registering in my head as familiar because of some rock star's biography I read a while back. After wandering the area for a few days, letting myself become part of the landscape and routine of the neighborhood and the hotel, I start going to shows along the Sunset Strip. Rock shows, weird new electronic bands, even some stand-up here and there. I dance and I laugh and I still don't talk to anyone, the crowds too big and too raucous to infiltrate.

It's the closest thing I have to a routine—I arrive in a new city, pick a neighborhood, and soak up as much of it as I can. Now that the chaotic loudness of Halloween is over, Los Angeles reveals itself to be livelier and brighter than anywhere I've ever been. I'm entranced by the mismatched buildings, the sparkling hills, the scents of interesting food wafting down the street. But it's as overwhelming as it is enticing, and like with every other city I've been to, I have a hard time seeing how and where I'm going to fit into it.

Not even a week has passed and I can feel myself getting restless. This is the problem with getting everything you want, with going to see some of the best bands for free, being seated at the front of the most famous comedy houses, having bottomless bottle service wherever you go. When I was first on my own, the novelty of it kept me busy for a while. The unfettered freedom, and then, the necessity of figuring out how to actually survive, was an activity. I guess most people my age are in school or have a job, but both of those options seem like a waste of time. So I read books and go to shows and spend an entire day in my villa watching TV and subsisting off of minibar food just because I can before I realize I haven't gotten the bartender's tattoos out of my head. I didn't get a good look at them and I want to.

So I do.

"You came back," Indah drawls, and I shrug sheepishly as I slide onto a bar stool.

"I can't find another good vodka bar in this city to save my life." I grin and I see the moment she melts. No hostility, no revelation. Simple acceptance.

Something inside me deflates, just a little.

She should be pissed, she should be annoyed, she should be *something*. I barreled into her life, haven't apologized for stealing her vodka and making her take me home, and she finds it adorable. My desire to be liked overcomes everything else and I try not to hate myself too much for it.

"I don't know what it is"—she shakes her head—"but you are some kind of charming. Especially for a kid," she adds pointedly, and I just shrug again.

She's already pouring me a double. I don't even really like vodka that much. But I drink it down as I examine her tattoos. On the back of one forearm is horizontal writing in a language I don't recognize. The other arm is covered in delicate vines that wind from her wrist to her shoulder, snaking around her light brown skin. Small flowers bloom along the vines, the largest one in the center of her wrist.

Suddenly feeling self-conscious about staring at her, my cheeks warming in a blush, I swivel my stool to take in the early evening crowd populating the bar. A few loners but mostly pairs. Couples on a first drinks date, work friends swapping stories, bespectacled hipsters no doubt discussing their nauseatingly basic screenplays. I don't need to talk to any of them to know that Indah is the most interesting person in here.

I turn back to tell her so, only to find her frowning at me, vodka bottle still in hand.

"You shouldn't have just up and left the other night," she tells me, a crinkle in between her eyebrows.

"What, were you worried?" I tease.

"Yes," she says humorlessly, and I stop smiling. "Look, this is a pretty safe neighborhood but you're just a kid and you're new in town and people get weird on Halloween. With what happened to Blaze . . . I just, I came back with the dustpan and you weren't there and I panicked, okay?"

"I'm not a kid," I snap, a knee-jerk reaction. Her face softens, my unconscious need for her to not be mad at me doing its work.

"Who's Blaze?" I ask, knowing Indah won't ever call me a kid again.

"A friend," she says, dropping the bottle back on the shelf. "He's a year older than you and he . . . sort of went missing last week."

"Oh," I breathe, not knowing what to say. "Sorry."

"No, I'm sorry." Her big brown eyes stare earnestly into mine. "I didn't mean to scold you. I just . . . I *care*."

The word is like honey rolling off her tongue and I want her to mean it so badly. That want twists in my gut, carving out ugly shapes of need that I know will be met regardless of what the other person truly feels. But does it matter? Does it matter if Indah really cares? Or is it enough that I want her to care? Either way, I can feel my restlessness settling, being replaced with a bubbling curiosity I haven't felt in a long time.

"So what is there to do in this town?" I ask, not wanting to linger too long on the question of if she means it when she says she cares.

"What do you mean?"

"I mean, besides drinking at a kitsch Russian bar," I clarify, and she glares at me, but there's no heat to it.

"Depends," she says. "What kind of scene are you looking for?"

"Something different," I tell her. I want her to peel back the layers of shine over this city and show me the underbelly. There's no reason to bet on her knowing where the underbelly is, but she's the only source I have, and besides, if tattooed bartenders don't know the more fringe scenes, who would?

"Actually . . ." She smiles, leaning forward on her elbows. "There's somebody you should meet."

Later, Indah will wonder what compelled her to bring a boy she just met to meet her best friend/sometimes-more-than-friends friend. She doesn't introduce Neon to a lot of people, too worried about revealing Neon's secret, too selfish to want to share her with anyone else, and yet she gave both away so easily to the odd teenager who smiles so well she poured him an entire bottle of their finest vodka on the first night they met. She didn't know a thing about him, she *still* doesn't, and yet, it seemed like the thing to do. He sat there smiling, not at all contrite about ditching her a few nights before, making her worry, and she suddenly wanted *desperately* to show him the most interesting parts of her life.

Later, Indah will wonder how she didn't see it. How *she*, of all people, didn't see *him*. She'll wonder if it would have made any difference even if she had.

Indah will wonder where she'd be if he hadn't walked into Lubitsch that night. If she hadn't introduced Robert and Neon. Maybe things would be different. Or maybe she, like Robert, was doomed from the start by something given to her at birth.

"Sup," the woman says, extending her arm to me. I go to shake her hand, but she just slaps my hand, open palmed, twice, like we already have some kind of established handshake.

"This is my friend Neon," Indah laughs, rolling her eyes. I smile like I'm in on the joke, but I'm already distracted by the fact that Neon seems to be one of those effortlessly cool people who never feel self-conscious about doing anything. A small but built black woman with long locs, she's wearing an enormous leather jacket that doesn't look ridiculous even though it's clearly three sizes too big and heavy black combat boots to match. There's something electric about her. Magnetic. I'm immediately pulled in.

"Aw, come on, babe," Neon purrs, curling herself around Indah, "'friend'? I think we're a little more than that."

Neon nuzzles Indah's neck and Indah laughs some more, pushing her away.

"Well, *you* say we're not girlfriends, so if we're not that, we must be friends," Indah throws back.

"There's plenty of space between friends and girlfriends," Neon says, stepping closer to Indah, putting her arm around her again.

"Not to me." Indah shakes her head, smiling, and playfully pushes Neon's head away gently with the meat of her palm.

I have no idea what to do with myself. I take the moment to look around the room. We're back on Sunset, in one of the music clubs that speckle the strip, but one I haven't gotten to yet. There's booming bass coming from the main room, but we're ensconced in a run-down, but oddly cozy, backstage room. In my nights out since I got here, it never occurred to me to come backstage, where there are fewer people and you can actually hear yourself think. My veins thrum in time with the distant music, so many wants rushing through me that nothing has a chance to come to the surface. I stick my hands in my pockets, uncertain about what else to do.

"Aw, I think we're scaring the poor choirboy," Neon observes.

"He's from Kansas," Indah teases, eyes sparkling at me, and I shrug in what I hope is a self-deprecating and charming move. The hope alone tells me it will be received as such.

"Well, Kansas, nice to meet you." Neon smirks, pulling away from Indah and lighting a cigarette. The flame of her lighter makes her dark skin glow, highlighting the bright blue eyeliner and glitter that cover her eyelids. On anyone else it would look ridiculous. On her, it's mesmerizing.

She steps toward me as she exhales, her brown eyes peering up at me through the smoke. They rake up and down my body, scanning me like she's looking for weak spots. I stand my ground, refusing to cower, and the ghost of a smile moves over her lips.

"It's Robert," I say, "Robbie. That's what—that's what people call me."

I'm already mentally kicking myself for saying that—after leaving Nebraska, I swore I'd never go by Robbie again. It shouldn't matter that I've given her that name—if I don't want her to call me that, she won't. But something compelled me to say it, so maybe—

"Right . . . Robbie." Neon nods before cocking her head to the side and giving me the once-over again. "You know, it's funny, you don't look like a Robbie."

"What do I look like?" I flirt, feeling bold.

"Trouble." She smirks.

"You have no idea, babe," Indah says, huffing a laugh, from behind her.

"Oh yeah?" Neon looks over at Indah, smoke curling between her lips. "He give you problems already?"

"Mm-hm." Indah nods, smiling. "He crashed on my couch, broke one of my glasses, and fled the scene."

"You took him home with you?" Neon's eyebrows rise as she looks between us. I have the strangest urge to apologize for a nonexistent betrayal of a relationship that doesn't seem exclusive in the first place.

Eight years of being the way that I am and I'm pretty confident in the power I hold over people. It's imperfect, intangible, but I know how to command attention. A single minute of being in Neon's presence and she's somehow overridden all of that. She has the same intangible quality. Except she's not like me. She can't be. There's no one in the world like me, but Neon has bottled power in a way that makes even me want to do what she says. It sets my brain on fire in the best way and the thought flickers across my mind that maybe this is what people mean by love at first sight. But suddenly

I'm thinking of Them, the only people to ever say that word to me, and Neon starts to fade away as I begin to sink into memory.

"Poor kid needed a place to crash," Indah says, her now familiar voice bringing me back to the present. "I don't even know how he convinced me to let him stay over."

"I can be pretty persuasive." I shrug, showing my teeth in a mockery of a smile. I brush off the strange new feelings of a moment ago, focusing on my need for Neon to know that I'm not going to fall at her feet like she expects. With her short but strong body, the ends of her hair dyed an electric blue, piercings on her nose and eyebrow and cascading down her ears, she cuts an intimidating figure next to my doughy, pale body. But looks can be deceiving.

"So, Robbie—" Neon starts.

"Robert," I demand, making a decision. "Or Rob, if you really have to shorten it."

"Of course." She smiles. "Robert."

Her acquiescence is like dopamine straight to the center of my brain and I smile a real smile. It's one thing to have Indah or the hotel clerks do what I want. They're easygoing. They're in service, trained to believe that the customer is always right. But Neon . . . I know immediately that Neon is a hard sell and I just bought her respect. The thrill of my satisfaction at this is only slightly dampened by my desperation to keep it up.

"What're you doing in our glorious city, Robert?" Neon asks, collapsing back on the worn couch, and I take her cue, sitting on the even rattier couch opposite.

"I don't know yet," I say honestly. "I've only been here a week."

Neon laughs, so different from Indah's big, beautiful laugh. Neon's laugh is sharp and demanding, like she is. The kind of laugh where you never know if you're being laughed with or laughed at.

"Wow, one week and you already have Indah wrapped around your little finger," she teases. "I'm almost too impressed to be jealous."

"From the looks of things, you've got nothing to be jealous of." I give a small nod toward where Indah has settled in at Neon's side. "I get the impression I'm not Indah's type."

"Wow, you really are from the middle of nowhere," Neon quips.

"What do you mean?" I ask, not liking the sensation of feeling a step behind.

"You can like more than just one, you know," Indah explains, and Neon grins and tightens her arms around Indah. I try to smile back like I know what she means.

"But you're right, emo white boys aren't really my type," she teases sweetly. "Especially ones who are eighteen."

"No shit?" Neon's eyes widen. "You're eighteen?"

I shrug.

"Eighteen and fresh off the bus from the Midwest," she goes on. "Lemme guess: you're an actor."

Now it's my turn to laugh, though it's not as big and unself-conscious as the laughs of the two women sitting across from me.

"No way," I scoff. "I'm a . . . a nomad." I smile at Indah, borrowing her word from the first night we met.

"Well, nomad"—Neon leans back—"what brought your wandering feet our way?"

"Seemed like as good a place as any," I say.

"Ha, yeah," Neon laughs around her cigarette, "I guess worse has been said about LA. People never appreciate our fair city. But you give it a chance, and you'll learn to love it."

And she's right. Two weeks here and I'm sold.

There's a thrumming in this city. The buzzing of neon. The desert heat in the air. The smell of exhaust mixed with the distant scent of salt water. The desperate, cloying sound of people trying to impress each other. Los Angeles isn't relentless but it is *demanding*. It whispers promises in your ear, tells you sweet lies. It says, "You can have everything you've ever wanted, just sign here. Sign here and don't look too closely at the fine print and all your dreams will come true."

Those are the whispers that everyone else hears. The sly seductions that the foolish and the ordinary fall for. I don't pay those sweet nothings any mind.

No, instead, I'm the one whispering to the city. "You're mine. You'll do what I want, *be* what I want. I'm here now. I'm where I should be and everything will be better."

The porch light flickers above me. I'm looking out, out, out, over empty fields and big, black sky. Everything is empty. Emptiness everywhere.

The house behind me is empty too. Empty and silent. The fields are louder than the house—the sound of the breeze through the corn, the crickets. There's life there. The house stands behind me like an animal carcass. Only bones.

They'll come back, I tell myself. *They have to.*

"They'll come back," I tell the fields. The fields don't answer. There's nothing but silence.

The music is loud and punishing. I went to some punk shows in Lincoln before I left Nebraska—trying to find my people in all the shouting and moshing—but I couldn't stand how the blown-out speakers made my teeth rattle, how the press of sweaty bodies was impossible to predict, impossible to control. The sound here is a little better—a little more balanced, I guess, it being an actual music club as opposed to the bar basements where semitalented men my age would scream into cheap microphones. But the claustrophobic crowds and sticky floor are the same.

Neon is somewhere in front of me, jumping up and down, slamming her tiny body into the mosh pit like she's something that can't be broken. Indah and I are leaned against the bar in the back, nodding our heads and watching Neon bob in the sea of people. I'm taking a break from dancing with Neon, out of shape and out of breath, while she seems to have an endless well of energy, but I can't stop smiling while trying to suck in more air. Being in a huge crowd I can't control isn't as daunting with these two by my side.

"You don't want to get in there?" I shout to Indah over the noise.

"Not really my scene," Indah calls back, her eyes and smile directed toward Neon the whole time.

"Why are we here then?"

I've only known them two weeks, hanging out at bars and going to shows, and they've already folded me nicely into their pairing. I never feel like a third wheel, never feel unwanted, and I'm genuinely uncertain if that's due to my nature or to the fact that they're not really a couple. Maybe they're just good at making and having friends. I don't know what that's like, what making friends is even supposed to look like, so it's a difficult thing to measure against my ability.

"This is Blaze's favorite spot," she shouts, a complete sentence that doesn't invite more questions. A closed door has never kept me out, so I'm about to prod when a particular loud clang of guitar and beating of drums signals the end of a song. There's indiscernible talking from the stage, the cheer of the crowd, and then Neon is in front of us, blue and electric, the sweat glittering on her forehead and her smile big and open.

"Set's over," she pants, smoothly swiping the drink from Indah's hand and taking a large gulp before handing it back. "Come on."

She whips around, her hair thwacking me in the arm, and starts marching back toward the stage. Indah follows without question and I down my drink before trailing behind, curiosity thrumming in my bones as we skirt the edge of the stage and go through a black curtain to the side.

On the other side of the curtain, things are muffled and calmer. An enormous bouncer, larger than the three of us combined, looms in the narrow hallway, peering down his crooked nose at us.

"What," he grunts, arms crossing in front of him, somehow making him even larger.

"Cory here?" Neon asks, matching the bouncer's stance.

"Who's asking?"

"We're Blaze's friends," she says, absentmindedly looking around the bouncer into the hallway behind him, like he's barely worth her attention.

"Blaze isn't here."

"I know." She rolls her eyes. "That's why we're looking for Cory."

Even though I don't know what I'm doing here or who we're looking for, I want this bouncer to let us pass. I want to find Cory, and I want to find out what makes Neon able to face a man a foot taller than her with biceps as big as her torso like he's a lamppost in an unexpected place and not a potentially dangerous person.

"Do you mind," I say, not a question, as I step forward, my shoulder brushing Neon's. I try to emulate her nonchalant attitude, her effortless confidence, but I feel like a little kid stepping into my dad's shoes. Which is ridiculous, because I know exactly how this is going to go. I can feel it, that focused desire forming inside of me and pushing outward. I haven't actively used my ability in days—haven't wanted or needed to while hanging out with Indah and Neon—but now I wish I could tell them what I do, have them fully appreciate how useful I could be, how powerful I am.

"Right, yeah," the bouncer mumbles, stepping aside.

Yep, exactly how I knew it was going to go. I try not to smile too broadly.

Neon turns to me, raises her eyebrows in confusion and admiration before a pleased smile takes over her face. Without a word, she marches past him, taking a sharp left when she gets to the end of the hallway. I nod at the bouncer in mock thanks and look behind me at Indah, who is staring at me with narrow eyes and a question on her face. I shrug and follow Neon's path, hearing Indah's soft, cautious footsteps behind me.

By the time we reach Neon in one of the back rooms, she's finishing what looks like an elaborate handshake with a pudgy guy about her age with tan skin and floppy, bleached bangs that swoop in front of his eyes. A huge smile overtakes his face the moment he looks over Neon's shoulder.

"Indah!" He rushes toward her, wrapping her in a hug as she laughs, bright and easy, a sound that brings sunlight into my brain.

"Hey, Cory," she giggles into his shoulder. "Guess it's been a minute, huh?"

"Sure feels like it," he says, releasing her from what seemed like a bone-crushing hug. "Who's this guy?" he asks a second later, look-ing at me for the first time.

"This is Rob," Neon tells him, "a stray that Indah picked up."

"She fed me vodka and took me home," I say, smirking, and Cory laughs.

"Sounds like Indah," he says, smiling big. "Nice to meet you, Rob. Cory Alvarez." He extends a hand, which I shake, warm and friendly.

Once again, I wonder if this is how you make friends. If it's as easy as saying your name and making a joke and shaking a hand.

"'Sup," I say after a moment, following a script I've seen other people perform. I want Cory to like me, want anyone in Indah and Neon's orbit to like me, but it's so quiet, low stakes, that I wonder if my power is doing any work at all.

"Is Blaze with you?" Cory asks, looking toward the doorway like this mysterious figure will suddenly appear.

"We were actually hoping he was here with you," Indah says, her smile fading into worry.

"No, I haven't seen him in a few weeks," Cory says, face crum-pling. "He missed a gig last week and hasn't been returning any of my calls. I had to get my cousin Ricky to play drums tonight. Are you guys sticking around for our set?"

"Yeah." Neon shrugs. "I think we were planning on it."

"Oh." Cory deflates. "Well, then you should know that my cousin isn't really that good. He's definitely no Blaze."

"When was the last you heard from him?" Indah asks.

"Um . . . ," Cory starts as he looks down at his shoes. "I guess the last time we played? So, like, a month ago maybe?"

Neon's mouth twists in disappointment and Indah sighs. This isn't the answer they were looking for. I don't know *what* we're looking for, but I have a feeling that this guy isn't telling us the whole truth.

"Are you sure?" I ask casually.

"What?" Cory looks confused and takes a quick glance at Neon and Indah to see the look mirrored on their faces. Annoyance surges inside of me—if they didn't want me to take part in whatever Nancy Drew–ing they're doing, then why did they invite me along at all?

"The last time you saw Blaze," I continue, the name sounding foreign on my tongue. I don't even know what this guy looks like. "Are you sure that it was when you played?"

Cory's brow is furrowed, sweat gathering on his face. He's nervous, hiding something. I want to break him open and see what comes tumbling out.

"Yeah." He gulps. "We played a show at the Three Clubs and I called him the next day but he never called me back. I just assumed he ran out of minutes but then he didn't show up for our gig, so . . . have you guys not heard from him either?"

Cory looks properly worried now, eyes darting back and forth between Neon's and Indah's wincing faces, but I don't want to let him off the hook that easily.

"What happened at the gig?" I ask, keeping my voice level and easy, the focus rising back up in me.

"What do you mean?" Cory looks back to me and I just stare him down, wanting to know whatever it is he's keeping all locked up. And then:

"Okay, so"—Cory exhales, looking at the ground—"we were packing up the gear and the other guys were inside and I think Blaze was a little drunk because he tried to kiss me."

Neon's eyebrows shoot up, both in surprise and as a challenge to whatever Cory will say next.

"And like"—Cory swallows, still staring at his shoes—"that's totally cool or whatever, I don't really care. But, you know, it's not my thing."

"Oh no . . . ," Indah mutters, a realization breaking on her face.

"Yeah," Cory says, sneaking a look at Indah, "you know how Blaze gets. I kinda pushed him away—not mean or anything—but he got so embarrassed and he ran off. I tried to call him to tell him everything was cool with us but I just figured he still needed some space. I didn't know that he liked me like that and I didn't want to . . . I don't know, I wanted to give him time, I guess."

My shoulders drop and I let go of the thread I strung between me and Cory. That wasn't as exciting of an answer as I hoped. And, taking a look at Neon's face, I see it wasn't the answer she was looking for either.

"So . . . you guys haven't seen him?" Cory's eyes dart between the three of us, the furrow in his brow getting deeper.

"You know Blaze." Neon half smiles. "He's probably just blowing off some steam."

And that's what we do for the next few weeks—we blow off steam that I'm not sure I had in the first place, but that Neon seems to have an endless supply of. Punk shows, vodka shots, and strange parties at odd after-hours bars tucked into residential neighborhoods like pockets of nocturnal activity. I feel alive and vital and like I never know what's going to happen next. I've never felt that before, never felt that there were so many things to do and see, so many possibilities laid out in front of me that I'm overwhelmed in a positive way, overwhelmed with choice and desire. I begin to learn the city, to learn the differences in Neon's laughs and how to draw them out in her; I learn that the way Indah looks at Neon is the way I wish she would look at me—the way I wish they would *both* look at me—but I also learn that there are some things my wants can't manifest.

I also learn why Los Angeles is so quiet at four in the morning: all the bars close at two a.m., a cockeyed choice for a city that revels in its degeneracy. But scattered throughout the urban sprawl are run-down houses with big yards that don't seem to belong to anyone. It's in these pop-up gatherings where Neon knows everyone and everyone knows Indah that I, the complete unknown, start to find my rhythm with the couple I've found myself sandwiched between.

"You're Neon and Indah's boy, right?"

I pull my eyes back from searching the darkened yard for Indah's warm skin to look down at the petite and pretty woman in front of me. She's got short, spiked hair, piercings all up and down her ears, and I've already forgotten her name.

"What?" I ask, thinking I must have misheard her question. There's no way they'd consider me theirs, make that claim to other people. Not even They felt that degree of loyalty or possessiveness, and those things were supposed to be hard-wired into Them.

"I work at the shop with Neon," she says, smiling, "and she keeps talking about a stray puppy they've adopted."

"I am *not* a puppy," I snarl, suddenly defensive in my disbelief, and the easy smile on the woman's face drops.

"Right. Sorry," she says sarcastically, eyes widening.

She turns on her heel and walks into the party, leaving me blissfully alone in the shadows on the edge of the yard. The glow of a heat lamp warms my face and I close my eyes, tilting my head toward it and soaking up the artificial sunlight. I've been here for a month and already I feel addicted to the daylight. I've spent so much of my life in darkness—the shadows of corn stalks, the hollow shade of a house when the electric bill hasn't been paid, the inky black of the desert—that the triplet suns of Neon, Indah, and the Los Angeles sky have warmed me so thoroughly I never want to slink back into the blackness.

Just as the rays from the heat lamp are starting to singe my eyelashes, a shadow crosses over my eyelids, a solar eclipse. I blink open my eyes, expecting to see Neon's grin, ready to make fun of me for falling asleep standing up, but instead I find myself staring at a narrow chest wrapped in a black button-down. My eyes roam upward, until I'm looking into the face of a tall, thin man, his bright green eyes peering silently at me.

"Uh, hey, dude," I say dumbly, shifting from foot to foot. "Can I help you?"

"What's your name?" he asks, his head tilting unnaturally to one side. The hair on the back of my neck stands up. I catch Neon's eye across the yard. She tilts her head at me as well, but it's fluid and human. A question—a friend checking in on a friend. I widen my eyes at her, the "rescue me" look I've seen Indah give her from behind the bar when we hang out at Lubitsch during her shift and a slimy agency bro won't stop hitting on her. I see Neon start to walk toward me before my eyes snap back to the man, who has repeated the question.

"Um, Cory," I lie, wanting this guy to leave me alone and wondering why he hasn't. It's chilly out, the kind of desert winter cold that ignores how bright and hot the sun is during the day, but the long black coat hanging from the man's shoulder seems more decorative than utilitarian. He's standing perfectly still, except for the tilt of his head, like there's no air around him, like he's not even inside his own skin.

"Nice to meet you, Cory." He smiles, the gesture stretching the tight skin across his gaunt face like a Halloween mask.

"Yeah . . . you too . . . ," I say, feeling distant and disassociated. I try to reach out, push my desire for him to leave onto him, but it's like he's a moving target and I can't get a grip.

"So . . . *Cory*," he continues, chewing the name like it's in a foreign language, "what do you do?"

"What do I do?" I echo, before switching tactics. "Listen, I should—"

"Hey, Rob, you okay?" Neon's voice pulls my eyes away from the man's rubber face and I internally curse at the sound of my real name. Even though I'm now looking at Neon, I can feel the man's gaze narrow at me.

"Rob?" he asks, his voice smooth and expressionless.

"Gotta go, man," I say, not looking at him. I grab Neon's hand and she pulls me out of the spotlight of the heat lamp and into the different warmth of the crowd. I didn't notice how cold I got with the man blocking the lamp, and between the hum of the people milling around and the heat of Neon's hand, I come back into my body.

"Who was that guy?" Neon asks, dropping my hand now that we're a safe distance away. I only take a moment to mourn the loss before she grabs it again, intertwining her fingers with mine. The surprise nearly stops me from answering before I remember to relish the comfort she's giving me, asked for but unverbalized.

"I have no idea," I say, gripping her fingers a little more tightly. "But I think he brought the end of the party with him. What do you say we find Indah and get out of here?"

"I bet he was an agent," Indah suggests lightly, her eyes on the road. We're in her car, Neon in the passenger seat, feet up on the dashboard, me in the middle seat in the back. Despite Indah's insistence that everyone wear their seat belt, I've unhooked mine so that I can lean forward between the front seats and regale the two of them once again with my impression of the creepy tall man, now a lot less scary in my overdramatic retelling.

"You think every creepy guy is an agent," Neon teases.

"Well, it's usually true!" she says, sending Neon laughing in a way that I haven't unlocked yet. "I bet he was trying to get our dear, handsome Rob to model for him or something."

She smiles at me through the rearview mirror, somehow both genuine and teasing. Neon turns to make cooing kissing noises at me and I playfully push at her shoulder, the close atmosphere and late hour making me more confident. I don't touch people much and people don't touch me. But Neon held my hand earlier, so pushing softly on her shoulder feels safe, and when she smiles and pushes back, it feels like sunlight brightening on my face.

"What do you think, Rob?" Neon asks. "Think you'll become a model?"

"What, with a face like this?"

"It's a good face." She shrugs and I realize that she's not teasing me.

I know the truth about how I look—soft, blank, and unremarkable. I've seen the billboards that line the streets of LA and know that I don't measure up to the most generic of models, know that I'm too short, too chubby, too speckle-faced to be one of LA's glamorous residents. But without my focusing on it, I clearly want Neon and Indah to think I'm attractive. It's not the first time something like this has happened, but it's no less embarrassing than it was the last time.

"I don't really think the lifestyle of the rich and famous is for me," I say, trying to change the subject.

"What *is* for you, then?" Indah asks.

"What do you mean?"

"Like, what do you want to do next?" Neon clarifies. "You've been here a few weeks now, you must have some reason for being here."

They're both looking at me with open and interested expressions—Neon twisted in her seat to face me, Indah glancing through the rearview mirror every few seconds. I haven't been thinking about next steps. I've been driving from place to place for so long, looking for a place to settle but finding that so impossible that I stopped trying to settle a while ago. But I've also never met people like these two before.

"I've never seen the ocean," I say, reluctant to reveal anything more than that, reluctant to even *think* about anything more than that that I might want. "I hear surfing is big out here," I add.

"Ugh," Neon groans. "Don't tell me you're staying in Venice."

"Uh, no," I say, confused. "What's wrong with Venice?"

"Anything west of the 405 is another planet," Neon explains.

"Wait," Indah interjects, "where *are* you staying?"

"You're staying *here*?"

"Not too shabby, huh?" I smile, walking farther into the villa, leaving Indah boggling in the doorway.

"What were you saying about not wanting the life of the rich and famous . . . ?" Neon asks, looking around in awe.

Pleasure rushes through me at their faces—they're impressed. And I don't think they're even impressed because I *want* them to be. They're impressed because this is impressive. *I'm* impressive.

Suddenly I want desperately to tell them both what I can do. Show them just how powerful and impressive I can be. But, if past experience is anything to go by, people's knowing about me doesn't make them more inclined to like me. In fact, it sometimes makes using my ability on them that much harder.

Still, the tall, pale man continues to loom large in my head. Joking about him in the car was one thing, but now that I'm back in my own space, which is in a hotel with dozens of other people and big glass doors that lead to the courtyard, I remember the powerlessness I felt in his shadow. It makes me want to prove what I can do. I flex my hand as I flop down on the couch, the phantom sensation of Neon's grip and the feel of her shoulder beneath my palm both still lingering on my skin. I'm not broken, not too buzzed to have my ability work—that much was proven by Indah and Neon's complimenting my looks in the car—so why did that man linger when I wanted him so badly to leave?

"Yo, catch me up here," Neon says, stepping toward the baby grand in the corner. "Are you secretly loaded? Are you actually some trust fund kid on their gap year or something?"

"Ha, definitely not," I scoff.

"Then . . ." Neon sweeps her arms outward, gesturing to the grandiose surroundings.

"I have my ways." I shrug, mock humble.

"You know, you say that a lot for someone who doesn't even have a wallet," Indah murmurs, still standing in the doorway. There's that crinkle between her eyebrows, like she's looking at an optical illusion, trying to find the cracks in the image. I guess that isn't far off—me, a dumpy eighteen-year-old kid in beat-up Converse sneakers and a too-big hoodie, staying in a lavish rock star hotel, is its own kind of optical illusion.

"Do you guys want anything to drink?" I say, deflecting. "The fridge is pretty well stocked."

"Ha, I can imagine." Neon snorts. "And probably insanely overpriced. Sure you can afford it?"

"I wouldn't worry about it." I grin and Neon grins back. She takes another look around the room, whistling low, before moving to the fridge, only to whistle again when she sees the contents.

Meanwhile, Indah is still standing in the open doorway, narrowing her eyes at both me and Neon. I suddenly realize how far the couch I'm on is from the door—Indah might be out of range. There's plenty I still don't understand about what I can do, but proximity seems to be a factor. Without the magnetic pull of my ability enticing her into the room, she has space to think about all the pieces of this that don't make sense—space to make out the shape of the duck when I want her to see the rabbit.

"Do you want anything, Indah?" I say smoothly, rising from the couch and moving slowly toward her as if she's a spooked animal. "There's soda and stuff too."

"Yeah, real fancy shit!" Neon yells, her head still in the refrigerator.

"Robert, what's going on here?" Indah asks.

Crap, she's taken a minuscule step back, putting her weight on her heels like she's ready to spin on them and run at any moment.

"What do you mean?" I put my hands in my pockets, show her I'm not a threat. But I keep moving toward her, slow step by slow step, hardly picking up my feet. Neon seems plenty occupied with the drinks, and hopefully my desire for her to have a good time will keep her there. But even as I inch closer, I can't feel Indah, can't tell how much closer I'll need to get to her to convince her that there's no reason to ask more questions.

"There's something . . ." Her brow crinkles more and her gaze becomes unfocused, giving me the chance to slightly speed up my steps. "There's something strange about you, Robert," she finishes, and I fake a chuckle.

"Yeah, that's been said before."

"No, I mean, there's something . . ." She trails off again and I feel a click inside my body, like I'm finally picking up the tune of a song playing far away.

"Something . . . ?" I prompt, knowing I'm out of danger for now.

"Nothing." She shakes her head. "I can't—I don't remember what I was going to say now." She smiles at that, like she's laughing at herself, and her whole body relaxes as she steps into the room.

"Holy shit."

I turn around to see Neon staring at us from the kitchenette. She's got tiny bottles of liquor in both of her hands, but based on her ashen face and wide eyes, I don't think that's what she's swearing about.

"What?" I ask, heart beating fast. Crossing the room to work my magic on Indah might have put Neon out of range, but there's no way. There's no way she could suspect something about me, other than the general suspicion that I'm some sort of criminal. Which I could hardly criticize her for—the evidence is fairly damning, even if it isn't strictly true.

"You're one of us," she breathes.

One of *us*.

Chills run down my arms.

"One of who?" I ask, doing my best to keep my voice steady.

"You can do something, can't you?" she continues. "I don't know what it is, but Indah—I know what Indah looks like when she senses—and you just—you just made her totally calm without saying anything. Indah, babe, are you okay?"

Indah's eyes widen in confusion as she looks between Neon and me.

"I'm—" she starts, before shaking her head and starting again. "Nee, he's—"

"I'm nothing," I interrupt, starting to panic.

"No, you're *something*," Neon continues. "This place . . . everything you have, everything you're able to get . . . you do something, don't you?"

"Look, I don't know what you're talking about," I say, taking a step toward her.

"No, don't—"

She puts her hands up in warning, the mini bottles clattering to the floor. Light reflects off the rings on her fingers and the hair rises on the back of my neck.

"Don't come any closer," she warns.

"Neon, calm down," I say soothingly, trying to push my ability out as far as it will go.

"Indah, come here a sec," Neon calls. I look behind me to see Indah's eyes darting between us, torn between someone she trusts urging her over and the tentative hold I still have on her emotions. I don't want her to move—I want her to stay behind me, on *my* side—but reaching out to Neon has meant loosening my grip on Indah, and I don't know which is stronger: the trust or the power.

"Babe, come on," Neon pleads, and the endearment snaps the connection between us. Indah rushes to Neon's side, putting them both in the kitchenette and me still standing in front of the open door. There's one exit and they have to pass me to get there. There's still time for me to fix this.

"What did you mean, 'one of us'?" I repeat, slowly stepping backward to shut the door.

"Don't you dare close that door," Neon hisses, but I click it shut softly.

"It's okay," I assure her. "You really think I could hurt you? Look at me." I wave my hands over my body—soft and weak compared to her wiry strength—and give her my best innocent look.

"I don't know what you can do, Robert," Neon says. "And that means I can't trust you, no matter how unthreatening you look."

"How didn't I know?" Indah murmurs. "Nee, he's different. I couldn't sense anything from him. Not until tonight. That's why I—that's why I started asking questions."

"What are you—'couldn't sense anything'?" I echo. "What the hell are you talking about?"

"Who *are* you—" Indah shoots back, her voice sharp in a way I've never heard.

"Okay, okay," Neon shouts over us, "we clearly have some things we need to talk about. Why don't we all just calm down and start explaining."

"You first," I snap, crossing my arms.

"Nuh-uh, kid." Neon shakes her head. "You're the new guy in town, *you* explain first."

"Don't call me 'kid,'" I mutter, annoyed that I have to say it out loud.

"That's what you are though," she continues. "You're eighteen, you somehow got Indah to serve you the moment you met her, you're staying here without paying a dime, and—and weren't you running from something in Vegas? There's a lot you haven't told us and you better start."

"Why should I? I barely know you two, why would I tell you anything?"

"Because in the past month, it's become pretty clear that you're a curious kid and I have a feeling you'll do what you need to to find out what I meant by 'one of us.'"

"Yeah, you're right," I concede, clenching my jaw. "But, as you've guessed by now, I'm not in the habit of playing by other people's rules." I start to stalk slowly toward them. These two are clearly no strangers to conflict, but even if they wanted to fight their way out of this, by the time they try, they'll be in range for me to do my thing. "So if you'll just do me the very kind favor of telling me exactly—"

I take another step and Neon's hands go up again. There's a flash of blue light, searing pain, and then darkness.

She was sixteen when it first happened. It started small. A static shock on her fingertips. A current up and down her spine when she held her tongue. The smell of lightning in the air that comes before a storm, except there never was a storm. The storm was her all along.

It didn't stay small. The more upset she got, the more she held in her feelings—tried to fit in, tried to appease her parents, her friends, her school—the higher the static would rise. She didn't know it needed a release. If she had, she would have found an outlet, somewhere safe to discharge all the electricity, before it was too late. Instead, it burst out of her like a supernova. She never let it build up again. She couldn't risk it. Couldn't risk being found out, hurting someone, burning another building down. She couldn't risk any of it.

The moment she could, she left her small Arizona town and moved west. To somewhere she wouldn't be looked upon as strange. Her town had always seen her that way and they didn't even know about the electricity. She stuck out like a sore, sparking thumb. At least in Los Angeles, her run-of-the-mill weirdness—her love of punk, her hair, her sharp wit and steel spine—would be just that. Run-of-the-mill. Los Angeles could accept her. Los Angeles was a place for lost people to find themselves.

She found herself, all right. She found Neon.

". . . he'll be fine, Indah. Don't treat me like an amateur."

"He's been out for five whole minutes. You know that's not good."

"He spooked me, okay? I didn't mean to discharge that much."

"Is he—"

"Oh shit—"

"Robert? Robert, are you okay?"

"What the fuck happened?" I groan as I blink open my eyes. I'm lying on what I assume is the floor, Indah and Neon bent down on either side of me. Indah's eyes move around my body, while Neon squints at me with a guilty grimace.

"Sorry, kid," she says, and I cringe internally. I wish she'd stop calling me that. And it's a little weird that she is when she's right next to me. My ability should be taking care of that, even if I am still half-conscious.

"Here, let me help you up," she continues, and Indah nods in agreement as they both grab on to my arms. Something is off. There's a low hum in my ears and my skin feels overly sensitive, like it's been sunburned. I shake my head back and forth, like that will clear it, as they lead me to the couch.

"Okay, really, what the hell just happened?" I croak, settling back into the couch.

"I shocked you," Neon says, sitting down on the coffee table across from me. Indah settles on the arm of the couch, crossing her arms and looking down at us like a disapproving schoolmarm.

"What do you mean, you shocked me?" I ask.

"Like I said: you're one of us. And people like us . . . well. We can do a lot of different things." She gives me a small, soft smile, like we're in on a secret. "I still haven't figured out exactly what it is you can do, though."

"I can make people do what I want."

I don't know what compels me to tell her. Maybe it's feeling like I've been microwaved and then struck by lightning; maybe it's that, for once, I feel completely powerless, and even worried and shaken, Neon radiates that commanding confidence that I want to bend to. Maybe it's just because I think it's the only way she's ever going to give me more than vague statements.

"Huh," she says, not at all the reaction I expect. "I thought it might be something like that. But how does it work?"

I'm thrown by the question, expecting an outcry of disgust or disbelief or *something*.

"I, uh . . . I don't really know," I admit. "I've been able to do it a really long time and it's just—I just want something and people around me want it too. I don't really think that much about it most of the time."

"What do you want right now?" Indah asks softly from her perch.

"I want you to explain who the hell you are, but . . ." I concentrate on the part of my feelings that always feels like an old bruise. The place I poke at when I do what I do. The bruise is silent, un-aching.

"It's weird," I continue, "I can't—you're *not* explaining. And I can't really feel the want."

"Does that happen a lot?" Indah asks.

"Never," I say, moving my gaze back to Neon. "What did you do to me?"

"What *I* do," she says, leaning back and lifting her chin in pride.

"And what exactly is it that *you do*?" I spit. "Knock people unconscious?"

"Sometimes." She shrugs. "I try not to make a habit of it."

"But you're . . ." I trail off. Not sure how to ask for it. Not even knowing what word to use. Feeling self-conscious about this conversation still.

"God, I need a smoke." Neon stands abruptly, digging into her pants pockets. "You got a light, babe?"

"Neon," Indah chastises.

"What?" Neon asks around her cigarette as Indah jerks her head toward me. "Oh, right, is it cool if I smoke in here? This whole situation is, you know, kind of stressful."

"What the fuck do I care?" I shrug, annoyed that the conversation is getting waylaid and I'm apparently completely powerless to control that. Neon should be sitting, telling me all of her deepest, darkest secrets, and instead she's kissing Indah on the cheek as she takes a lighter from her hand and completely ignoring me.

"Um, excuse me," I snap, "I think you were just explaining why I was unconscious on my hotel room floor a few minutes ago?"

"Right, sorry." Neon pulls the lit cigarette from her mouth and sits back down on the coffee table, leaning toward me, her elbows on her knees. She takes one more long drag before meeting my eyes as she exhales, face serious, the cigarette dangling from her fingers.

"I'm an electropath," she says, like I know what that means. "I can make things go all sparky with my mind," she explains, before I can ask for more clarification out loud.

She rests her cigarette on the edge of table, brings up her arms in front of her and suddenly the air crackles with electricity. Lightning comes from her hands, twisting around her fingers, kissing her wrists.

"No, it doesn't hurt," she says dreamily, gazing at her hands with affection. She's so calm, so comfortable in herself, that I can't tell if she's answering my desire—still distant in my body—or anticipating the natural question you have when seeing someone essentially electrocuting themselves.

"How . . . ," I breathe, not even knowing what I want to know.

"How long?" she ventures. "How does it work? How do I use it?"

"How did you know about me?" I blurt, my lips making the rare move of forming words without my brain's careful crafting of them first. "How did you figure it out so fast?"

"It took us a month. I wouldn't say that's exactly *fast*," she grumbles. Then, seeing my unsatisfied expression, she rolls her eyes and continues. "When you've been around the block as much as I have, you learn how to recognize other Unusuals."

The way she says it, I can practically hear the capital letter.

"Unusuals?"

"That's what I call people like us. No one I've met has ever had a word for it, so that seemed as good as any."

She picks the cigarette back up and takes another drag and I want to inhale the smoke she lets out of her mouth, like breathing in her exhale will give me all the knowledge she's ever gained about people like us.

"I—" I start, "I didn't know. I thought it was just me."

"In all your Kerouac-ing around the country, you never ran into another Unusual?"

"I, um . . ." I rub my hands on my legs. "I never really got to know anyone well enough to find out."

"God, that's sad."

I don't know what to say to that. I don't know how I could possibly disagree. So I don't say anything at all.

Another drag. We sit in silence as she exhales.

"You don't just . . ."

I sit up straighter, unused to Neon trailing off.

"What?" I push.

"Ask people?" She raises her eyebrows at me. "I mean, not ask people outright but . . . you know . . . ask in your unique way of asking. Want them to tell you," she finishes, like I didn't get the point.

"I can't ask what I don't know to ask," I tell her softly, embarrassed to admit that I don't know something.

"You never wondered if there were other people like you?" she asks, lips moving around her cigarette.

"I just never even thought about it," I say. "I never . . . I've never had a name for what I can do. At first I thought I was going crazy."

"Yeah, me too." She snorts, smoke curling out of her nose. "But, well, it's hard to deny this." The tips of her fingers crackle and spark in emphasis and I flinch involuntarily, making her smile.

"Don't worry, it can't hurt you," she says, smiling proudly as she takes the cigarette out of her mouth, the electricity briefly flirting with the lit end.

"I think I have pretty solid proof to the contrary," I retort, sinking farther into the couch.

"You're fine, aren't you?" she quips. "A little singed maybe, but . . . fine."

"I'm actually . . ." I search for the want deep inside of me and am uncertain about what I find there. Things usually just *happen*. But this conversation isn't going at all as I want it to and I don't know why. It's different from the unbalanced feeling I had standing in front of the tall man earlier tonight. This isn't being disoriented or frustrated. This is empty.

"I think maybe you did something to me," I finish, hoping Neon will fill in the blanks.

"You mean with your ability?" Indah asks, twirling a cigarette between her fingers. I've never seen her smoke but she always carries them with her. I don't know yet if Indah is an Unusual like Neon, like *me* I guess, but she's already an enticing enough mystery on her own.

"Do you guys . . . ," I start. As I struggle to find my words, I realize that I don't normally talk this much. My interactions with other people are often short and always dictated by what I'm feeling. I don't say much because I never have to say much. My wants find their way to the people around me so that I never have to voice them out loud. Even with Indah and Neon so far, the point has been to make *them* laugh, hear *them* joke, make them like me without revealing too much about myself. But here we are being *honest* and it's new and terrifying territory.

"What, kid?" Neon prompts, and I grimace.

"*That.*" I jab a finger at her. "That's what I'm talking about. If I was at a hundred percent, you wouldn't be calling me 'kid.'"

"You don't like it," Neon breathes, leaning back on her elbows and putting the cigarette back between her lips.

"No, I don't." I shake my head. "And I shouldn't have to tell you that."

"Maybe the electricity rewired things a bit," Indah suggests, looking at Neon. "It's happened before."

"Excuse me, what?"

"Chill," Neon says. "It's temporary. A lot of abilities are based in the brain, so sometimes my little light show gets in the way. Neurons and all that shit."

"Okay, seriously, who are you guys?" I say, exasperated, scooting to the edge of the couch. "How do you—I mean, how many people like us have you met?"

"A fair few," Neon says. "Indah here is our little bloodhound." She tilts her head toward Indah and smiles big. Indah just rolls her eyes.

"Explain," I demand.

"I'm not like you," she begins. "I'm not an Unusual. Or, at least, not in the strictest sense."

"Okay . . . ," I say, urging her along.

"But I *can* sense you guys," she continues. "I've always been able to. That's how I first knew about Neon, and then she introduced me to Marley and we picked up a few more along the way, though mostly it's just the four of us now. Well, when Blaze is around at least," she finishes darkly.

"A few—what—who's Marley?" I have a million questions and I can't tell which one is most pressing because they aren't answering before I can ask and it's been so long since I've had to closely examine my own wanting process. Sometimes wants battle themselves, but usually one rises to the top, and then most of the time things just *happen*.

"Oh, you'll meet Marley," Neon says. "And probably others too, eventually. But what I want to know is: Why couldn't Indah sense *you*?"

Neon pierces me with her dark brown eyes, leaning forward again and pointing her cigarette-laden hand at me. I guess it's better than a hand covered in electric current.

"I don't know." I shrug. "I'm clearly new to *all* of this."

"You've never told anyone about what you can do?" Indah asks.

"No," I say automatically. "I mean, there are a few people who . . . no, no one knows."

"And I'm guessing you'd like to keep it that way?" Indah prods.

"What, you think it'd be a good idea to up and tell people that you have the power to get them to do what you want?" I say mockingly. "How exactly would *that* conversation go?"

"I think *that's* why," Indah tells Neon, pointing at me. "If he didn't want me to sense it and his power works the way it does . . ."

"Then his need to hide what he can do would trump your sensitivity." Neon nods.

"You guys really *have* been around the block about this, haven't you?" I ask, unable to keep the drop of awe out of my voice.

"It's not all that different from an empath ability," Indah explains. "I mean, no, it's *very* different in terms of outcome, but—"

"Yeah, you could say that we know a thing or two," Neon finishes for her.

"Jesus," I sigh, collapsing back into the cushions. "This is . . ."

"A lot?" Indah guesses.

"Yeah." I huff a laugh. "Yeah, this is a whole goddamn lot."

Indah and Neon smile softly at each other and then at me. It makes me feel less alone and suddenly I need to know.

"Am I . . . ," I start. "I'm gonna be okay, right?"

"Yeah, kid." Neon slaps my knee and it makes me hate the "kid" a hell of a lot less. "You're gonna be fine. You'll be back to normal in no time. Or, at least, your version of normal. Sorry I overloaded your circuit board there."

"That's okay," I say, and mean it. "I'm just . . . you guys are cool with what I do?"

At that, they look at each other again, this time smile-less.

"It's definitely more . . . unique than we've encountered before," Indah says carefully. "But if all you're using it for is to get free booze and stay in some swanky hotel, then . . ."

"Then screw the fat-cat capitalists," Neon says, grinning. "Let's have some fun."

"Robbie, I just don't understand what's wrong with you."

My mother is crying and I don't know how to make it stop. I want it to stop. Why won't it stop?

"What do you mean, Mom?" I ask, tears gathering at the corners of my eyes. I'm too old to cry. I'll be in sixth grade in two months and middle schoolers don't cry.

"There's something not right with you, Robbie," she sniffs. "Your father and I love you very much, but you're scaring us."

"I don't mean to scare you," I say, tears running freely down my cheeks. She usually brushes them away. Why isn't she brushing them away?

"I know, baby, but then why did you make your father do that?" she pleads, and I wish that she would reach out and pull me into her arms instead of standing several feet away from me like I'm something toxic she's afraid to touch.

"It wasn't my fault." I shake my head. "I just wanted my Frisbee."

The tears are coming in full force now. I try to push them down, cry silently. I don't want to wake my dad, upstairs napping in his bed with a broken leg.

"It wasn't supposed to happen that way," I whisper. "I just needed him to get my Frisbee."

"But why did you make him jump off the roof?"

"Rob, this is Marley," Neon says, gesturing toward the genuinely terrifying figure next to her. I have a heart-stopping moment where I think it's the tall man from the party the other night. But after the initial double take, I realize that Marley is tall, yes, but broad shouldered and built. His blond hair is cropped close to his skull, making his unsmiling face strangely sharp in comparison to his impressively beefy frame. Add the extreme paleness of his skin to all that, and the result is like looking at the corpse of Frankenstein's monster.

"Hey, man," I say, shaking his enormous hand. "Robert Gorham. It's good to meet you." I want to bite back the words—the stupid Midwestern manners They instilled in me crawling their way out before I can come up with something cooler, more casual.

But for some reason the awkward, out-of-place politeness makes him smile, just a bit, and he keeps his eyes on me as he says to Neon:

"Where'd you find this one?" His voice isn't what I expected. Instead of low and gruff, it's strangely smooth and slightly higher than mine.

"At Lubitsch," Indah says.

"Ha, figures. You even old enough to drink, kid?" Marley asks before his face twitches and he course corrects. "I'm—I'm sorry." He sounds genuinely apologetic and I see Indah tense out of the corner of my eye.

"Down, boy." Neon lifts her eyebrows at me and I glare.

". . . What just happened?" Marley asks, squinting between us.

"What do you mean?" I blink innocently and Indah shoots daggers at me. I want her to chill out, but all my energy is focused on

Marley. On impressing him, figuring him out. I don't have desire left to spare for Indah.

"Robert here is one of us," Neon tells him.

"'One of us'?" I echo. "You mean, he's also . . ."

"Marley's the first Unusual I ever met," Neon explains, smiling up at him. Marley returns her gaze and something in him relaxes.

"Yeah." He nods. "We met years ago when we were both a lot less in control than we are now. We helped each other through it all, shared all our secrets. We're family."

He says it all without hesitation, my ability slowly sinking into him.

"What can you do?" I ask.

"See pasts," he says simply.

"What?"

"I can see into people's pasts," he sighs, like he's just telling someone about his boring accounting job or something. "Not like time traveling or anything," he clarifies. "But I get these little visions—well, full-on audiovisual hallucinations, really—that show me bits of someone's past."

"What," I say again, this time less of a question. Nervousness rises in my throat and my eyes flicker to the door, ready to escape at any moment.

"Give Rob a sec," Neon says, grinning. "He's still new to all this."

"Doesn't seem that new." Marley rubs the back of his neck with his massive hand. "Whatever you can do, seems like you know your way around it. Is it . . . like, a truth serum thing?"

"Wait," I say, deflecting, "you could tell I was doing something to you?"

"I mean, I think so?" he says. "I don't normally tell complete strangers everything about myself."

"That was you telling someone everything about yourself?" I scoff. "You said, like, three sentences."

"He's normally very reticent," Indah quips from the kitchen. "Marley, lend me a hand?"

Marley obeys, moving around the island separating the kitchen and living room. He joins her as she creates some sort of drink concoction that, having spent the past few weeks drinking with Indah outside of Lubitsch, I know is probably too strong to legally serve to bar patrons. Neon and I enjoy being her guinea pigs though.

We're in Neon's apartment, a space that's casual and haphazard in the way that Neon can be. Tonight, Neon is wearing her typical getup. Black leather pants, black tank littered with safety pins, black biker jacket, black combat boots. The only color in her whole ensemble is the bursts of blue at the ends of her hair and the edges of her eyes. Like a neon bar sign in the middle of a dark night.

"Wait a second," I start, a thought occurring. "Neon isn't your real name, is it?"

"You're just figuring that out now?" She snorts.

"No," I say, rolling my eyes, "I assumed it wasn't your real name but it's—it has to do with the electricity, doesn't it? And Marley . . . ghost of the past?"

I turn to Marley as I say this and he smiles, showing all his teeth. My stomach twists at the unexpected sight—it should be menacing, this towering man grinning, but instead, like his voice, it's soft and genuine and at odds with everything else about him.

"You got that pretty fast, kid," he says. "Neon's is obvious but it can take people a second to put two and two together with me."

"I like to read," I say with a shrug, and Marley smiles bigger and nods.

I smile back, warmth spreading through me at Marley's approval. And he called me "kid." So I'm not working my mojo on him. He's impressed because of me, not what I can do.

"What does 'Indah' mean?" I ask, raising my voice over the clatter of the cocktail shaker in her hand.

"'Beautiful one,'" she says after a moment, pouring the contents of the shaker into three glasses.

"I don't get it," I say. "I mean, not that you're not—I mean . . . it's accurate." I can feel my face heating but Indah laughs her big laugh and I think it's okay.

"Isn't it just?" Neon says dreamily, gazing up at Indah from her place on the couch.

"It's my real name, Rob," Indah explains, handing me a glass of something cold and slightly pink. I take a cautious sniff of it and, yup, definitely one of Indah's more lethal creations.

"We don't think I'm actually an Unusual," she continues. "I'm just sensitive to them. As far as I can tell, I don't have any other abilities and I'm not sure sensing people with abilities really counts as an ability itself. So I'm like the . . . caretaker of this ragtag group of weirdos."

She sits on the arm of the couch and brushes at Neon's cheek as she says this, Neon still gazing up at her lovingly.

"Jesus, this is efficient," Marley says from the kitchen.

"What is?" Neon says distractedly, stroking her hand up and down Indah's denim-clad leg.

"His ability," Marley expands, moving around the island and back into the living room. "I've never heard Indah explain any of that that quickly. But you wanted to know, didn't you?" He directs that to me, and I can't find judgment in his voice.

"Yeah." I nod. "Yeah, I wanted to know. I'm . . . curious. About how all of this works."

"All of what?" Neon asks, tearing her eyes away from the "beautiful one" to focus on me.

"*This*," I say, waving my hand over the three of them. "Like . . . what do you guys *do*?"

"You've seen what we do," Neon says. "We drink—well, not all of us—we go to concerts, we find other people like us when we can. Is there something we're *supposed* to be doing?"

"No, not at all." I shake my head. "I just . . . I haven't met a lot of other people who just live their lives and don't have to worry about all that other stuff."

"What other stuff?" Marley asks.

"You know—family, work, I don't know . . . taxes . . . ," I say eventually, uncertain what real people do in life.

"You think we don't worry about that stuff?" Neon laughs sharply. "Of course we do."

"Rob, you met me at my *job*," Indah reminds me.

"Well, yeah, but you're . . ." I trail off. She lifts her eyebrows in challenge and I decide I'm close enough to her that she's not going to get mad at me. "You're not one of us, not really. So you have to work."

"Yeah, so do we, bud," Neon says, waving her hand between herself and Marley. "I work in a bike shop. This"—her fingers spark blue—"comes in handy when you're fixing faulty engines." My mind flashes back to the spiky-haired woman at the house party, the one who said she works at the shop with Neon, and I curse myself for not asking for more information, for not interrogating that woman for every bit of information she has on Neon and what Neon has said about me.

"And I do security at bars—sometimes I bounce at Lubitsch actually—to pay for classes," Marley says. "I'm pre-law." He smiles again, the paleness of his cheeks warming.

"Oh," I say, a little dumbfounded.

"Yeah, not all of us can hop from place to place not worrying about money or any other damn thing," Neon says, leaning forward to grab her smokes from the coffee table. "Just because we're special doesn't mean we don't have to pay rent."

"It does for me."

"Well, nice to be you then," Neon teases, lighting her cigarette. I'm hypnotized by the way her lips wrap around the cigarette, the glow of the flame from the lighter reflecting in her brown eyes.

"Those things will kill you, you know," I say, tearing my eyes away from her and nodding toward the pack she's dropped back on the table.

"Not you too," Neon groans, rolling her eyes.

"Thank you, Robert," Indah exclaims. "I've been trying to tell her for two years and all I get is an eye roll and, yep, *that*." She lifts a hand to Neon's middle finger and Neon just grins around her cigarette.

"Marley's on my side," Indah continues. "And now with you, maybe the three of us can work on her."

"Blaze never minded," Neon says, exhaling.

"Blaze had too much fun trying to light your smokes from across the room," Indah retorts. "You still haven't painted over most of the burn marks!"

Indah sweeps her arm around the apartment and I follow her

hand. Now that I'm looking, there are several black streaks scattered on the walls of the living room. My eyes roam over the room with more intent and I see that the corner of the rug is singed.

"Blaze . . . I'm assuming he's one of us?" I ask, things starting to snap together. *Us.* I love hearing myself say that, love the way it feels on my tongue, love this easy rapport we're falling into. Like we really are an "us." Like I belong somewhere.

"Pyrokinetic," Neon says, nodding. "Pretty powerful, too. But, *god*, he hates it. That's why I let him experiment in here, even if it means the place smelling like a firepit all the time. Anything to make him see how cool what he can do is."

"So when you said you thought he was just blowing off some steam . . . ," I say, hoping my awe doesn't show through the question. The way they're talking about all of this, about being *Unusual*, makes it seem run-of-the-mill. But my brain is reeling with possibility, with the idea that there are people who can electrocute you, set fires, *see your past.*

"He does that sometimes," Indah says. "He gets so fed up with his power, with being an Unusual, that he'll go away for a little while, get some flames out at a lake or in the desert. Somewhere no one can find him and where he won't do too much damage. But he's never been gone for this long."

"I'm sure he's fine, babe," Neon says soothingly. "We always knew there was a chance that he would leave one day and not come back. It's not like Southern California is the best place for someone who sometimes accidentally starts fires. And if the whole thing with Cory really set him off . . . maybe he needed to go a lot farther and bigger this time."

"I guess that's true," Indah concedes. "I just wish he'd take the time to call, to let us know that he's all right."

"If this is something that he does a lot, then why were you so freaked when I left in the middle of the night?" I ask Indah. "It doesn't sound like he's *actually* missing."

"I just . . ." Indah sighs. "I had a bad feeling. And with you being new in town and only eighteen, I panicked. I don't like not knowing where people are."

"What's the worst that could happen?" I ask lightly.

"Like Neon said, Alex—Blaze—*hated* his ability most of the time. Sometimes I worry . . . well." Indah looks down at her feet and Neon squeezes her leg.

"I worried he'd kill himself," Indah blurts, and Neon flinches.

"Damn, Indah, no need to sugarcoat it," Neon says, withdrawing her hand.

"No, I didn't—" Indah blinks in surprise before turning her eyes toward me. "Robert."

"What?" I shrug.

"You can't—you can't do that." She shakes her head. "You can't just use your ability on us for everything. If you want to know something, you *ask*."

Indah has scolded me before, chastised me in the way an older sister would, but this is the first time I've heard real bite in her voice. With the mention of suicide, the mood of the room shifts and suddenly it doesn't feel like an "us" anymore as much as a "me" versus "them."

Behind the couch, Marley inhales deeply and crosses his arms. He's staring right through me, and I take a few steps back, feeling claustrophobic and out of control. I don't know how Marley's ability works, what exactly he sees, but I want to do everything I can to never find out.

"It's not like I *mean* to," I say defensively. "It just happens—I can't control what I want."

"Can't you switch it off?" Indah demands.

"Can you guys switch *yours* off?" I counter. "As far as I know, the only thing that benches me is having a couple hundred thousand volts pushed through me, and I don't exactly want to replicate that experience." I nod to Neon and she scowls.

Eventually everything went back to normal, but being shocked by Neon was the first time since I was ten that I was just . . . a completely normal person. Sure, sometimes when I'm tired or drunk or whatever, it can be harder to control, and I'm still turning over the whole experience with the tall man in my head, but Neon's electrocuting me straight-up put me out of commission. It was terrifying and weirdly liberating but there's no way I'm letting it happen again.

"Listen, Rob, we're your friends," Neon says, standing. "But you can't go prying into our heads."

"I don't get why you guys are freaking out about this," I groan, trying to keep my attitude casual in the hopes it will spread. "Clearly you have some stuff about your friend you need to talk about—"

"Don't," Neon interrupts, and there's a brief spark of blue around her shoulders. "Blaze is *our* business, not yours. Yeah, we worry, but he's probably somewhere getting the flames out and decided to take a detour and just forgot to up the minutes on his phone. It wouldn't be the first time it happened."

Ours. Not mine. Theirs. That stings more than I know what to do with, so I just cross my arms, mirroring Marley in stance and scowl, my heart beating painfully in my chest.

"I'm telling you, there's something different about this, Nee," Indah calls from the couch. I don't know if my ability is still working on her or if she's just choosing to be up-front. "I can feel it in my gut."

"Then we'll keep looking for him." Neon turns to her, raising a hand gently to Indah's cheek. "I promise. I'm not gonna let anything happen to that kid."

"Sounds like it might not be up to you," I jab pettily. "If he's gonna off himself, there's nothing *you* can do about it."

There's a beat of shocked silence before Neon rounds on me, her mouth opening, hands sparking, when suddenly—

"Leave off, Neon," Marley calls out. "It's a sensitive subject for the kid."

"What are you talking about?" I growl.

"I can see, remember?" His eyes narrow at me in a challenge that makes my blood boil.

"Don't—" I choke on the word. "Don't go looking in my past, *Marley.*"

"Not so fun, is it?" he says coldly. "Being on the other side."

My breathing becomes shaky as he stares me down and I know, I just *know*, that he can see it all.

"You mean . . . ," Indah starts, her voice soft and pitying.

"It's none of your goddamn business," I bark, but Marley doesn't flinch. Out of the corner of my eye, I see Indah and Neon go still.

"Sometimes you still wish you had," Marley snaps back before his mouth slams shut, his eyes widening. Without meaning to, I've shut them all up, but in that moment I don't feel a lick of guilt about it.

I don't know how he can know that, don't know how he could read *that* in my past, but I feel a sob rising in my throat and I can't bear to be around these people—standing silently, staring into me—any longer.

I slam my unfinished cocktail on the coffee table and walk out of the apartment without saying another word.

Marley tries not to look, he really does. He knows it's invasive, knows he doesn't have a right to peer into people's private lives like that. He's seen more in his twenty-five years than most people see in a lifetime and he doesn't relish the idea of seeing more. But sometimes an emotion, an experience, is just so strong that it rises in front of Marley's eyes unbidden.

He didn't mean to look into the newcomer's past like that. He didn't want to see all the darkness and sadness within this odd stranger. But before he could stop it, he saw the inky blackness of water, strong hands holding someone down, the desire to stop existing. That taste lingered on his tongue—lingers around Robert too—not strong enough to drown in, but so steady and persistent that it reminds Marley of waterboarding. And that brings up more ugly ghosts from the past, flooding his senses until drowning doesn't seem like such a bad option.

I tried once. Just once.

It was a month after my sixteenth birthday—a month after I left Ithaca, Nebraska, and never looked back. And because I didn't know shit about the world, I went north and discovered that Montana in March is one of the worst places you can be. Spring still hasn't come and there's absolutely nothing to do. I'd been on my own for years, been living with my ability for years, and I was just *done*. I hadn't figured out how it could be fun yet. I'd only ever used it to hurt people, even when I didn't mean to.

The next logical step seemed to be hurting myself. Get someone else to do the deed. Suicide by murder. Except the thing about my power—the fly in the ointment—is that I have to actually *want* it. I've wanted a lot of terrible things in my life, but the end of it just wasn't something I could muster up enthusiasm for.

I never tried again.

Screw those guys. Screw Neon and her seductive confidence, Indah and her kindness, Marley and his hard-edged/soft-cornered personality that I barely got to know. I don't need them to take over this city. I don't need them to find more people like them.

I need to leave the Sunset Marquis. Management hasn't made any kind of noise, but being in a hotel is too public. Getting up close and personal with the equivalent of the Ghost of Christmas Past has made me squirrely about my own. I don't want to be easy to find.

I don't bother checking out. I leave the meager possessions I did have in the room—consider it my tip to the staff. However, I *do* kindly ask the valet to please bring out my black 1967 Plymouth GTX—a nice convertible I spotted pulling into the hotel the other day. I'm sure whatever douchebag musician is staying at the hotel has plenty of other cars they can use. I have a little trouble navigating the boat-sized car out of the hotel's tiny driveway. After all, it's not like I ever got my license. All my driving experience has been, well, experiential. No taking the family car out for a spin with my dad in the local grocery store parking lot. Like everything else, I did this on my own.

I think about driving west—actually seeing the ocean I came

here weeks ago to see—but Indah lives nearby and Neon's on the east side, and there's something in me that doesn't want to be far from them. I don't know yet if I'm going to go back to Lubitsch. The thought of seeing them again makes my skin crawl. I don't want whatever pity or judgment or platitudes they're going to have for me.

But they're also the only people on the planet—other than Them—who truly know about me and what I can do. And they didn't reject it, or me, out of hand. Maybe I don't have to throw them out entirely. It'd be good to stay close.

I hear the Hollywood Hills are nice.

PART TWO

PART TWO

THE HILLS

"Three . . . two . . . one . . . Happy New Year!"

Raucous cheers come from around me as the tune of "Auld Lang Syne" starts blasting. People around me gather one another into hugs and kisses as they celebrate the arrival of 2007. I see a woman I was speaking to earlier kiss her boyfriend passionately, watch as he dips her until she laughs into his mouth. We had talked about a whole bunch of nothing—the polite conversation of two strangers at a party—but she was wearing a flowery perfume that reminded me of Indah's, and she touched my arm as she laughed at something I said. I find myself wishing she was kissing me instead of the anonymous man with his arms around her. But she's all the way on the other side of the room, so she keeps laughing, swaying in the guy's arms, as I stand alone in the cool January night air.

Another year gone by, the march of time beating unflinchingly forward, and it doesn't matter that I'm standing on a balcony that overlooks the Hollywood Hills, surrounded by bright and shiny people at a party I invited myself to. It doesn't matter that I'm in a house packed full to the brim with bodies. I'm alone.

I try to take comfort in that. Alone is better. Safer. The Hills have been a good place to lie low. Finding out that there are other people like me threw me for a loop that I'm still getting through. I've always been careful about not being found out, but I never had to think about it too much. How can people suspect you of something that shouldn't even be possible?

But if there are other people out there—other Unusuals—then that calculation becomes a bit more complicated. I typically try to steer away from complicated, but I haven't wanted anything as much as I want to find more people like me, like the friends I almost had. But I don't know where to start, so as a caterer with a tray of champagne glasses passes through the balcony doors, I quickly swipe one and try not to think about the Unusuals I already know and how they might be embracing each other in celebration, having forgotten all about me as quick as the woman who smelled like flowers.

Today marks three months in LA and I think I'm really starting to get the swing of things. I've got a spacious house—I think it would easily qualify as a mansion; it's certainly the biggest house I've ever stayed in or seen in real life—on the top of a steep hill and the Plymouth is still purring like the enormous cat it is.

Every morning I wake up. Well, *sometimes* I'm up before noon. I get up, eat breakfast, lunch, whatever, and go for a quick jog around the neighborhood. I tell myself it's because I want to get a look at the area, learn who lives there, but if I were honest with myself, I might admit that being in a city full of beautiful, fit people is starting to get to me. I think of Marley's broad shoulders and look at the way a leather jacket I got on Melrose Place hangs off my chubby frame and feel like I'm playing dress-up. Trying to be someone I'm not. Trying to be the person other people see, the person I *want* other people to see.

In the past, I've been anxious around neighbors. When people get used to seeing you, they start to ask questions. Questions inevitably lead to even more questions, and the re-upping of convincing someone there's nothing to see here is exhausting.

But in LA, people don't care. They see an eighteen-year-old driving around in a fancy car and they assume I'm the newest Hollywood heartthrob or the son of some exec. Hell, most of the neighbors are famous themselves and have no interest whatsoever in having chitchat with the Joneses down the street. It's perfect for lying low, for surviving, but pretty imperfect for having a life.

I'm starting to feel that restlessness again. I thought maybe trying to live life normally would be enough of a departure to keep my mind occupied for a while, give me space to come up with a plan to find more Unusuals. But now that I'm all settled in, no plan has magically appeared in my head. The house is mine for the foreseeable future—I signed a yearlong lease—and I changed out the plates on the car, so I should be good for a little while. I've never *stayed* in a place. Not since Nebraska.

There's a knock on the door. If it were my parents, they wouldn't knock. They have a key. They have *the* key. I never used to carry around a key. For the past week, I've had to. I went through every drawer in the kitchen before finding the spare.

The stranger knocks again. I assume they're a stranger. I suppose it could be a neighbor. Mrs. Henshaw from down the road—maybe her dog got lost in the cornfield again.

I creep toward the door, avoiding the windows that look out onto the porch. When I get to the front door, I press my ear against the wood, listening for any indication of who it might be.

The next knock is right against my ear and I fall flat on my back.

"Hello?" a woman calls. "Is anyone in? It's Ms. Crane from the school."

Shoot. My guidance counselor. I knew the school would eventually get suspicious but I wasn't expecting a home visit.

"Hello?" She knocks again. "Is anyone at home?"

I want her to leave. I want her to leave and forget about me.

She does. And she stays gone. Even when I don't want those things anymore.

———————

I don't know if it's the LA lifestyle, the loneliness I refuse to acknowledge, or the nightmare about Ms. Crane weighing on my mind, but when I pass a therapist's office with "Dr. Crane" on the placard, I find myself walking in. Thirty minutes later, I'm in the middle of my first—and almost certainly my last—therapy session.

"This is something I see a lot with my clients," Dr. Crane says sagely, leaning back in his fashionably modern chair. I should have expected a Hollywood therapist to be unfazed by my bemoaning the restlessness born out of getting everything I want, but his casual approach still bothers me. I'm not the typical Hollywood kid he assumes I am—I'm *extraordinary*. He should realize that.

"Achieving our goals can be a terrifying thing," he continues. "We expect to feel a sense of accomplishment, a sense of satisfaction, but getting things we want can leave us wanting *more* if we're not focused on wanting the right things."

"What does that mean?" I sigh, frustrated. "I don't want more, or the wrong things. I have everything."

"But it doesn't sound to me like you *do* have everything you want," he says, tilting his head in what I'm sure he thinks of as an inviting gesture.

"I don't think you understand," I say flatly, trying to spell it out for him. "Anything I want, I can have. That's the way it's been for almost ten years and it's never going to change."

"But the friends you made—you don't have them."

"What makes you think I want that?" I snap, my cheeks heating.

"The way you talked about them," he says, leaning forward on his elbows. "You said you'd never met people so interesting. Are you saying you don't want to see them again?"

"They're . . ." I fish for an excuse, for a reason to argue with him. The past twenty minutes have been like this—I'm trying to control the conversation, control *him*, but I don't know why I came in here, what I want from him, so he keeps getting the upper hand. But I don't want to use my ability on him, don't want him to acquiesce the way everyone else does.

"They're dangerous," I say finally. "They can find out things about me that I don't want them to know."

"You think they wouldn't like you if they found out certain things?" he suggests.

"No, it's not that," I say, not certain if that's actually the truth. "I just like to control what people know about me."

"You like to control other people," he says simply.

"What?" I snap, nervous. "That's not true, I don't want to control people. I'm not a bad person."

"I never said you were," he says soothingly. "It doesn't make you a bad person to want your friends back. That's a very human thing to feel."

"I'm not human," I mutter, not meaning to, and he blinks in surprise.

"Of course you are, Robert," he says.

"It's supposed to be easy, isn't it?" I ask quietly, half-hoping he won't hear me and we can just move on.

"What, being human?" he asks.

"Everyone else makes it look so easy," I say. "People know how to talk to other people, how to connect, how to be a person. No one ever taught me that. The rules don't apply to me so I never learned."

"Who says you can't learn now?"

"Because the rules still don't apply," I explain. "They're never going to. And no one understands that, no one understands that the things I've done, the things that have happened to me, are out of my control."

"We all feel this way, Robert," he says. "We all feel as if no one will ever understand us—"

"Listen, Dr. Crane," I say, scooting forward on the couch, suddenly irritated, "there's a lot you don't understand about me. You think you get it, think you know what kind of person you're dealing with, but you don't know anything. You could never really understand me. The only people who could were—"

My voice stops itself as Neon's and Indah's faces rise in my head. Suddenly sitting here in this office feels like a terrible waste of time, like an indulgence beyond the mansions and the cars and fancy meals. I don't need to talk things through with some quack; I need to go back to the people who actually *can* understand.

"Another?" the bartender asks, and I nod and give a wobbly thumbs-up. I shouldn't have another. I have had several. And then several more. But it's expensive and free and this bar stool is strangely plush, the wood warm beneath my arms, and I think maybe I'll just stay here forever. I chickened out on my way back to Bar Lubitsch, stopped over at a different bar instead, and started strategizing about finding more Unusuals. But that wasn't enough of a distraction from thinking about Dr. Crane's saying the one thing I wanted was my "friends," and now . . . well. Now I'm very drunk.

"You all right, man?" he asks, setting down the drink next to my head. Oh, I put my head on the bar. That's why he's asking. Not because he genuinely cares. But because he doesn't want some drunk teenager passed out on his bar. Not that he knows that I'm a teenager. But still.

"Yeah," I groan, lifting my head to look at him. He's young, handsome, and tattooed, like Ind—like *all* bartenders in LA. Like it's some code they have to follow. The League of Pretty Tattooed Barkeeps. I giggle at the thought and he lifts a perfectly manicured eyebrow at me. God, LA is such a weird place.

"No, I'm not—" I start to explain, before waving the giggling away with my hand. He takes the wave as a dismissal and starts to move away, but I stop him.

"I don't know what to *do*," I moan, flopping my arms down on the wood.

"Well . . ." He takes a slow step back toward me. "I would start with a glass of water and two aspirin before you go to bed. And then the greasiest breakfast you can find."

"Not *that*. I don't get hangovers," I sniff proudly. A bald-faced lie. I get brutal hangovers. I have no doubt I'm going to have a brutal hangover in about six hours. When it comes down to it, I'm just like everyone else. I can't wish away my pain.

"I mean, in *life*, you know?" I continue earnestly. "I can do whatever I want and I'm just. So. *Lost.*"

Whoops. I didn't mean to say that out loud. Maybe Dr. Crane should install a bar in his office. He might get further faster.

"Whatever you want, huh? Sounds like a pretty nice problem to have," he says, lifting one side of his mouth in a smile as he wipes down the bar. Most of the patrons have left already. It's just me and an old guy at the other end who may or may not be asleep. I have no idea what time it is. I don't even remember what bar I'm *in*. I really shouldn't drive home.

"Yeah, you'd think, right?" I slur. "Total freedom, no worries 'bout money or food or sleeping or—or—or *anything*. But it's not—it's not all it's cracked up to be."

"Yeah, I get it." He nods. "I see a lot of kids in here like you. People who get a lot of fame or money before they're twenty-five and feel all this pressure to do something with it. You just gotta keep working. Focus on your craft, or whatever. Focus on the thing that got you all the money in the first place."

A common misconception. He thinks I'm a celebrity, an artist. I can't take his advice, can't focus on the thing that gave me this life because that thing is *me*. It's just the way I am. There's no external component to it.

"I'm not a kid," I say, because I can't tell him anything else. "Especially not to you. How old are you, anyway?"

"Twenty-six," he preens, and I roll my eyes.

"Oh, and here you are waxing poetic about the experiences of people, like, a year younger than you?" I laugh.

"Well, not all of us have luxury in our twenties." He smiles. "Real life ages you quick."

"Don't I know it," I grumble into my drink.

"What's your deal, then?" he asks, leaning his arms on the bar.

"What do you mean?" I say.

"You a movie star? Rock star? Bel Air kid?" he jokes. "What's your deal?"

"None of those." I shake my head. "I'm just . . ."

He's smiling at me with his whole face, easy and open. There's no way this guy knows about Unusuals. No way telling him anything and then wanting him to forget all about it will harm me. The chances of my seeing him again—once I find out what bar this is and make a point to avoid it in future—are slim. The liquor and loneliness have made me care a lot less about the potential of being discovered, so I decide to let go of the act for a night.

"I'm just a kid from Nebraska who dropped out of high school." I shrug and something starts to catch in my throat. "I've got a tenth-grade education, no family, no job, and everything I could possibly want always at my fingertips."

The bartender has leaned back now, hands still on the bar, and he looks confused, his eyes squinting. It's not as endearing as the crinkle between Indah's eyebrows. I want to push his frown deeper until I see her face.

"And I don't know what I want to do with the rest of my life," I say, horrified to find that tears are gathering at the edges of my eyes. "I want . . . I want . . ."

"What do you like doing?" he asks when it's clear I'm not going to finish that thought, leaning in again, fulfilling my desperate need to be interesting. To be the object of someone's attention.

"I like people," I admit, before I can stop it. I didn't mean to say that. I never would have thought to say that. And yet, there it is, floating on sound waves toward a handsome stranger.

"But me and people . . . ," I continue, swirling the brown liquid around my glass again, "that's a bad mix."

"I don't know," he says, "I think you're doing okay so far."

I look back up at him and see that easy smile on his face. Must be nice. To be handsome and kind and carefree. Getting to talk to different people each night, a bar between you, never having to commit to anything, never having to give too much away.

"Yeah?" I breathe, and his eyes sparkle. What it must be like for him—to know that he's desired, that he has something people want. To see women bat their eyelashes at him for quicker service and then for his attention when they see his face, and to never have to say yes or no. I want that. I want people to try to catch my eye the way that you try to catch the eye of the person pouring drinks at a busy bar.

"Yeah." He nods, moving in closer, and suddenly his lips are on mine. I keep my eyes open, watching his close, as he leans into the kiss. I press back slightly, closing my eyes a bit, seeing what it feels like. It's calm and sweet and warm and not nearly enough. I can smell his aftershave and feel his breath on my skin, and nothing about it feels quite right but it feels like *something*. I wanted connection and here it is. This is playing by the rules of the world, isn't it? This is what people do?

"Whoa." His eyes widen as he pulls back. "I'm not—I mean, not that there's anything wrong with . . . but I'm not *gay*."

"Yeah, neither am I, dude." I shrug, covering up my blush by taking a swig of my drink.

"Oh." He blinks. "Then what was . . . what are you then?"

"Fuck if I know," I snort, feeling strangely sobered by the kiss. "I've never given it much thought to be totally honest." I look into my drink and swirl it around in my hand, feeling a rare self-consciousness as Indah's words—*You can like more than just one*—echo in my head.

"Oh," he repeats. "So, then, was that . . ."

I turn my focus back on him and he looks panicked, bracing for a blow.

"It was nice." I shrug and he relaxes. Ha, guess "not gay" doesn't mean he doesn't have an ego. "But, I don't know, nothing special.

"You didn't really want it," I add quietly, uncertain if that's true. All the wants are jumbled up inside me and I want to fit them into neat boxes but I don't know how.

"What do you mean?"

"Forget about it," I say, and he does. "But I guess *I* wanted it," I mutter. "I must've, on some level, but it wasn't right, you know?"

"Not really . . ."

"Yeah, I guess you wouldn't," I mumble. I shouldn't drink. All my wants get tossed around and distorted and control flutters away.

"So . . . what *do* you want?" he asks, and for a moment I feel like he actually wants to know.

I think of the girl at the New Year's party, the touch of her hand on my arm, her smile pressed into her boyfriend's lips. I wanted her and I didn't. I wanted to *be* her, or him. There are a million desperate people in LA—I could have any one of them, but that doesn't mean I want to. Sometimes I feel like I'm supposed to, but "supposed to" doesn't make my ability work.

"I want it to *mean* something," I say honestly, after a moment.

"Then maybe you should go out and find someone it'll mean something with." He shrugs, pulling up the bottle to refill my glass.

"Yeah . . . I guess I should," I say. "It's just that most people aren't very interesting. They'd have to be interesting."

"Well," he says as he pours me another, "who's the most interesting person you know?"

Ms. Crane really never does come back. But eventually the principal shows up, and I'm so close to choking on the loneliness that I can't keep him away. I don't want to be alone enough.

There's no good reason for me to stay in school. But it's something to do. And there's still a small part of me that thinks if I just stay put, if I stay in Ithaca, They'll come back. They'd want me to stay in school. Or, at least, They would if They ever thought about me at all.

It was fun at first, when my ability first started. When I didn't know what it was or how it worked but I just seemed to always get what I wanted. Dessert before dinner. Then dessert *instead of* dinner. All the toys I could possibly ever want for Christmas. Except then my dad had to sell his truck because suddenly we were in debt. Too many years of buying too many things that I wanted. And he broke his leg trying to get my Frisbee back because I wanted him to come off the roof *right now*, shouting and crying directly under the eaves, barely having time to move out of the way as he plummeted to the ground. And then Mom was mean to Mrs. Henshaw because I was afraid of her dog and wanted Mrs. Henshaw to stay away. Wanting something should be a binary equation—you should either get it or not. There shouldn't be *con-*

sequence. And even when I realized that there was, I didn't know how to *not* want things.

I wanted Them to leave, so they did. But I didn't want Them to stay away. That They chose on Their own.

"Indaaaaahh," I singsong, throwing my arms out and nearly toppling off the bar stool.

"This your boy?" the bartender asks from behind me.

"I guess so," she drawls, coming toward me. She's wearing Neon's leather jacket, which perfectly matches the frown on her face, the familiar crinkles in her brow lighting up my brain.

"I'm glad to see you," I slur.

"Mm-hm," she says, crossing her arms.

"I've gotta lock up—"

"Yeah, I can take him from here," Indah says over my shoulder. "How many have you had?"

"Lots." I grin. "I had some and then he kissed me"—I sweep an arm back in the direction of the bartender—"and it was just okay and then we started talking about who I thought was interesting and I got sad about missing Neon and so I had some more and here you are!"

"Why didn't you call Neon?" She glowers.

"I don't have her number," I tell her. "I don't have *your* number either. I don't have a phone. But I told him you work at Bar Lubitsch and—"

"And here I am," she sighs.

"You came for me." I smile, spinning slowly on the stool. Nope, bad idea. I stop the motion by slamming my arm on the bar and Indah flinches.

"I don't know why," she mumbles.

"You came for me," I talk over her, "and I wasn't even there to make you want to do it! You came all on your own." I'm grinning big at her and she sighs again before taking a few steps toward me.

"Come on, Robbie," she says, reaching an arm out. "Let's get you home."

"*Robbie*," I spit. "Ugh, I hate that name. You know I hate that name, why would you call me that?"

"To annoy you," she says simply.

"But you shouldn't be able to." I blink blearily, sliding out of the stool and into Indah's open arm. I trip a bit over my own feet and Indah catches me, looping her arm around my torso in a half hug. It's nice.

"What?" she asks, guiding me to the door.

"Nice talking to you, man," the bartender calls. "Get home safe."

"Yeah, s'nice," I slur in his general direction.

"Oh," Indah says, catching up, "because of your power. Yeah, how's that work out for you when you're this trashed?"

"I dunno." I shrug, nearly toppling us as we exit the bar. "Never been this trashed before."

"Trust me, after tomorrow morning, you won't get this drunk again for a *long* time."

"It's gonna be bad, huh?" I grimace as Indah leans me up against her car.

"Oh yeah." She nods and I groan. All this walking from the bar stool to the door to the curb has made me dizzy, and the next thing I know, I'm sitting in the passenger seat, and thankfully Indah takes it upon herself to put the seat belt around me.

"'Beautiful one' . . ." I giggle. "You're so pretty." Her face is only a few inches from mine as she reaches across me and the orange light from the street is warming her brown skin in a way that makes her seem even more touchable than usual.

She huffs a laugh as she clicks the seat belt, and the wry smile she's wearing pushes up her cheeks and creates new shadows on her face. I want so badly to kiss her in that moment, to have something that matters, so I do.

"Whoa." She's pushing at my chest seconds after my lips touch hers, tearing me away from the tantalizing warmth, the smell of her perfume. I flop back into the seat as my eyes try to focus on her confused expression. "What the hell do you think you're doing?"

"I'm sorry," I slur. "I just—you're so beautiful and you're so nice to me and I just wanted—I wanted it to matter."

She sighs, shaking her head, that familiar furrow pulling down her eyebrows.

"Wrong tree, remember?" she says simply, her voice and smile tight as she pats me on the chest before moving to put her own seat belt on.

"Am I really not your type?" I ask, settling back into the chair and wondering how I can convince her to let me kiss her when I don't have the sobriety to use my ability.

"You're a man, so . . . no," she says, sounding irritated as she turns the engine on and shifts into drive.

"Wait . . ." I blink a few times, adjusting to the sudden movement of the car. "I thought you said you didn't just like one."

"I said it's *possible.* And I meant it when I said emo white boys weren't my type." She glances over at me, the ghost of a laugh on her lips. "But boys in general aren't my type."

"Oh," I say, wrong-footed and disappointed.

"Even if I did like both, you can't just go around kissing people," she says, the familiar scolding tone bringing me back down to earth.

"I'm sorry," I say again, and I think I actually mean it.

"Just don't do it again," she tells me sternly, and I nod enthusiastically, wanting to do whatever I can to avoid Indah's looking at me the way she is right now, like she's both disappointed and angry.

We drive along in silence, the streetlights flashing by my eyes, making me dizzy. I'm about to ask Indah to pull over, afraid I'm going to get sick, when she speaks again, her voice distracting me from the roiling in my gut.

"I was talking about Neon," she explains. "Neon's the one who likes both. She likes everyone really," she grumbles.

"And that's a problem?"

"No, not at all." She shakes her head. "It's not a problem for Neon. It's sometimes a problem for me."

"The 'not girlfriends' thing?" I guess, leaning my head back against the seat.

"Yeah." She nods, glancing over her shoulder before she merges left. "Neon is sort of impossible to tie down. And it's hard not to get jealous when she's had a thing at some point with basically everyone we hang out with."

Indah's voice is sharp, cutting through the fog gathering in my brain.

"You mean . . ." I flounder. "Her and Marley?"

"Mm-hm." She nods, lips pursed. "Mostly before I met them, but every now and then . . ."

"Huh," I say, because it feels like it's my turn to make sounds. I get the feeling that Indah wants something from me in this moment but I'm not sure what it is. I'm not used to the wanting going the other way.

"Maybe you should find someone who just likes girls then," I offer. "Less . . . competition."

"Don't let Neon hear you say that," Indah scolds, and I shrink into the seat a bit more, feeling like I did something wrong without meaning to again. Indah clocks it and rolls her eyes and sighs.

"Neon's problem isn't that she likes everyone," Indah explains. "That's not a problem. People can like whoever they want to like. Her problem is that she's too terrified to commit to *anyone*."

I nod like I know exactly what we're talking about.

"And," Indah says, sighing again, "maybe that's not even a problem. I don't know. But she's always the one that's calling the shots and sometimes I just wish . . ."

Indah is talking mostly to herself at this point, and I want to reach out and comfort her but the motion of the car is starting to get to me and moving at all seems like a bad idea at the moment.

"Maybe *I'm* the problem," she mutters. "Neon's allowed to do what she wants. Just because it doesn't match up with what *I* want doesn't mean it's a problem."

She shakes her head and flexes her hands on the steering wheel, sitting up straighter.

"You're in love with her," I say, not even a question.

"Yeah," Indah sighs.

"And she's not in love with you?" I ask, and she winces.

"I don't know who Neon is in love with," she says softly.

"I'm sorry," I say, trying to follow a script I've never performed before.

"Eh." She shrugs. "I knew what I was getting into with her. Falling for a free spirit only ends in heartbreak."

The first time she saw her, Indah knew Neon was trouble.

It was like something out of a movie. Indah was sitting on a café patio when a motorcycle pulled up to the curb. The driver took off their helmet to reveal the most beautiful face Indah had ever seen. As the stunning, leather-clad figure walked past and into the café, she noticed Indah openly staring and threw her a lopsided smile. Goose bumps appeared over Indah's arms.

It was the instant attraction that masked Neon's nature from Indah at first. Not until Neon chose a table on the patio a few feet away from Indah did she realize that the goose bumps weren't just because a gorgeous girl looked her way—it was her unique sensitivity, her sixth sense, telling her that Neon was special. That's what ultimately drove Indah to be bold enough to go talk to her. She didn't usually approach strangers with gifts, but she had a feeling deep in her gut that whatever Neon could do, it wasn't dangerous.

Indah was wrong. Neon's power is one of the most dangerous she's ever seen. But Indah has never felt threatened by it. For her, the most dangerous thing is that lopsided smile.

I hear the whoosh of the corn stalks before I see them. I'm running through the fields, chasing something. The stalks are high and I'm surrounded by them on all sides. The only sounds I can hear are the crinkling of the ground beneath me and the whisper of the plants as I brush past them.

"Robert!" my mother calls from far away. I'm running, running, running, running, farther and farther, faster and faster. I'm miles from her. Leagues. Light-years.

"Robert!" she calls again, somehow closer than before. This is a game we play. I go running, my parents come chasing. They always find me.

The sun is setting and the moon is hiding. It's growing dark, the stalks so high I can't see the stars.

"Robert!" She's so far away now and I'm not sure I can get back to her. Her voice is coming from all sides and from no side at all. If I stop running, I'll be lost in the dark. So I keep running.

"Robert!"

I snap awake to find Indah's face hovering over mine.

"Robert, you were, like, thrashing around, I wasn't sure—"

I sit up on my elbows, swinging my legs to the living room floor.

"God," I groan, "what is it about sleeping on your couch that gives me nightmares about my parents?"

"Your parents?" Indah sits down next to me and I put my head in my hands. "Sorry," she says, backpedaling. "Sensitive subject?"

"No, it's—my *head*," I moan into my hands. Now that the adrenaline has worn off . . . "God*damn*, what did I drink last night?"

"The whole bar as far as I could tell," Indah says dryly.

I just groan again, words too difficult to form.

"Come on." Indah gently pats me on the back. "Let's get some food into you."

Two hours later and I'm clawing my way back to feeling a little bit human. I am never drinking again.

"I'm never drinking again," I say aloud to Indah, who is lying on the ground next to me. After pouring me into her car and picking up breakfast burritos while I sat in the passenger seat and tried not to throw up, Indah took me to Barnsdall Art Park, handed me an enormous bottle of water, and told me to "lie in the sun, motionless, like a cat, until the pain stops." I don't love being told what to do—as I'm the one who usually does the telling—but, goddamn, she was right.

"People always say that," she says into the sky, eyes closed behind her sunglasses.

"Yeah, well I mean it."

"What spurred the great binge-drink of 2007 anyway?" she asks, turning onto her side and propping herself up on her elbow to peer down at me.

"Nothing." I shrug, my shoulders digging into the grass. "It was just something to do."

"And what exactly *have* you been doing these past few months, Robert?" Indah asks, unable to keep the sharp edge of judgment out of her voice.

"Oh, you know, just using my horrible ability on unsuspecting people," I snap. "The usual stuff."

"Don't give me that, Robbie," she says, and I barely stop myself from flinching. My ability is dulled by the hangover, my innate distaste for the nickname buried somewhere it can't reach Indah. "*You're* the one who reacted badly," she continues, narrowing her eyes at me. "We were just trying to get used to what you can do and you decided to paralyze all of us and storm out. You never even gave us a chance."

"I didn't have to," I say, closing my eyes to the sun above me and the heat of Indah's stare. "I could see how things were going to play out. You would have turned on me eventually."

"Have you ever told anyone about your ability before?" she asks.

"No," I admit begrudgingly. "But, c'mon, it doesn't take a genius to figure out how most people are going to react."

"We're not most people," she retorts. "We're *exactly* the kind of people who are going to understand. We'd understand *all* of it," she finishes pointedly, and the specter of talking about what Marley saw makes me snap.

"Please," I scoff, throwing her a look, "just because you can sense people like us doesn't make you one of us."

The pain in my head flares again as silence rings between us.

"Wow," Indah breathes after a moment. "You really have no idea how to be someone's friend, do you?"

That stings more than I'd care to admit, so I just turn my eyes away from Indah and resist staring directly into the sun.

We lie there in silence for the next hour or so—at first tense, then slackening into something less loaded as Indah drifts in and out of sleep and the sun starts to dry the alcohol out of me—until Indah abruptly sits up and proclaims that it's time to go.

"You're too pale to be sitting out in the sun for too long," she elaborates.

"Where are we going?" I ask, climbing gingerly to my feet.

"Are you still at the Sunset Marquis?"

"Not exactly."

The look on Indah's face as we pull up to my house is one I've never seen from her before. Part disgusted, part impressed.

"You've got to be kidding me," she murmurs under her breath, and then, louder, "*This* is your house?"

She spins around to look at me, hands clenched on her steering wheel. I shrug.

"You are a piece of work, Robert Gorham," she mutters, shaking her head but unable to keep a small smile from blooming across her face.

Marley is having a bad day. And when Marley has a bad day, there's only one person in the entire world he wants to talk to.

"Neon, let me in," he calls, pounding on her apartment door. He should have texted her before showing up out of the blue—things have been tense between them since Blaze went AWOL and they had that weird scuff-up with the new guy, and Marley feels like he's not automatically entitled to her space anymore—but he's out of minutes, with no money left to buy more this month. Maybe he could have called her from the library pay phone, but he didn't think of it in his urgency to see her. Marley really just needs Neon to let him put his head in her lap while she runs her hands over his buzz cut.

"Neon!" he shouts louder, and finally, *finally*, Marley hears the click of a lock.

"What?" she snaps before the door is even open. "What the *hell* do you want, Marley? I was *sleeping*."

Marley pushes past her and flops onto the couch—now that the door is open, he has free rein. They're family, after all.

"I completely bombed my midterm," he moans toward the ceiling, head leaned back on the cushions. "I just really can't go back to my horribly empty apartment and think about how I can't call Blaze to come over and how he's normally the one that does flash cards with me and how the fact that he wasn't there to do that this time meant that I failed and that's the least of our worries because the kid hasn't called in two months and I'm pretty sure he's dead."

Marley doesn't really mean to say that last bit.

Marley is having a *really* bad day.

Much to my surprise, Indah stays the night. She sleeps in one of the three bedrooms that the house has. One slightly higher on the sloped plane of the house, overlooking the tops of trees, sunlight always streaming in in the mornings. I played Goldilocks for the first two weeks after I moved in, sleeping in each bedroom for a few nights at a time, trying to find the one that was *juuuust* right. Indah's room—somehow already *her* room even though she's only slept in it for a few hours—was my nightmare for exactly the reason that it was her dream.

"Rob, that bedroom is a *dream*." She yawns, walking into the kitchen, still sleepy and even more pliable than usual. Something in me softens at the sight. I like how comfortable she seems in my space, how comfortable she seems with *me*. Not at all afraid.

"Really?" I ask. "I couldn't stand that room. Too much sunlight."

"You're crazy," she says. "Waking up to natural sunlight is *such* a luxury. If I could do that every day, I just know I'd be a better person. But no, my bedroom window just looks out onto a brick wall."

"Indah, you work at night," I argue. "Don't you sleep until noon like the rest of us?"

"Is that why you don't like that bedroom?" she laughs. "Because you're sleeping until noon every day?"

"I'm a nineteen-year-old who doesn't need to work or go to school and gets to do whatever he wants. Of *course* I'm sleeping until noon every day."

Indah just laughs some more again, and that's its own kind of sunlight.

"Wait," she says, interrupting her own laughter, "did you have a birthday?"

"Oh," I say dumbly. "Yeah. It was last week."

"Oh, Robert," she breathes, and I can hear the apologies, the platitudes coming, and immediately change the subject. I'm not ready to tell her how I spent my nineteenth birthday eating a grocery-store cake and letting the darkness close in on me because I was too paralyzed to get up and turn on the lights once the sun went down.

"Want an omelet?" I offer, turning away from her to open the fridge, and also so I don't have to look directly at her bright, pitying face. I'm feeling soft and vulnerable, and on top of all that, I'm still embarrassed about trying to kiss her the other night. She hasn't said anything about it and I sure as hell am not going to, so I want to make sure we steer as far away from serious subjects as possible.

"You cook?" she asks skeptically.

"It's one of the few things I actually know how to do," I admit, rooting through the fridge for the eggs, ham, and veggies. "When you live ten miles from the nearest grocery store and your feet can't reach the pedals of a car, you learn how to fend for yourself. I can make about fifty different recipes just using corn."

I close the refrigerator door to find the light of the sun snuffed out. Indah is looking at me with an expression I've never seen on her. The pity is still there, but also what seems like genuine, delighted surprise at my sharing something of myself unprompted.

"How do you feel about Denver?" I ask, deflecting again, uncertain how I managed to move from pathetic birthday to tragic backstory. I focus all my attention on wanting her to not ask about any of it. So, of course, she doesn't.

"Never been," she says, a flicker of annoyance flying across her face before it smooths over. She's starting to notice the moment my ability finds its way to her. But then, of course, the knowing washes away with the annoyance and she continues like nothing happened. "Why?"

"Denver omelets," I say, tossing the ingredients on the counter, and Indah's eyes light up, pleased. I put a pan on the stove and light one of the burners, the motions second nature.

"So," I say as I start cracking eggs into a bowl, "who were you talking to this morning?"

My heart beats faster as I ask, not wanting Indah to think I was listening in on her conversation. But as I crept into the kitchen to make coffee, I could hear a low murmur coming from her room. I want to know if she called Neon, if she and Marley know that I'm back in their orbit now.

"What?" Indah asks, and I turn around to see genuine confusion on her face. I'm about to clarify, tell her I overheard her without making it sound creepy, when it seems to click for her.

"*Oh.*" She nods. "I was praying."

"What?"

"Praying," she repeats. "You know, that thing that people of faith sometimes do . . ."

"Oh, right," I say blankly. "Praying. Of course." I turn back to the eggs, wanting her to say more. And, lo and behold:

"Five times a day," she continues. "It's hard to pull off sometimes at the bar, or to get up at dawn, what with my hours, but I do my best."

"Five times *a day*?" I ask, aghast, turning back to her and leaning against the counter behind me.

"Yep." She smiles, unfazed by my bug-eyed expression.

"So you pray five times a day, you can't drink, but you don't wear the . . . the—" I make the clumsy gesture I made when we first met, all the more humiliating in my sobriety.

"The hijab?" Indah quirks an eyebrow at me and I'm horrified to find myself blushing. "No, I don't. I used to, but I haven't for a long time."

"Why not?" I ask.

"Let me guess," she starts, staring me down. "You think that Islam is all about oppression and terrorism and—"

"No, no, of course not," I hurry to say. "I don't think you're a terrorist. I mean, I never thought that. Ever. You don't even look, you know . . ." I trail off awkwardly and now Indah is the one with the red face, but I have a feeling it's not because she's embarrassed.

"Good lord, Robert," she says, jaw tightening. "Are you saying I don't look like a terrorist because I'm not Middle Eastern?"

"No," I say, floundering, "no, I just meant . . . well, because you're . . . you know . . ."

"I'm what?" she says, and I want to shrink back into the counter-top and disappear. I'm trying—trying to understand, trying to learn more about her—but I'm terrified to ask.

Indah sighs heavily before inhaling deeply and flatly giving me all the information I could want.

"I'm Indonesian, I was raised in a very religious household and departed from it pretty strongly when I was a teenager. No hijab, drinking, smoking, a lot of stuff that's haram—that means 'sinful, forbidden,'" she explains before I have a chance to ask. "Then I moved here and grew up a bit and reconnected with my faith in my own way. I still pray, I don't drink, but I also work in a bar and have sex with women, so, you know, my faith is not the same as a lot of Muslims' faith."

I swallow, childishly self-conscious at the mention of sex, and nod like I completely understand. After a moment, I pour the eggs into the now-hot pan, the sizzling filling the awkward silence between us.

"You know," Indah continues after a moment, the same tighten-ing in her voice that I heard last night, "if you had just asked—actu-ally had a conversation with me about it—I would have told you all of that. In my own way. My own time. You didn't need to use your ability on me."

"I can't control it, okay?" I say sheepishly, but her eyes flash at the excuse.

"Is that really true, Robert?" she asks.

"I . . . I don't know," I answer truthfully.

"That's not good enough, Rob," she says, shaking her head. "It doesn't—it's *confusing* and scary when that happens, don't you get that? It feels like going into a trance."

"It does?" I ask, horrified at the idea that she can feel it. "Well, I don't—I don't always notice when it's happening. I just—I wanted to know more about you, so . . ."

"So I gave you the CliffsNotes version of something incredibly personal and private." She's scowling at me now, arms crossed as she leans back in her chair.

"Yeah . . . ," I say, mad at myself for opening this can of worms and wishing we could just move past this thorny subject. But my curiosity about Indah overrides my discomfort.

"How does it work for you?" I ask, a direct question for once.

"How does what work?" She narrows her eyes at me suspiciously.

"The thing you do," I explain. "You said you know when someone is an Unusual. How does that work?"

"I don't really know," she says, shrugging. "I've always been this way. My grandma always said I was touched by God."

"Do you think that's true?" I ask, dubious and completely out of my depth. *They* believed in God, so when They left, They took Him with Them.

"I think that there's a reason I can sense people like you," she says serenely. "I think it's part of my purpose. Neon, Marley, and Blaze—and now you—I think it's my job to protect you all. To love you."

My throat tightens at her words, so close to coming right out and saying that she loves *me*, specifically. I focus on the stove in front of me, completely unequipped to respond to Indah's certainty and goodness.

"It feels like God," she continues softly, answering my want for her to keep talking so I don't have to. "I've thought about trying to seek them out—go around and try to find more Unusuals—but you can't seek out faith. Faith finds you. Just like you did."

She smiles warmly at me and I'm filled with a deep need to touch her, to be touched by her, wrapped in her arms and soothed. But after the disastrous kiss attempt, I don't know how to want it well, so I want for her to change the subject instead.

And she does. We move on, like nothing ever happened. We cook and eat and talk about what she's been doing the past few months—

more of the same, it sounds like—and we avoid all the heavy subjects. Indah seems to have forgotten all about my clumsy invasion of her private life, because she brings up Neon completely on her own.

"We were supposed to get lunch today," she tells me. "It's both of our days off, so . . ."

"Date night?" I ask. "Or, rather, date *day*, I guess."

"I don't know," she sighs. "She's been spending a lot of time with Marley recently."

"Don't the three of you always spend a lot of time together?" I ask, still baffled by the dynamic of the group. I'm baffled by the dynamic of *any* group, having never really been in one myself, but one that contains a whole bunch of Unusuals seems like it would be even more complicated.

"Yeah, we do," she says, nodding. "Marley and I have never really clicked though. He's a nice guy, and really reliable, but . . . I don't know," she finishes, looking sad.

"Well, it's gotta be kind of weird, right? With you and Neon and him and Neon . . ."

"That's part of it, I guess." She shrugs. "But honestly, Neon might be the one thing Marley and I *do* see eye to eye on. She's about the only thing we have in common."

"How about Blaze?" I ask. "What's his deal?"

"Pyrokinetic, like we told you, a bit of a temper. Has been on his own about as long as you have, I think," she says, turning her gaze onto me. "But, um, how long would that be exactly?"

"What?" I ask, pretending I don't know the question.

"How long have you been on your own?"

She asks it casually, moving her eyes away from me and focusing on taking another sip of coffee. But I can feel the tension in the air, the stakes of asking about my past.

I wonder if she knows. I wonder if she knows that I'm barely using my ability on her right now, that there's nothing I really want from her in this moment. After we sat for a while and she filled up on caffeine and eggs, Indah was beginning to relax again, and I started to relax in kind. But tension is starting to creep into her shoulders, like she's ready to get up and run off at any second. That idea hurts me more than I'd ever tell her. I don't think she's wrong for being afraid of me, of what I can do, but the fear still hurts.

"A while," I say finally, choosing something I've never chosen before: vulnerability.

"What's 'a while'?" she prods.

"Since I was thirteen," I tell her, and her eyes widen.

"Oh," she breathes. "What . . . what happened?"

I could tell her. Even though I haven't seen her in months and was just barely beginning to become friends with her before I ran away, I feel like I know Indah. I know that if I told her the whole sob story, she'd listen attentively, nod along at the right parts, and then her heart would bleed all over me. She would be sympathetic, would maybe even touch my arm, give me a hug, tell me how sorry she is that I've been alone for so long. And the whole time, even if I were wrapped in her embrace, having soothing words whispered into my ear, I would wonder if any of it was real. I want that affection so badly, but in the cold light of day, that desire feels unseemly. I hate that dark little part of me that craves comfort, craves a soft hand and a warm body, but as much as I despise it, I can't destroy it. It rules me, and I rule everyone else.

So I say nothing at all. I turn around to put my coffee mug in the sink, hiding my face and trying to bury that ugly desire for pity somewhere deep. When I look back at Indah, her face is blank, waiting.

"Come on," I say, forcing a smile, "let's get you to your date."

Indah drops me back at my car, still haunting the bar I left two days ago, before driving off to meet Neon. Before she goes, she gives me her number and tells me to call.

"Neon and Marley still talk about you, you know," she says just as I put my hand on the car door to step out. "They'll be happy to know you're okay."

"I don't know why they'd care," I snap, having a hard time believing that she's being honest. There's no way Marley is still thinking about me—that's wishful desire on my part, and nothing else.

"I know you don't, Rob," she sighs, and I wait for her to say
something else. But she stares silently through the windshield, her
foot still on the brake, ready to drive away the moment I get out of
the car.

So I do. I go to sit in my own car, where I stare through my
windshield, wondering what she meant by that and why I didn't ask
for more. Why I didn't stick around for the unvoiced questions to
be answered.

"Why won't you talk to us, Robbie?" my mother coos.

I don't answer her. She does this every night now. Stands in the
doorway of my room like she's afraid to cross the threshold. Like
she's afraid that if she comes too close to her son, he'll open his
mouth and swallow her whole. So I've kept my mouth closed, not
said a word in almost an entire week, terrified of what might happen if I express any thought or feeling out loud.

"Please, darling," she pleads, "just tell us what's going on."

But I can't. I can't tell her because if I speak, she might end up
doing something like stepping off a roof and breaking her leg, and
I don't want to hurt anyone else. I just want to be left alone. I want
my parents—I want *everyone*—to leave me alone.

I didn't know it at the time, but saying it out loud wasn't the
trick. It was simply wanting it at all. If I had known that then, I
would have done everything I could to stop myself from wanting
to be left.

As it was, I got my wish.

"I shouldn't have just up and left like that," I say, head bowed in con-
trition. I don't know that I completely believe the words I'm saying,
but I want *them* to believe it, so they will. "I just . . . I've never had anyone know about me—the whole truth about me—so I got spooked."

We're back at Neon's apartment, Indah perched on the arm of

the couch, looking at me encouragingly, as the yin-yang pairing of Neon and Marley sits silently, arms crossed, giving me twin blank stares.

"I'm sorry," I finish, the words feeling misshapen and foreign in my mouth.

A long silence follows in which I see everyone's shoulders and faces soften—my desire for them to forgive me, to let me back in the group, is working, when suddenly—

"Jesus!" I cry, jumping at the sudden zap that hits my arm.

"Sorry, kid," Neon says, unrepentant. She stands, hand still crackling with blue electricity, and pats me on the shoulder. I try to flinch away but when she makes contact, nothing happens.

"It's purely decorative at the moment," she says. "I'm not going to shock you again."

"Why did you have to shock me in the first place?" I ask, rubbing my arm, which is still buzzing with a phantom sensation.

"I needed to make sure you weren't using your power on us," she calmly explains, walking into her kitchen.

"So you *electrocuted* me?"

"It worked the first time," she calls out. I look at Indah for support. She just rolls her eyes and follows Neon into the kitchen, pushing her aside to take over drink-making duties. Marley is smiling to himself, the first time I've ever seen him look amused. It doesn't make me any less nervous to be in his presence.

"Everyone's just cool with this then?" I throw my hands up in the air before flopping down on the couch next to Marley.

"It's not real forgiveness if you force it," Marley says.

"Well, how about me?" I snarl, wanting to back away from him any time his gaze shifts to me. "You hurt my feelings too and I don't see anyone apologizing for it."

I want to take back the words the moment I say them, but unfortunately my ability doesn't serve as time travel. If it weren't for Neon's electricity still coursing through me, maybe I could make Marley forget that I've said them, but instead, unprompted, he gives me something I want even more, saying, "I'm sorry," and sounding like he means it.

"*Genuinely*. I'm sorry," he says again, shaking his head and closing his eyes. "I shouldn't have used your past like that. As a weapon against you."

"Can you . . . can you stop looking?" I ask, a genuine question.

"Mostly," he says. "But there are times when it just appears before I can stop it. I can keep it to myself though."

"Yeah." I nod. "Yeah, that'd be good. Thanks."

"Can you try to not use your power on us?" Neon says from behind me. I tilt my head up to find her upside-down face looking down at me, her hair falling around me like a curtain.

"I can try," I say, not sure if I'm telling the truth or not.

"That's good enough," she proclaims, handing drinks to Marley and me. "For now," she adds ominously.

She and Indah come around the couch, Indah taking up her perch on the armrest and Neon plopping down on the coffee table.

"Look, you're one of us, Rob," she says seriously, staring straight into my eyes. "There aren't a lot of us in this world and we need to stick together. But being an Unusual isn't a free pass, okay? We all still have to do our best to be good people."

"Okay," I agree, even though I'm a little annoyed that Neon, a woman maybe five years older than me, is talking to me like I'm her kid. But the annoyance is crowded out by gratitude that I get to have this again. People who know me—*actually* know me—and seem to want me around anyway. Getting shocked by Neon from time to time (which I have a feeling is going to be happening semi-frequently) doesn't feel like such a bad price to pay. And I think that, maybe, deep down, I actually want to be good.

"To the Unusuals," Marley says with a grin, raising his cup.

"To family," Neon follows, her signature smirk replaced by a grave expression.

"To family," I echo, my arm rising as I swallow around the words. I look over at Indah, who is smiling softly at me, and I pledge to myself that I won't make the same mistakes with this family as I did with my other.

––––––––––

Neon isn't sure she trusts Robert. He smiles sweetly and says sorry and it sounds like he means it, but she's still not sure she can trust him. Anyone else and the little scuff-up they all had would have been long forgotten. Hell, Neon's said worse things to Blaze's face, gotten into it way worse with Marley, but they're her family. They fight and they scrap and they forgive each other.

Neon doesn't know how to be family with the kid. She likes him, thinks he's clever and funny, unpredictable and smart, in a way that makes him feel like a kindred spirit. But she's lived in LA for years now, has met plenty of charming, quick young men who don't have to face the ugliness of the world. She knows what that can do to a person over time.

Still, when he apologizes, contrite and so clearly wanting to be forgiven, Neon can't help it. She was a lost soul too once, angry and alone, and it was only Marley's acceptance that started to soften her edges. She could have written Marley off—a stoic white guy three times her size with a skinhead haircut and silent, unwavering stare—but she didn't. She didn't write him off because he was special, like her, and trusting him turned out to be the best decision she'd ever made.

If she could accept Marley despite his menacing appearance, simply because he was Unusual, surely doing the exact reverse with Robert is another good decision.

Tentatively, I'm folded back into the Unusuals' lives. It occurs to me that I really didn't know anything about them before blowing the whole thing to hell—I walked out on the very first night I even met Marley. That same night, I found out that Neon didn't actually make a living from looking badass and smoking in back rooms of music clubs, so I start spending time at the bike shop, watching her do repairs.

"You like doing this?" I ask, watching the grease climb up her arms over the course of an hour.

"Hell yeah, dude." She grins. "I've always loved taking stuff apart and putting it back together, and then when my, you know"—she looks around to make sure no one's listening—"*thing* started up, I figured out how to use it to fix the things that no one else could."

"But it's so . . ." I crinkle my face in distaste at the scene around me. We're in a garage, its large door open, a cool breeze fluttering in, carrying dust and leaves with it, that mingles with the smell of oil and exhaust. Neon's hair is bundled at the back of her neck, tied with a bandana, and the grease on her arms has left trails on her neck and face and clothes. She's a mess and she looks thrilled about it.

"Ooh, I didn't realize I was dealing with such a dainty young man," she teases.

"I just don't like getting my hands dirty," I say.

"Didn't you grow up in the Midwest?" she asks. "Doesn't everyone there, like, milk cows or whatever?"

"And you guys think *I'm* ignorant," I joke, and she huffs a laugh. "No, we didn't all 'milk cows or whatever.' There's plenty of cities in the Midwest, you know. The coasts didn't invent urban living."

"You know what I mean," she says, rolling her eyes. "I thought you grew up in the country."

"What made you think that?" I ask.

"Everything about you," she says, her voice getting lost in the inner workings of a motorcycle as she leans forward to reach her hands back inside.

"Well . . . ," I start, not sure why I contradicted her in the first place. "Yeah, you're right," I sigh in resignation, and she pauses her work to look over the bike at me. "I grew up in a little nowheresville in Nebraska. My family didn't have cows, but we did have acres and acres of cornfields."

"See?" She smiles. "I knew you were a country boy. Here, come down and hold this for me."

The clinking of metal starts up again as she dives back into the bike, and I breathe deep, swallowing in relief and surprise. In the past thirty seconds, I told Neon more about myself than I've ever told anyone. And she took it all in stride like it was nothing. Maybe it *is* nothing. The circumstances of my upbringing aren't at all extraordinary. I recognized that on some level, but to have my biography so casually received, especially by someone who knows the truth about me, is comforting all the same.

I join Neon down on the floor and she hands me a bent bit of metal, covered in grease. I grimace and she laughs, which makes the slippery oil on my fingers easier to bear.

"Hey, sunshine."

Both Neon and I look up to see a handsome, impeccably dressed man grinning down at us.

"Hey, Nick," Neon replies, turning back to her task.

"Nice to see you," he says, and Neon just "mm-hm"s in response. He glances quickly at me, the smile still on his face as he runs his hand through his floppy blond hair.

"Do you know if my bike is ready?" he asks, staring at the back of Neon's head like that's going to will her to pay attention to him. God, to be an ordinary person. I might have a complicated relationship with my ability, but sometimes I really do feel bad for the suckers who don't have it.

"I think so. Check with Cal."

He nods and moves through the garage and into the shop behind us to talk to the owner, a burly man who seems to communicate exclusively in two-word sentences but whom Neon speaks fondly about.

"Who's that?" I ask, jerking my head toward the back of the man, Nick.

"One of our regulars. He has a vintage bike that he does *not* know how to take care of, so he's in here a lot."

"Hm."

"What?" Neon asks, squinting at me.

"Nothing." I shake my head. "I don't know, I don't like the way he was looking at you."

"Whatever." She snorts, her attention centered on the motorcycle in front of her instead of on me.

I sit back on my now-dirty hands, watching Neon use tools I don't have names for like they're extensions of her own limbs. Every now and again, I catch sight of a tiny blue spark, lighting up the inside of the bike and the smirk on Neon's face when she sees me noticing. With every lift of her mouth in my direction, my stomach swoops and my heart rate picks up. Suddenly, I don't mind the grease on my fingers so much.

Eventually, Nick comes back—apparently his motorcycle needs another day before it's fully repaired—and starts to ask inanely about what Neon is doing. I may not know anything about motorcycles, but even I can tell that this guy knows less than me.

"It's pretty sexy, you know," he says, smiling slyly at Neon. "A woman who looks like you *and* knows her way around a hog."

My body is grappling with the warring impulses of gagging, rolling my eyes, and sticking my leg out to trip Nick when Neon responds.

"Yeah, my girlfriend thinks so too." She grins up at him and I'm disappointed to see that it just makes Nick smile more.

"Girlfriend, huh?" he croons. "Does she look anything like you?"

"She's the pretty one," Neon says, refocusing on the bike, and Nick takes a smooth step toward her. I'm suddenly keenly aware of the fact that we're in a pretty vulnerable position—both seated on the floor, Nick older and bigger and stronger. Neon doesn't seem at all concerned, but she's also not looking at his leering eyes and sharklike smile.

"You don't say," he flirts. "Well, how about you and your *girlfriend* . . ."

Neon's shoulders are tensing, her jaw clenching, and I suddenly remember exactly who we are. Nick may be towering over us, but we're *us* and we have no reason to be afraid.

Just as I'm about to stand up and tell the guy to get lost, I realize the garage has gone silent. Nick trailed off without saying whatever slimy thing he was about to say, and Neon's looking at me with inquisitive eyes.

"I, uh," Nick stammers, "I don't remember what I was going to say. I think I should probably go."

"I think that'd be smart." I grin back, showing him all my teeth in a mockery of his smile that I know he probably considers to be charming.

Nick just nods and turns on his heel, walking toward the edge of the garage. But before he crosses out of the shade of the garage door, he pauses and calls back.

"I'm sorry for being such a dick all the time," he says flatly. "I'll try to do better." And with that, he walks away, his increasingly distant footsteps only interrupted by Neon's bursting into laughter.

"Oh my *god*, Rob," she cackles, "that was *priceless*. Did you make him do that?"

"I wanted him to leave," I say simply, shrugging one shoulder.

"You know that's not what I meant." She sighs happily, the laughter loosening her whole body.

"He was being a creep," I explain. "And I have the feeling that's not the first time he's done that to you."

"It definitely was not."

"So, yeah, I figured you deserved an apology."

Neon stares at me, a small smile on her face, an unreadable look in her eyes. I can't tell if she knows that I'm bluffing, that I didn't *want* Nick to apologize, that it just happened, either a response to some deep-seated desire even I'm unaware of or an active choice on his part. I don't know if any of that makes a difference, if Neon would be mad about my taking credit for something I'm not sure I did. But she must not care, because her shoulders relax and she says:

"You're something else, Robert Gorham."

"Thanks . . . ?"

"You know, I could have taken care of it," she tells me, rattling the wrench toward me in mock menace. "I don't need a white knight."

"I have no doubt," I say, smiling.

"You really can make anyone do anything you want, can't you?" she asks after a moment, her eyes moving down to the wrench still in her hand as she twirls it around.

"I mean . . . yeah." I'm looking at my own hands now, scared of what comes next. The rejection, the fear, all the horrible things my own brain tells me people would say if they knew.

"That's wicked cool." She laughs again, softer this time.

"Yeah?"

"Yeah." Her eyes come back to meet mine and I think I can see electricity in them. "And it gives me an idea."

———

Neon has been dealing with men like Nick her entire life.

She knows that it's not about being pretty or cool or able to "hang with the boys," even though that's what everyone tells her. She knows that if she didn't have the face she had, if she didn't wear leather jackets and ride motorcycles, there would still be the same bullshit to deal with. Maybe from a different source—she does seem to attract a very particular kind of sleaze—but life would never be quiet. Not for a woman who refuses to be anything but her loud self. Not for *any* woman in this world.

It used to scare her, the attention. She's always been too small and too black and too queer besides—life was never going to be easy for her. It was never going to be safe. She walked through the first fifteen or so years of her life with armor around her and one eye always looking over her shoulder. And then the lightning came and there was a bigger thing in her life to be afraid of.

But once she got *that* particular monster under control, she realized it wasn't something to fear at all. And it helped the other fears too. When she was sixteen and a boy at a house party tried to take things farther than she wanted, he got three thousand volts sent through him. She knows there are still people out there who could overpower her, but most of the time, she stands up squarely to the men who try to intimidate her, and she smiles with the knowledge that she could bring them down with a flick of her wrist.

Neon knows that there are plenty of people who look at her and assume she's nothing to fear. She knows that the men who know the truth and stick around anyway are men she can trust. Sometimes it doesn't feel like there are many good men in the world, but Neon knows that she's found at least a few of them.

And she knows when you do find the good ones, it's important to keep them.

". . . and that's where Rob comes into play," Neon finishes, and I see matching expressions of concern on Marley's and Indah's faces.

"You want us to use Rob's ability to get information from people?" Indah asks. "Is that . . . legal?"

"It's not like there's a law *against* it. What would that even look like? 'The law prohibits a superhuman from using his powers of persuasion to coerce people'?" Neon laughs at her own mock-officious voice like the whole idea is ridiculous, but Marley's frown deepens.

"Actually, yes," he says. "If the law recognized Unusuals, I think that's *exactly* what it would say."

"But the law *doesn't* recognize Unusuals," Neon says.

"Rob, you're okay with this?" Indah asks me softly.

"Yeah, of course I am. Why wouldn't I be?"

"I don't know, you don't feel weird about using your ability to manipulate people?" Indah asks, shifting on the armrest.

"That's not what this is," I say, defensive. "I'm not using my ability to manipulate people, I'm just . . . being myself. Which sometimes means that people tell me stuff they wouldn't usually share. If we want to know where Blaze is, then I can find him."

"I'm game," Marley says, shrugging, and I'm surprised and pleased he's on our side. I haven't spent much time with Marley—choosing instead to actively avoid him—but there's still a big piece of me that wants his approval, that wants to show him I'm more than what he thinks.

"Really?" Indah turns toward him. "What about what you *just* said?"

"Neon is right: the law doesn't recognize Unusuals. Yeah, Rob's power is ethically . . . a bit tricky, but so is mine."

"Exactly." Neon nods. "I'm the only one with an ability that's pretty cut-and-dried. I don't use it on people—"

I make a sound of disbelief.

"—*unless I have to*," Neon emphasizes, looking at me pointedly. "Physically hurting people is a big no-no—we can all agree on that—but looking into their pasts or making someone want something is a bit . . . gray."

"I think making someone want something is a pretty big no from me too," Indah says, crossing her arms, her brow furrowed.

"What if the thing they want is to tell the truth?" I ask.

"It's still coercion," she says, scowling.

"Look," Neon says, stepping toward Indah, "I don't love it either, okay? We've all been on the other side of Rob's power and it's . . . it doesn't feel that great."

"Wow, thanks, Neon," I deadpan, trying to keep the genuine hurt out of my voice.

"It's not your fault, kid," she says soothingly, and I flinch. "We know that you don't mean to do it, but it is *weird* when it happens."

"Really?" I ask. "What does it . . . what does it feel like?"

There's a three-way significant glance and I suddenly very much do not want to know the answer. Before I can even voice that thought out loud, the conversation has moved on from my question, my silent wish granted.

"This might be the best shot we have at finding Blaze," Neon pleads.

"Getting the truth out of people won't matter if no one knows anything," Indah points out.

"True," Marley concedes, "but you know Blaze. He hung out with some . . . weird folks."

"You mean weirder than a bunch of superhumans?" I quip, but no one laughs.

"He's a really lost kid," Marley says, acting like he's a hundred years old and Blaze is his son. Like he's responsible for him—for his well-being, his happiness. Is that what this is? Is that what Neon meant when she toasted "to family"?

"He's never been a big fan of being an Unusual and sometimes would take out that frustration in . . . other ways," Neon adds. "Could be some of those people know more about what he's been up to recently than we do."

"But you don't think they'd tell you?" I ask. "Wouldn't they want to know what happened to him too?"

"Not necessarily," Indah says darkly. "That crowd isn't the most nurturing bunch."

"But with you, Rob, we might be able to get something out of them."

I nod, swallowing around a suddenly dry throat. I've never had a job before—something to *do*. A purpose.

"Ugh, '*Rob*,'" Neon scoffs, interrupting my mini crisis. "'*Robbie*,'" she says emphatically. "That name doesn't suit you at all."

Indah laughs at that for some reason, and a smile starts to curl its way around Neon's face.

"Think it's time for a name?" Marley asks, mirroring her smile.

"Mm-hm." She nods, leaning forward on her elbows. Suddenly I'm nervous in a different way. I'm excited, leaning forward as well, the air between me and Neon full with a kind of electricity she can't make from her hands.

"A name?" I ask, unable to keep the smile out of my voice. "Like the ones you guys have?"

"Mm-hm." She grins, cocking her head at me. "And I think I've got it. You know who you are? You're like a little Damien."

"From . . ." I search, the name ringing a bell somewhere deep in my mind. "From, what, *The Omen*?"

"Ha, yeah, that's the one," she laughs.

"Isn't he the antichrist?" I ask, trying not to be offended.

"What, you think that doesn't fit?" Neon teases. I'm about to rebut when—

"'To tame.'"

We both turn our heads toward Indah.

"What?"

"'To tame,'" Indah repeats. "'To subdue.' That's what the name 'Damien' means."

"God, Indah," Marley laughs. "Why do you *know* that?"

"Maybe we did some poking around online." She shrugs innocently, and my heart flutters at the idea that Indah and Neon have been thinking about this for a while.

"'To tame' . . . ," I echo, the words rolling strangely off my tongue.

"I mean," Neon starts, "that *does* kind of work for you, kid."

"So, what," I say, "you want to change my name to Damien?"

"You need a name." Neon shrugs.

"I have a name," I argue, wanting to be christened an Unusual but wondering about the weight and history of the name that Neon wants to bestow on me.

"Rob, you told me the very first night we met how much you hate your name," Indah calls out.

"Yeah, well I was very drunk at the time," I retort.

"So you *do* like your name?" she asks skeptically.

"Of course I don't fucking like my name," I admit. "*They* gave it to me."

"Ooh, who's 'they'?" Neon sits up, eyes wide in excitement.

"No one," I say.

"It doesn't sound like no one," she taunts. "If they gave you your name, I'm going to assume they're your parents?"

"Wow, top-notch detective work," I deadpan, and Neon sticks her tongue out at me. The sight warms me, even though we're edging toward a subject I'd really rather avoid. But this is what friends do, isn't it? They learn about each other, share the gripes of childhood, hopes, dreams, petty thoughts, crushes. They give each other responsibility, a purpose. They rely on each other and tease each other and they don't leave.

Robert Gorham could never quite manage all of that stuff. But maybe Damien can.

I know I'm not the most sociable person in the world, but Blaze's roommates seem particularly heinous as far as people go.

The next time the four of us all have an afternoon free—which doesn't happen as often as I would like, though *I'm* free literally *every* afternoon—we go to Blaze's loft, where he lived with three artist types who appear to be stoned at two p.m.

"You rented out his room?" Indah asks incredulously. All of Blaze's possessions have been hastily boxed up and stacked against one wall of the enormous and practically empty shared living space.

"He hasn't been here in months," a Twiggy-looking girl drawls.

"Months?" Marley clarifies.

"Yeah." She sounds bored. "And it's not like he left a rent check or anything . . ."

"Months . . . ," Neon murmurs. "I thought he just lost his cell or got a new boyfriend or something . . ."

"Why didn't you guys come to his apartment until now?" I ask.

"We don't exactly love coming here," Indah answers, her eyes widening, and then glances sideways at Twiggy.

"Though it is a pretty great place," Marley comments, looking around. He's right. The apartment is on the top floor, with high, beamed ceilings. The part of the loft we're standing in is an enormous open space, the living room leading to a dining area leading to the kitchen. "Too bad you guys don't do anything with it."

"Whatever, dude," Twiggy drones.

"Where's Blaze?" I ask pointedly, looking straight into her dead eyes. I want to know what she knows, what she could be hiding, but I suspect that it's probably nothing.

"Listen," she says, staring straight back, and I feel the tether between us click into place. It's working; she's going to tell me the truth. "No one gives a shit about that guy. He was barely here when he *was* paying rent and when he was, he was always so . . . weird. It honestly took us a little while to realize he was gone."

Her flat words fall with a thud in front of the four of us and I'm afraid to look at the others. This isn't what I wanted—I was supposed to be helping them find their friend, not proving that the people in his life didn't care about him.

"Well, *we* give a shit," Neon snaps, stepping toward the girl menacingly. "So if he comes back—*when* he comes back—you're gonna give him his room back. In the meantime, we'll be taking his stuff with us."

"Whatever," she says again, rolling her eyes, the link between us slackened. "So . . . are you guys gonna get out of here or what?"

We do. We go up to the building's roof, after dodging one of Blaze's other ne'er-do-well roomies asking for money. Indah says that Blaze liked to come up here to let out small flames when he needed, but there doesn't seem to be any trace of him.

"At least they didn't toss his stuff," Neon says, kicking a rock across the wide and empty rooftop.

"Why does he live with these people?" I ask. "Why don't you guys all live together?"

Marley just shrugs.

"I don't know. It'd be nice. *This* spot would be great, but there aren't a ton like it in LA. These creeps have been here since long before Blaze. Guess the rent was cheap and he wanted something with a rooftop."

"I get that," I say, looking out at the view. We're a few miles from downtown Los Angeles, one of the only parts of the city with anything remotely resembling skyscrapers, and the vista is not too shabby. It's not an overly tall building, but because everything in LA is so low, we can see the high-rises of downtown, the mansion-speckled hills, the sprawl of the city that I know eventually reaches out to the ocean, somewhere beyond what we can see, hidden behind the distant sheen of smog.

"Okay, so he hasn't been home in months, hasn't answered any calls or texts . . ."

"Where did he work?"

"Fry cook," Marley says. "I already checked, he quit a few months back."

"That's not unusual for Blaze though," Indah says. "He wasn't very good at holding down a job."

"So where else is there?" I ask. "Give me someone else to talk to and I'll figure it out."

"Can't you just . . . ," Indah starts, looking nervous.

"Can't I just what?" I ask.

"Look . . . ," she says, stepping close to me. I can see the worry in her eyes and smell her perfume—light and flowery—and it warms my face. "I know you don't know Alex," she says, and I don't think she even realizes that she's used his non-Unusual name, "but can't you just . . . want him to be back?"

Her eyes are pleading and I want so badly to lie to her. I want to tell her that, yes, that is how it works. I can reach across cities and states and countries and oceans and want someone to come back so badly that they do. But I lived with that sour hope for too long and I would never poison anyone else with it.

"I'm sorry," I whisper. "It doesn't work like that. It's a proximity thing, I'm pretty sure. I need to be close to the person to have it work." Even as I explain it, I'm not 100 percent certain that it's true. What if *that's* the lie and what Indah hopes is the real truth? What if I've been living with a hope that could be met but never was because They were too stubborn to let my wanting bring them back?

"Are you sure?" Indah insists. "Have you tried?"

"Yes, he has," Marley says, his soft voice even softer in the light breeze that's sailing over the rooftop. I let his response hang in the air, all at once angry and embarrassed he's seen my past again and relieved that I don't have to explain to Indah why what she wants won't work.

The four of us stand in silence, looking out over the city where Blaze might be. I can practically feel the longing coming off of each of them, like they're the ones who can project their desires onto me, and I try to pretend I can't relate to what they're feeling. I don't know Blaze. I have no investment in this other than wanting to help my fellow Unusuals. My friends. This isn't like it was when it happened to me. When Blaze doesn't come back, it won't sting as much.

"We should go to Void," Marley says after a moment, breaking the tense quiet.

"Shit," Neon sighs.

"What's Void?" I ask.

"It's a bar that Blaze used to go to a lot," Indah explains.

"It's where he used to buy . . ." Neon trails off.

"Where he'd buy what?" I prompt, feeling dumb and out of the loop.

Marley gives me a significant look and the penny drops. I guess Blaze had bigger problems than just being a pyrokinetic.

The pain is extraordinary. It defies description, defies logic, defies all the known laws of the universe. He's not sure when it started, can't fathom it ever stopping.

He's felt pain like this before. When everything first started, he could feel the fire building in his blood, in his skin. He thought he was sick—full of fever and bile—and he wasn't completely wrong. This *is* an illness. But one that he can't sweat out or treat with painkillers, as much as he's tried. The stuff he's gotten from his roommates, from the people at Void, it's supposed to be able to knock anyone out, keep anyone under. But the fire still burns.

It's burning worse than ever now. The pain should be coming from somewhere else, should be a response to something that someone is doing *to* him. The human body shouldn't be able to create pain like this on its own. But then again, he might not be human. Maybe he's some sort of devil and not actually a person at all. It would explain the hellfire in his veins.

But devils are supposed to be at home in the fire. Instead, the fire has made a home out of him. It's going to keep raging through his body, burning everything inside, and leaving nothing but ash behind.

Dust to dust indeed.

Void lives up to its name.

Even though the sun set hours ago, entering the bar, I feel like my eyes have to adjust to the darkness, as if I just came inside from a bright day. The small windowless club is a few miles from Blaze's apartment, in a somehow even worse part of town, and filled with thumping bass and frantic strobe lights, and I immediately want to be anywhere else. But we have a mission to complete.

"All right," Marley shouts over the music, his large body like a battering ram parting the crowd for us, "we gotta find Kenny. He's usually on the dance floor."

Kenny, I've been told, is Blaze's sometimes-friend, sometimes-dealer, and an "all-around mess," as Neon put it. What Marley generously called a dance floor is really more a mash of sweaty bodies slamming into each other. I glance behind me to see Indah rolling her eyes at her surroundings and Neon with her hands tense, probably ready to shock anyone who gets too close. But no one will. Even without Marley's enormous frame creating a pathway, everyone in here is going to give us a wide berth. I'll make sure of it.

"There he is!" Marley calls, his stature giving him the advantage of picking the messy pale purple curls out of the fray.

"Wazzzzuuuuuup," Kenny cries when he sees Marley, launching his squat, teddy-bear body into Marley's arms for an enormous hug that involves Kenny's wrapping his legs around Marley's hips. Marley looks bored by this, simply patting Kenny on the back before setting him down.

"We need to talk," Marley yells.

"Huh?"

"We need to talk," he shouts harder, but Kenny just cocks his head, confused. Marley grabs him by the shoulders and starts to steer him out of the crowd, the three of us trailing silently behind.

Keeping my eyes on Marley's broad shoulders and my mind on wanting everyone in the club to pretend like we're not here, I soon find myself stepping through a back entrance and into an alley, the cool, silent night air almost oppressive on my ears after the relentless assault of the music inside.

"Yo, Marley, what gives?" Kenny says, his voice tinny and raw. "Things were just getting good in there."

"'Sup, Neon," he adds when he takes a second to look around. "Who're your friends?"

"This is Indah and Damien," she says, and I feel a thrill up my spine at the use of my gifted name.

"Good to meet you, bros," Kenny says cheerfully, giving a cock-eyed salute in our direction. "So, what, you guys looking for some fun? I don't have a lot left, but I bet I could dig something up . . ."

Kenny looks down and unzips the fanny pack around his waist, reaching a hand in and rooting around.

"No, Kenny, we're not trying to buy," Marley sighs.

"Right, right." Kenny keeps nodding, craning his neck to make eye contact with Marley. "That's never really been your scene, huh, Marley boy?"

"Have you seen Blaze?" Neon asks.

"Mr. Bonfire himself?" Kenny smiles. "Nah, I haven't."

"When was the last time you saw him?" I ask, stepping forward to come face-to-face with Kenny. I feel the trio around me go silent and still—it's my time to go to work.

I stare Kenny straight in the eyes. He's small—smaller and rounder than me, his face sallow and sunken. He's probably only a few years older than me, but he looks prematurely aged, like he's been left out in the sun for too long, right down to the unnaturally dyed hair that's lost so much of its color.

Kenny's dark brown eyes dart around before settling on me. I can feel his nervous energy, his desire to move away from me, to go back into the safety of the club, but I quash that with my own desire to know what he knows. I can sense the connection between us, a strong, thin string tied from my brain to his. A one-way connection—like rolling a ball down a ramp until it hits the first domino.

"Lemme think," he begins, high pitched and frantic, the dominoes falling. "I haven't seen him in a month probably. Two months? Maybe more. I don't remember a lot of days these days, you know? He was *supposed* to come to our Halloween party but he never showed. I remember that much. Which is kinda weird because he was pretty stoked about it. He said he was gonna do up some pretty good fireworks, if you know what I mean. So I guess the last time I saw him was, like, September? Oh yeah, it was definitely September, because we had a birthday party for Max and I got *so* twisted and got sick and Blaze took care of me. Oh wait! I saw him after that too, here, for eighties night. That was a really good night too. I was dressed like Marty McFly and there was this really cute girl dressed like Cyndi Lauper and—"

"Wait, you know about what he can do?" I ask, distracted from the purpose of this interrogation for a moment. "You know that he's . . ."

"What, a pyro?" Kenny grins. "Yeah, of course. 'S fucking awesome. Way better than what I can do."

"What?" I balk. "Wait, what can you—you're an Unusual?"

"Course I am," he laughs. "It's how Blaze and I met. He happened to catch me when I was stone-cold sober—early in the night, you know how it is—and I was able to read his thoughts and yeah, he was thinking about his power. He was always thinking about it, whenever I managed to overhear."

"Wait, wait, wait," I say, hearing my friends shift impatiently behind me. They can keep it together for a few more minutes—they're the ones who brought me right to another Unusual and didn't seem to think that was relevant information to share. "You can *read minds*?"

"Sure can! Oh, don't—don't get that scared look on your face, I can't read anything *now*. That's kind of the point of rolling, ya know? Makes everything else so loud that the inside of my head goes quiet. The music does too, and the dancing—hey, we should go back inside and dance, I don't know what we're doing out here—"

"Have you heard from Blaze since eighties night?" I interrupt, wanting to get Kenny back on task. I have a feeling I'm not going to get a more coherent explanation from him about his ability, as much as I might want it.

"No, not since he left with that guy," Kenny says, shrugging. "And I was mad about that too because I wanted to know what the whole deal was with him. He didn't seem like Blaze's usual type, you know? Way too old."

"What guy?"

"I don't know, it was some guy that was talking Blaze up at the bar for, like, an hour. Real buttoned-up type, you know? Wearing a long black coat. Indoors. Which is a bad idea, let me tell you, especially if you're already buzzing. I don't know, maybe he was dressed up as, like, a white Shaft? Whatever he was going for, I'm not totally sure it was working, it just made him seem really creepy—"

"What did he look like?" I push, a bad feeling starting to creep up on me. "Exactly."

"Uh, I don't know, your standard older white dude. Dark hair. Boring face. Kind of a Cryptkeeper vibe. Tall. Really, really tall."

The hair on the back of my neck rises.

"Did you talk to him?" I hear Marley ask from behind me.

"Not really," Kenny says. "He seemed pretty into our guy Blaze. And, listen, that's not my bag so I don't know what Blaze would have seen in him, but I wasn't about to interrupt, you know? Bro code."

"Bro what?" I ask, unable to keep up with Kenny's drugged-out ramblings.

"But you watched them talk," Marley clarifies.

"Yep."

"Do you have it?" Neon asks, and the way she says it, I know she's not talking to Kenny.

"I got it," Marley says, sounding certain.

"Let's go." I hear Neon's footsteps on the pavement behind me and look back to Marley.

"Thanks, Kenny," Marley says, and Kenny smiles. I drop the thread I've woven between us and Kenny's smile drops a few centimeters.

"What was I just saying?" Kenny tilts his head and squints his eyes at me, still standing a few feet away from him. Marley raises his pale eyebrows at me and I shrug.

"Force of habit," I tell Marley. "Usually I like when people forget they've talked to me."

"Cool move," Marley deadpans, and I blush under his hard stare, feeling like I got caught with my hand in the cookie jar.

"Take care of yourself, Kenny," Marley calls over my shoulder.

"Yeah, you too, Marley boy." Kenny waves.

With that, Kenny pulls a lollipop out of his fanny pack, unwraps it, and sticks it in his mouth before reentering the club. Marley and I stand side by side watching him, and the music from the open door fills the space between us for a moment.

"Come on," Marley says when the door swings shut. He starts walking toward the street, where Neon and Indah are leaned up against Indah's car, talking.

". . . not like him," I hear Indah say.

"It's exactly like him to go home with someone he just met," Neon says, lighting a cigarette.

"Not someone significantly older," Indah counters.

"I don't think it was like that," Marley says as we reach the car.

"What do you mean?" Indah asks.

"I don't think it was a hookup."

"What'd you see?" Neon asks.

"See?" I wonder aloud before realizing. "Oh . . . you looked in his past, didn't you?" The thought still makes my skin crawl, but I guess Marley's ability has its uses.

"Yep." Marley nods. "That's why I needed him to think about it specifically—it can help sometimes, kind of like conjuring up a memory. The way Blaze was talking to that guy . . . it didn't seem like a hookup."

"Someone he was buying from?" Neon suggests.

"Maybe . . ."

"But you got a good look at him?" Indah asks. "You'd recognize him if you saw him?"

"Definitely." Marley nods.

"Well, thank god for that." Neon exhales a plume of smoke. "Maybe now we can find him."

"Especially since we've got *two* people who have seen him," I say, trying not to sound too satisfied with myself. Three heads swivel toward me.

"What?" Neon asks, the cigarette hanging limply from her mouth.

"The tall man. I think I met him."

Marley thought he was tripping the first time it happened. Which is strange, because Marley has never done any drugs in his life. But, despite that fact, when he was seventeen he started seeing ghosts.

He was grabbing a late-night burger with his friend Rachel when he suddenly saw her brother sitting next to her in the booth. Her brother who had died a year ago. And then suddenly there were two Rachels, overlaid on top of one another, both drinking a milkshake, one laughing at her brother, one pouting at Marley. It was over as quick as it began, and Marley wondered if maybe there was something in the burger.

The next day he had the wherewithal to realize that it was probably just sleep deprivation—midterms had him pulling all-nighters and his mind was beginning to crack. He knew that Rachel and her brother often hung out at the diner that had become his and Ra-chel's post-study late-night spot—a bit of an odd image for his tired mind to conjure, but not completely out of left field. He did his best to brush it off and refocus on his studies.

But then, a month later, it happened again. And then again and again and again, and Marley realized he wasn't just hallucinating. It wasn't that he was seeing things that weren't there, he was see-ing things that weren't there *anymore*. He was getting echoes. It stayed location specific for a while—he could only see the past of someone when they were in the spot where the memory occurred in the present—but Marley had always been an overachiever. Once he understood what was going on, he started perfecting it. Well, no, that's probably skipping a stage. Once he understood it, Marley had to work on *believing* it. From there, he could hone. He wasn't sure if seeing these echoes—seeing people's pasts—was something you *could* be good at. Can you perfect something that's just inherent in your nature?

Marley was still waiting for an answer on that. He hadn't per-fected it, but that didn't mean it couldn't be perfected. It didn't mean *he* couldn't be perfected.

Because Marley and I are the only two people who have gotten a good look at the Tall Man (as we've come to call him), the group decides that it makes sense for us to pair up and go looking for the guy. Which strikes me as a bad idea in every sense. I don't know how wise it is to hunt down a potentially dangerous creep, and I also wasn't exactly looking for an excuse to spend more time with Marley. But having a purpose, a goal, is a strange and compelling thing, so I find myself agreeing to it before I have too much time to think.

We play private eye for a few days—going to all of Blaze's old haunts, talking to everyone and anyone that ever knew him, ask-ing about the Tall Man—but we keep coming up empty. It's not as simple as it looks on TV. There isn't a break in the case right at the moment that things seem lost. We hit dead end after dead end, and we're fresh out of leads.

"We're not cops, Robert." Marley snorts when I say this to him. "We don't have 'leads.' We're just trying to find our friend."

"I know that," I sigh, flopping down on Marley's couch. This is the second time that we've come back to his apartment post-investigating, and I'm beginning to feel comfortable here. I never realized how much someone's space could be a reflection of who they are. Indah's apartment is soft edged and homey, the living room just generic enough that you know it's shared by multiple people. Neon's "crash pad," as she calls it, is exactly that—a place to crash, hastily thrown together. I've gotten the impression that Neon is a bit like me—transient and noncommittal—but her apartment still has her flair. Bits of blue everywhere, an amp in the corner that doesn't seem to hook up to anything, a fully stocked bar, motorcycle parts in the silverware drawer. I think she spends most nights at Indah's—even though Indah is the one with the roommates—but Neon's apartment is where she can fully be herself. Where she can be *messy*.

I'm learning that, for Marley, being fully himself seems to mean the opposite. His tiny downtown studio apartment is sparsely but purposefully decorated—quiet in the way that Marley is quiet. It isn't that he doesn't speak—that he doesn't *want* to speak—it's that he doesn't say anything unless he has something to say. Marley doesn't mince words, and he doesn't blow hot air, and I want so badly to crack him open and see what he would say if he expressed every thought that ran through his head.

"I don't know what we're going to do," Marley sighs as he collapses on the couch, the dense weight of him jarring me out of my reverie. "We've looked everywhere, talked to everyone, and we're not any closer than we were a week ago."

"Have you looked through his stuff yet?" I ask, jerking my head toward the boxes stacked along the far wall, completely at odds with the fastidiousness of the rest of the space. Given his proximity to Blaze's loft, Marley took all of his possessions home so that Blaze's vulture roommates wouldn't pawn them.

"Yeah." He nods, leaning his head back against the couch. "Nothing in there. Mostly just random odds and ends, some journals . . . his passport, which I thought was kind of weird."

"Why?" I ask, realizing that I have no idea if a passport is even something most people have. It's never occurred to me to travel outside of the country, to go somewhere They couldn't track me down.

"Well, if he was going to leave for a while, it seems like an important thing to bring with him. Plus," he adds, softer, "I didn't even know that he had a passport."

"Is that weird?" I ask. "Don't you have one?"

He shakes his head, digging his neck into the cushion behind him.

"Yeah, but I *had* to . . ." He trails off, sounding sad. I want to ask more but he quickly deflects. "What about you? You seen the world?"

I don't answer right away. I've noticed that this is a thing that Marley does—any question I ask him, he immediately turns around and puts it on me. I don't know if he thinks it's an effective way to deflect my ability's influence on him, but as far as I can tell . . . it's not. I indulge him anyway, feeling confident that he won't go looking into my past to see the truth of why I stick around—it's easier to want him to keep his nose out of my business when it's just the two of us.

"Nope," I say. "Seen most of this country though. Or at least most of what's west of the Mississippi."

"Why so much moving around?"

Marley has tilted his head toward me, the side of his face lying on the cushion and yet still somehow so much higher than my own. He has an open, vulnerable expression that I'm not sure I've ever seen from him before, and I wonder how much of that is just the normal process of getting to know someone and how much of it is some underlying wish I have for him to show his true self to me. I try not to think about what the likely truth is and focus on the question he's asked me. Maybe if I match his vulnerability with some of my own, we'll start to form something more like friendship and less like a hardened cop and a rookie forced to work together.

"I think you know why," I mutter, chickening out at the last second.

"It doesn't really work like that," Marley says, voicing what seems to be the motto of the Unusuals. "I don't get the full biopic when I meet someone."

"Then how does it work?" I ask, genuinely wanting to know. Neon's ability is pretty easy to understand—and Blaze, even though I don't know him, haven't seen him in action, I can imagine it. Pyrokinesis is one of those things you see in movies and comic books. But what Marley can do seems nuanced and complicated in the way that my ability is nuanced and complicated, and I both want to talk to someone about that and am terrified to in case they tell me that no, actually having that kind of power is really manageable and easy and *you're just bad at being a person, Robbie.*

"Well," Marley breathes, and I shift on the couch to face him more fully, "it's strongest and easiest when I'm seeing an echo of something that happened in the same spot that I'm in. So, let's say a year from now, you and I are sitting on this couch: I might see an echo of you as you are now—a little piece of your past that's tied to a specific time or place."

I get momentarily waylaid by the casual suggestion that Marley and I will still be hanging out in a year. Is that what all of them think? That I'm now just a staple in their lives who will be there for holidays and family dinners and late nights sitting on the same couch we've always sat on?

"But you see stuff that happened in a different place, right?" I ask, distracting myself. "Because the first time we met . . ."

In an effort to derail my own thoughts, I didn't think about where that sentence was going, and now I've acknowledged the six-hundred-pound gorilla in the corner that I've very successfully been avoiding until now. I start to think about the fact that I want Marley to steer us out of the conversation, forget I said anything, but he's already talking.

"It can be tied to specific emotions too," he explains. "I think because we were talking about Blaze and some of the stuff he's been through . . ."

The implication hangs in the air and I decide to change the subject myself, unsure of what I actually want in the moment and what my ability might be trying to accomplish without my knowledge.

"Did you read his journals?" I ask.

"What?"

"You said there were journals in his things," I say. "They might have information—something that could help us figure out where he went."

"I'm not gonna read his journals—" Marley starts before cutting himself off and telling the truth. "I skimmed them. Nothing really new to learn—Blaze's been in a bad spot, wanting to hurt himself, wanting to tear his ability out of his body . . . that's how he described it anyway. But that's the way Blaze is—he describes things dramatically and violently because his ability is dramatic and violent. I'm just glad to see those things on the page. If he gets it out on paper, he's not taking it out on himself."

There's a long beat and then Marley brings his hands up to rub his face.

"Goddamn it, Damien," he sighs, and I thrill at hearing my new name from his mouth. "Don't tell the others. Worried as they are, they'd be *pissed* if they found out that I went digging in Blaze's private stuff."

"Your secret is safe with me," I say, smiling.

"And yours are safe with me," he says, dead serious and staring into my eyes. "I know that the first time we met . . . well, I was thrown off. By what you can do. But anything I see in your past is not anyone else's business. I'm not even going to bring that stuff up with you unless you ask. I care about people's privacy.

"The journals being an exception, obviously," he adds guiltily after a moment.

"Why does Blaze hate his ability so much?"

"Because it hurts him sometimes," Marley says, sadder than I've heard him. "It gets him in a lot of trouble—most of us have gotten in trouble at one time or another because of what we can do—but it also *hurts* him."

"What, like . . . physically?"

"Yeah." He nods. "Apparently just a low-level pain, like a chronic burning he says, but that can't be fun to live with."

"No shit," I mumble, horrified by the prospect. My ability doesn't feel like anything, other than when I'm using it. Even then, I can only feel it when I'm really concentrating, when I'm *trying* to do something. Most of the time it just happens and I don't think twice about it.

"It doesn't hurt for me," Marley shares. "I mean, sometimes I see pretty sad stuff in people's pasts, which hurts in its own kind of way. But I can't imagine having an ability that caused me physical pain."

"So you'd never give it up?" I ask, even though I can't imagine why.

"No, definitely not," he says. "Yeah, it's weird sometimes, but it's a part of me now. Like breathing."

Marley doesn't get to "what about you" this time. I don't want to think about what my answer to this question would be, and I definitely don't want to share it with Marley. I guess my will is stronger than his.

We sit in silence for a few minutes, both leaned back and staring up at the ceiling, lost in our own thoughts.

"Hey, Damien?" Marley asks quietly.

"Yeah?"

"Are you . . ." Marley trails off awkwardly, something I'm not used to from him. As a man of few words, he picks them all very carefully.

He pauses before starting again.

"You have a place to stay, right?"

"What?"

"I mean, Neon said you were at some swanky hotel back when you first got here but you've crashed on my couch a few times and you haven't invited us over anywhere . . ."

"I didn't realize I had to." I sniff.

"So you *do* have a place to stay," he says, voice serious as he turns his head back toward me and stares me down with pale eyes.

"Yes, I have a place to stay," I say mockingly, rolling my eyes. I'm surprised that Indah didn't tell them. If Marley doesn't know, then that means Neon doesn't know. I'm beginning to learn the chain of information within our little group—if Neon knows something, everyone does. I guess Indah keeps as much to herself as me.

"And I'm betting that it's nicer than this place." Marley sweeps his arms toward the rest of the tidy living room.

"Not really," I say, surprised to find myself being honest. "It's way bigger for sure," I continue, and Marley snorts beside me, "but, I don't know, it's not as . . . this is a *home*."

Suddenly, I can feel tears welling up in the corners of my eyes and blush in embarrassment. I sigh and clear my throat, closing my eyes as I dig my head farther into the couch cushion behind me— trying to pass off the emotional wave I'm experiencing as settling in for another night spent passed out on Marley's couch.

"What do you mean?" I can feel Marley turning his face toward me again and I swallow around the rising lump in my throat.

"I don't know, man." I shrug. "It's just . . . you know. You have your stuff and things on the walls and it's just . . . it's you. It feels like you live here."

"Well, yeah, I *do* live here." I hear him huff a laugh and I open one eye to peer at him. He's still staring at me, a curious expression on his face. I want to know what he's thinking.

"I can't quite figure you out, Rob," he says, my ability winding its way under his skin. "You have this power that can give you everything you want and yet . . . it's like what you actually want most are things not even your ability can get you."

"I don't really know what you're talking about," I say, my heart rate rising.

"You want a home, don't you?" he asks, and I already regret letting my power loose on him. Maybe I *don't* want to know what he's thinking—Marley sees me too closely, too fully, for me to want true honesty from him.

"Whatever, dude," I scoff. "I live in a mansion in the Hollywood Hills. I don't *want* anything."

———

I want them to come back. Even though I hated being around them—was so afraid of what I might do to them, what they might do to me in retaliation (though they never did anything, why did they never do anything, why didn't they stop me)—I want them to come back. It turns out, a house isn't much of a home without anyone in it.

Their smiling faces still stare down at me from the framed photos lining the wall of the main entryway. The blanket my mother knit for me still sits on the back of the couch—casually flung over the cushions one day when I got too hot. I've barely touched the couch since they left. For three years, I've gone straight to my room the moment my feet cross the threshold. When I'm alone in my room, I can pretend that the house creaks because there are other people in it, not just because it's starting to fall apart. I can pretend that I'm not alone.

But I am alone. I'm as alone as any person can be. On the outskirts of a town of two hundred, ten miles away from the nearest grocery store, with no family coming to keep me company. I tried calling my grandparents—the only people left who might give a shit about me—but the phone just rang and rang and rang. It rang every single day for two weeks straight. Either my grandparents were dead, or my parents had already gotten to them—warned them about their horrible, monstrous son. I don't know which version of events to hope for.

I have to leave this place. I know that, in my gut. I'm sixteen today, a grown-up now, and it's time for me to move up and out. School is an empty shell of what it once was—no conflict, no interest. Whatever is inside of me is getting stronger and there's no one in town who's immune. I don't want to be around them. I don't want to look at the blank faces of my classmates giving me their homemade lunches, packed with such love and care; I don't want to see the blank faces of my teachers as they give me an A on every paper, every test, every final exam, even when I didn't turn anything in.

It's time for me to see the rest of the country, the rest of the world. Maybe whatever poison is inside me will be sucked out by leaving Nebraska. Maybe the world outside of me will be stronger-willed.

Maybe I'll find people who understand me, who aren't afraid of me. Maybe I'll find people *like* me.

Even as I think it, I know it's a hollow wish.

Like a lot of things in my life, it happens when I'm not actively trying.

Neon and I hit up another one of Blaze's haunts last night and came up completely empty, and now the Scooby Gang has taken the night off. Marley has class, and Neon is at some show that neither Indah nor I wanted to go to, so it's just the two of us hanging at Bar Lubitsch. I haven't spent much time here in the past few weeks—getting more comfortable being in the Unusuals' space, their homes—but I'm struck by how familiar it feels to sit at the bar and watch Indah work on a particularly slow evening. It brings me back to the night we first met—barely half a year ago, even though it feels like a lifetime.

"Maybe I should learn how to bartend," I say as Indah mixes a complicated cocktail that a suited bro with perfectly coiffed hair just ordered.

Indah laughs as she sets a coaster down on the bar in front of the guy, but doesn't say anything. This is how Indah operates when she's got a customer, I'm discovering. She's aware of me, pays attention to me, but doesn't speak directly to me if there's someone else at the bar. I know that I could have her ignore everyone, put all of her focus on me, but I'm enjoying watching her tattooed arms stretch to reach the top shelf, her nimble fingers spinning a glass. There's a simplicity to this—to just sitting with her, thinking aloud and watching her work—that keeps me grounded. Satisfied. Wanting anything else seems unnecessary when I have this.

"Thanks a lot." Indah's voice cuts through my musings and I look up from my drink to see her grimacing at me.

"What?"

"That guy just left without having his drink *or* paying for it," she snaps.

I spin on my bar stool to look around me. She's right: the suited douche is gone, the bar practically empty, except for a guy on his laptop in the corner and the old woman from the first night in her usual spot with a glass of clear liquid.

"Oh." I wince. "Oops."

"Oops?" I spin back to look at Indah, whose eyes are bright with anger. "Robert, I make my living from tips and you keep driving business away."

"I'm not trying to," I say. "It's not my fault that people don't want to stick around."

"Yes, it is," she sighs. "It *is* your fault when they leave because *you* want me to pay attention to you."

"Jeez, fine, I can leave," I say, starting to move off the stool.

"Wait, no—" Indah shouts as she grabs my arm with a warm hand. "I want you to stay."

"You do?" I ask, knowing what answer she's going to give me and hating myself a little for wanting to hear it out loud anyway.

"Of course I do." She smiles sweetly at me, and just like that, everything's fine again. That is, until seconds later, when the door swings open and a tall, pale man walks into the bar.

"Please don't scare this one away," Indah mutters to me before moving to the end of the bar to greet him. I want to respond but my blood is turning to ice in my veins and my hair is standing up like I've had a run-in with Neon and her electric fingers.

"What can I get you?" Indah croons, and the Tall Man doesn't seem to hear her. He stands straight and still, gazing around the bar like he's looking for a friend. I try to imagine what kind of person would be friends with such a man—looming and expressionless, his jaw and cheekbones like knives on his face—when he turns his face to me. I quickly move to look back down at my drink. Does he recognize me? Did he follow me here somehow?

"Information, if you please," comes the smooth but sharp voice, like boiling water thrown on a block of ice.

"I'm sorry?" Indah asks politely, and I see her out of the corner of my eye leaning her arms on the bar in front of her as if the problem is simply that she didn't hear him.

"It is my understanding that a young man, Alex Chen, frequents this establishment." I grip the glass in front of me like it's the only thing that's keeping me tethered to the earth and take another sideways glance at Indah. She's no longer leaning toward the Tall Man, her arms now crossed in front of her as she narrows her eyes at him. I'm grateful for the width of the bar separating them, but it doesn't feel like enough.

"I don't know what you're talking about," Indah says coolly.

"Have you seen him?"

"I think you're in the wrong place, sir."

I'm suddenly very aware of the new, deadly silent atmosphere in the bar. The typing from the guy on his laptop in his corner has ceased and—even though she's been silently sipping her vodka for forty-five minutes—the old woman is sitting stiffly, clearly paying attention to the tall newcomer.

"I don't think I am," he purrs, and I see Indah clench her jaw. I want him so badly to leave; why isn't he leaving?

"We've been watching you, Indah Indrawati," he says, and Indah takes a step back, the blood draining from her face. I'm not even trying to hide my face from him anymore, trying instead to stare him down, pushing my power as much as I can, hoping he'll leave. Wanting desperately for him to leave. But he just keeps talking.

"We know that you're friends with Alex Chen," he says. "And we very much would like to know where he is."

"Who's 'we'?" Indah snaps.

"People who have his best interests at heart."

Indah snorts, a move that strikes me as foolishly bold.

"Sorry, can't help you." Indah turns her back on him, grabbing a dish towel and moving along the bar to wipe it down. For the first time since the Tall Man came in, Indah's and my eyes meet, hers growing wide at me, as if she's saying, "Do something, help me."

The Tall Man's pale eyes follow her along the bar until they land on me. I feel my heart start racing a mile a minute, my head dizzy, and I turn back to my drink, downing what's left of it in one go. By the time I set the glass back on the bar top, the Tall Man is a foot away peering down at me.

"Hello, Cory." He smiles wolfishly. "Or was it Robert?"

"Excuse me?"

"We've met before," he says, sliding onto the bar stool next to mine. I should get up and run out the door but something is keeping me planted where I sit.

"I don't think we have," I say, not looking at him.

"Oh, I'm sure of it." I glance over to see that his mouth is stretching into a mockery of a smile—like he's attempting to show his teeth rather than express an emotion.

"Sir, if you're not going to order anything, I'm going to have to ask you to leave," Indah interjects, now standing next to me, her arm leaned on the bar between us, nearly touching mine.

"I'll have a ginger ale, please. No ice," he says without turning to speak to her. He's still staring me down, the light from the windows behind him like a halo around his dark, closely cropped hair. For the first time in a very long time, I feel small.

Out of the corner of my eye, I see Indah begrudgingly grab a glass, loudly and pointedly scoop the glass full of ice, and fill it with ginger ale out of the soda gun. The sound of the blasting liquid fills the bar, highlighting the tense atmosphere.

With a clunk, she sets it on the bar, ice rattling in the glass as she stares at the side of the Tall Man's head and says:

"That'll be eleven dollars."

A truly ridiculous amount for a soda—even in Los Angeles, a soft drink isn't *that* expensive—but the Tall Man doesn't seem offended by the fact that she's very obviously and intentionally overcharging him.

His green eyes still staring into mine, the Tall Man reaches into the inside pocket of his long black coat—the same one he was wearing the first night we met—and pulls out his wallet. The gesture pushes his coat open slightly and I see a gun holstered to his hip. I can't breathe.

I watch his long, white fingers gingerly place a twenty-dollar bill on the counter and hear the rustling of the paper as if my hearing is heightened. The ring of the register as Indah puts the cash away feels abrasive and shocking and I do my best not to flinch. She slams the cash drawer shut and my eyes twitch in an involuntary blink. I see the corner of the Tall Man's mouth lift slightly as he revels in my discomfort.

A moment passes in which Indah very much does not give the Tall Man any change. He makes no move to ask for it or to take a sip of the drink he just paid twenty dollars for. Instead, he just keeps staring.

A second later, I find myself standing—whether I intend to leave or to fight him, I'm honestly not sure. He's not saying anything, not *doing* anything, but I'm spinning out, feeling trapped and baited.

My standing brings me closer to him and seems to spur him into action.

"My dear," he says, smoothly turning his body to address Indah again, "do tell me where Alex Chen can be found."

Indah starts at his voice and his eyes now boring into her—I see the glass in her hand slip before she deftly catches it.

"I told you," she snaps. "I can't help you."

She puts the glass back on the shelf and has started to walk to the other end of the bar when the Tall Man extends his long hand, unnaturally quick, and grabs Indah's arm, stopping her in her tracks. Fear climbs its way up my throat as I stand, paralyzed, wishing uselessly that Neon were here.

"Ah, I don't think that's true," he clucks. "I think you *won't* help me."

"What's the difference?" Indah says through clenched teeth, keeping her body turned away from him, her arm frozen in his grip.

"There's a whole world of difference between 'can't' and 'won't,'" he says. "'Won't' can be altered."

"I think you should leave."

"I haven't finished my beverage."

"You heard her," I find myself saying, "*leave.*"

His eyes swivel back to me, squinting and peering into my skull.

"Strange attack dog you have here," he says, looking me up and down. "Doesn't look like much but . . . looks can be very deceiving."

"So you looking like a low-rent hit man means what exactly?" I spit back, sounding far braver than I feel, and his mouth twitches again, like he's amused every time I speak.

"I promise you," he purrs, "I am anything but low-rent."

The implication sends shivers down my spine and I look over his shoulder to see the color drain from Indah's face.

"Alex isn't here," she blurts. "We haven't seen him in months."

The Tall Man slowly pulls his hand from her arm and leans back in his seat, smooth and silent, like a shark moving through water.

"Hm . . . so he hasn't run back home then."

"What?" Indah takes a step forward. "What do you mean?"

"Very well," the Tall Man sighs, "I can see that you'll be no use to me for the time being."

He reaches into his jacket again and I flinch. This is it. Somehow I've stumbled into a genuinely dangerous situation—after so many years of carefully sidestepping—and now this tall, pale man is going to pull out his gun and end everything.

I have a brief moment to realize that I'm not all that bothered by that prospect before I see that he's simply pulling his wallet out again. He takes out a few bills and tosses them onto the bar.

"For the charming service," he drawls, and Indah just clenches her jaw more. The Tall Man then turns on his heel and leaves through the door, like nothing ever happened.

"What the *fuck*," Indah exhales, collapsing her arms onto the bar and staring at the door into the bar.

"Yeah."

"I mean, honestly, what the *fuck*."

"Yeah."

She whips her head toward me and barks: "Is that really all you have to say, Robert? 'Yeah'?"

"What do you want me to say?" I snap back.

"You've seen that guy before—"

"Yeah, I have—"

"And your response to seeing him again and him remembering you is just 'yeah'?"

"I'm still processing it, okay?" I say, wishing I had a drink in front of me.

Just like that, Indah pushes herself up and goes about fixing a drink. She sets a glass of whiskey in front of me—something I've discovered (thanks to Neon) that I like a hell of a lot more than vodka. I knock it back and Indah starts to wipe down the bar, keeping her hands busy until, a few silent seconds later, her actions catch up to her and she pauses.

"Damn it, Damien," she hisses, and the gifted name sounds sharp on her tongue. "Can't you just give me a break for one second?"

"I needed a drink," I say, shrugging, and she shoots daggers at me. But then her eyes relax and fill with affection, the danger of the last few minutes momentarily forgotten.

But wanting to keep Indah calm and happy doesn't do anything for the adrenaline still coursing through my body. I think of the gun holstered to his hip, his hand on Indah's arm, and feel powerless for the first time in a very long time.

"Why didn't you ask him about Blaze?" Neon demands after we've recounted the entire Tall Man experience to her and Marley.

"He didn't exactly seem like the chatty type, Nee," Indah says.

"But it sounds like he knows where Blaze is," Neon protests.

"Or at least, he *knew*," Marley clarifies.

We're sitting in Indah's apartment, huddled in her small living room a few hours after her shift ended at Lubitsch. Marley and I are sunk into the couch—the standard position we've fallen into in our weeks of searching for the Tall Man—and Neon is slouched in an armchair, but Indah isn't perched on the armrest like usual. Instead, she's pacing up and down in front of the couch, running her hands through her hair, and breathing deeply.

"Look," I say, "it wasn't exactly a casual chat. We thought he was gonna kill us—"

"What?" Neon's eyes go wide. "He threatened you?"

"Yes," Indah snaps.

"Well, not exactly," I clarify. "But he had a real creepy vibe." I don't tell them about the gun—having not mentioned it to Indah, who didn't seem to notice—or the fact that he grabbed Indah's arm. I don't know why I stay silent, knowing that we all might be in real danger, but the fact that I'm not sure I could have stopped the Tall Man from doing anything makes me feel like a failure. I'm not ready to admit that.

"No offense, Rob, but *you* have a real creepy vibe sometimes," Marley sighs next to me.

"Gee, thanks," I snap.

"I'm just saying—"

"Him having a creepy vibe is not an excuse for just letting him go without finding out who the hell he is or what he's up to," Neon finishes.

"Exactly," Marley agrees.

Indah has stopped pacing and our eyes meet. I can tell she's trying not to burst open when—

"You two don't always have to be some sort of two-headed monster!" she shouts, starting to walk in circles again. "We get it, you've known each other for years, you share a brain—and everything else," she adds scathingly, "but that doesn't mean you have to gang up on us! You weren't there, you don't realize how frightening he was—how *unnatural*—and you always think you know everything just because you're special but you don't."

Indah exhales sharply and stops walking, facing all of us sitting as the color drains from her face.

"I . . . ," she starts, but she doesn't seem to have any idea of where to go next. I cast a furtive glance at Marley and Neon and see them both slack-jawed and wide-eyed at Indah's outburst. I'm a little slack-jawed myself until—

"Robert," Indah breathes, like a curse, "this was you, wasn't it?"

"What?"

"I would never have said that stuff—"

"Except you just did," I hit back.

"Because *you* wanted to say it and were too scared—"

"Don't put words in my mouth!"

"You're the one putting words in *my* mouth, making me say things—"

"I just wanted you to stand up for yourself for once!" I shout, surprised at the volume and intensity of my own voice. "Just because you're stupidly in love with Neon doesn't mean that she should be able to walk all over you, but she does! She's always calling the shots, and you've told me yourself that you wish she wouldn't. Don't blame me for the fact that you've been bottling all that up."

The apartment is so quiet that I can hear the low hum of traffic on Santa Monica Boulevard, several blocks away. Indah is scowling at me and Neon and Marley are still sitting stiff and silent.

"What I do or do not bottle up is none of your business, Robert," Indah says, deadly quiet. "You don't get to decide when I'm honest with my friends."

"Shouldn't you always be honest with your friends?" I ask.

"Oh, because you're so honest?" she retorts, stalking slowly toward me. "Because we know *so much* about you? You've barely told us anything about yourself, Robert Gorham. Don't pretend you know what being friends with someone is really like."

"I've never lied to any of you," I say, though I can't actually remember if that's true. "You know everything you need to know. Everything else is just . . . it doesn't matter."

Indah is standing over me now and suddenly I feel the three of them like meteors trapped in my orbit. Using my ability with multiple people is difficult—my wants ping between targets, sometimes not settling long enough to have an effect. But now, in this moment, with the three of them turned toward me, suspicious looks on their faces, my desire is clear and equally targeted. I want this argument to not be happening. I want the tense atmosphere to disappear, for us to go back to being friends who don't worry about tall men and missing people and the secrets that each of us is hiding from the others. I want everyone to love me.

And they do. I see three sets of shoulders drop, three brows unfurrow; triplet exhales cascade over me and I feel each of their minds in my grasp. It's a tonic—a rush of dopamine, of adrenaline, of pure, addictive control—that brings me back to earth after the confusing and off-putting encounter with the Tall Man. I'm more aware of these three people—of myself, of what I can do—than I ever have been, and it feels like having the strings to a theater's worth of puppets. Like knowing the answer to every trivia question. Like having a key to each of their apartments.

"We're gonna be okay," I breathe, and each of them continues to look at me with big, trusting eyes. Indah finally sits, perching on the arm of Neon's chair, and something inside me surges with warmth. This is the way it should be. Neon, the king of all of this, in her throne, her queen by her side; Marley next to me—stoic and steadfast in the way a knight should be—and me, outside and inside all at once. The one with the silent power.

"We're gonna be okay," I say again, relishing the silence, no longer awkward but instead respectful. Deferential to the one person who always has all the cards—all tall, pale men aside. "We just have to stick together."

The three of them nod in an uneven unison and I smile, feeling comfortable and at home for the first time in weeks. I can feel the desire to keep them calm coursing through my veins, can feel their minds flush against mine.

"Stick together," Neon echoes, like she's trying to understand a phrase in a different language.

"Yeah." I nod. "Stick together."

This makes Marley smile, his chiseled jaw softened by the curve of his mouth. Neon and Indah look at each other lovingly—despite Indah's frustration and Neon's indecision, it's clear they want to be together. That can be arranged.

"We should all move in together," I say, like it's a suggestion. Like it's a question I'm posing, a discussion I want to have. But the decision has already been made. They may not know that right now, but I do. I know that if I said "jump" right now, they wouldn't even ask how high. They would just leap, not even looking at what's below, damn all the consequences, even if it left them splattered on the pavement. It's more power, more satisfying control, than I've ever experienced in my life, and it is completely intoxicating. I want to see how they fall, how they fly. All I have to do is ask.

I tell them to jump.

Indah should have stopped the whole thing in its tracks. She shouldn't have agreed. She didn't have a choice *but* to agree, but there's always a small part of her that wonders if she could resist. When she's free and clear of him, it seems so simple, so harmless. She becomes herself again and thinks that maybe he's not as strong as she supposes.

But every time she's wrong. He comes back around and *wants* something and the next thing she knows, she's behaving in ways that she never could have anticipated. She's agreeing to move her whole life; move in with the woman she can't get to commit— who somehow, suddenly, has now decided *to* commit—with that woman's best friend and sometimes lover, and with a boy she barely knows with a power too big to comprehend.

Indah doesn't like it and she thinks maybe, *maybe*, she should just go. Maybe she should take this moment of being alone—of being out from under Robert's influence—and start over somewhere else. She'd done it before. But then she thinks about Neon and Marley and the still-missing Blaze, and, if she's honest, Robert, whom she's come to care for in spite of what he's capable of. She knows she can't leave all of them behind. Especially not when there's a dangerous man—potentially a dangerous "we" if the Tall Man is to be believed—on their tails.

Indah doesn't like it, but she knows she has to live with it.

PART THREE

THE LOFT

"I don't know that I like this, Nee," Indah's voice echoes in the huge space.

"What's not to like!" Neon shouts, spinning around in the empty living room. "We've got four bedrooms, no landlord, a *roof*! We're in the lap of luxury now, baby."

She grabs Indah by the waist and starts dancing her around the loft, singing an off-key tune and attempting a truly terrible waltz. I laugh at the sight and it stops both of them in their tracks.

"Did you just . . . giggle?" Neon asks, a huge grin spreading across her face.

"What?" I say. "No!"

"Yes, you did!" Indah laughs, stepping out of Neon's embrace and toward me. "I don't think I've ever heard that sound come out of your mouth."

"I laugh," I say indignantly.

"Not really," Neon says. "You chuckle. Maybe. But you're kind of a serious guy, *Damien*."

Her eyes widen at the use of the name she bestowed on me, and I laugh again.

"See, there"—Indah is smiling and pointing at me—"*that* was a giggle."

"Whatever." I roll my eyes and start walking across the big open space, looking for something to do.

"You're *happy*," Neon singsongs as I walk past her.

"Maybe I am." I shrug.

Neon swats at me and I dodge, and before I know it, the three of us are running around the empty loft playing a disorganized game of tag where Neon tags Indah by kissing her on the cheek and then I start doing the same, and soon Neon and I are chasing Indah, who is laughing louder than I've ever heard her, threatening her with affection.

As Neon and I capture Indah between us, each pecking a cheek and teasing her with coos of "oh great, beautiful one," I think about being happy and whether that's something I've ever felt. I'm not sure it is, but I think it must be something close to this. Whatever this feeling is—this free, light, careless, invincible feeling—I want to chase it until I find the other end of the rainbow.

It's been like this ever since I said we had to stick together and the three of them melted like butter in my hands. My desire for all of us to be inseparable, for us to be a *family*, has had some unexpected, though not unwelcome, consequences. Everyone agreed to live together, much to my surprise—the want clearly deeper and more powerful than even I knew. Moving us all into Blaze's old loft is a brain wave that I'm proud of. It will be easier to keep them here, in a familiar place, with the specter of their friend hanging over us, than it would be to keep them in an entirely new spot, like my house in the Hills. It was a little more trouble securing this shabby apartment than an anonymous mansion, but the smile on Neon's face tells me it was worth it.

Our giddy group-hug bubble is burst by Indah's moving away from between us and bringing us back down to earth.

"What *exactly* happened with the old roommates?" she asks, and I roll my eyes, not giving one shit about Twiggy and the rest.

"They all mutually decided that it would be best to live elsewhere," I say with a grin. "I hear the Valley is nice this time of year."

"Don't be a dick," Indah says, and I burst out laughing—not a giggle, but a big, hearty laugh that comes from my gut and warms my insides. That kind of language is exceedingly rare for Indah, and those sounds coming from her beautiful lips are enough to send me cackling.

"'Mutually decided' like the super and landlord mutually decided they didn't want to look after the building anymore?" Neon asks, her eyes glittering.

"Maybe," I say, shrugging innocently. "Though the super isn't going to leave us *totally* alone. It's nice having someone look after the place—I learned that lesson the hard way, trust me."

"And what about your house?" Indah asks. She was the only one who ever saw the place in the Hills and after the first night she stayed there and made a bedroom her own, I realized how much I loathed the place in her absence. Sure, we could have all moved in there, but the Hills was where I spent two listless months without any connection to the Unusuals. I didn't want to hang around there anymore.

"I was getting tired of the upkeep," I lie. "It's so much nicer to have a building where you're not responsible for the utilities."

"Mm-hm." Indah sounds unconvinced.

"Besides," I continue, "Marley and I thought it would be nice for Blaze to come back to his own home." I try not to preen too much at this claim, but being a team with Marley has sanded down his edges, made being around him less terrifying, and a not-small part of me wants to show that I get along with him just like Neon does.

"*If* he comes back," Indah says glumly, and Neon walks over to wrap her in a hug.

"He's coming back, babe," Neon coos. "That kid is so strong. He's gonna be fine and he's gonna get back here and be *so* surprised that we've just up and moved in."

"*You* haven't moved in at all," someone pants from the doorway, and I look to see Marley carrying a stack of boxes in his tree-trunk arms. "Last I checked, *I* was the one doing all the moving."

While still taking the time to tease Marley for his "woe is me" attitude, the rest of us start to settle in. I'm not about to go and get all sweaty lugging boxes up the stairs, and I don't have any possessions to contribute to the loft anyway, so I make myself busy by stacking Blaze's stuff in the corner, ready to be moved into a room if he comes back. I'd never say it to the others, but it doesn't sound like his return is all that likely, and it's definitely not happening that soon.

Alex wakes up sweaty and gasping, like he always does. He automatically pats himself down, checking for scorched clothes, for bits of flame. All his hands find is his damp, un-singed T-shirt.

For a brief moment, Alex wonders if maybe he's finally fixed. Maybe they did it. All that pain—that blinding pain he wasn't sure would ever stop—was worth it.

The wondering is interrupted by the realization that Alex doesn't have any idea where he is. It's dark; he seems to be lying on the ground. There's a vaguely familiar smell—dust and metal and mold. Did he light up somewhere? How long has it been since—since—

The last thing he remembers is meeting the strange, tall man in an alley and then . . . burning. Pain, so much pain. But there's hardly any pain at this moment—a dull smoldering in his torso, but he's used to that by now. He's dealt with far worse.

Alex needs to go home.

Life settles. Marley pops in and out in the way he always has, though we all see more of him than before now that he lives closer to his classes. Neon continues to work at the bike shop, to which she very happily commutes on a nice Kawasaki triple, a bike she mentioned she'd always wanted and that I managed to procure for her after some sleuthing on the Internet with a public library computer. Indah has quit Bar Lubitsch at all of our requests and with a little extra coercion from me. Though we try not to talk about the Tall Man—about how close he came to finding out about all of us, about how he seemed to know about Alex but not where he is now, hardly a positive sign—his presence looms over every conversation until I steer us toward happier things. But we all agreed that Indah's staying employed at the place he had tracked her down to was a bad idea.

So now she's working at a strange, dark downtown dive where, as she describes it, the patrons don't tip nearly as well and the floor is always sticky with beer. But she also isn't paying rent and is finally, *finally* happily settled into a committed relationship with Neon, which I feel partly—and proudly—responsible for.

The first few days in the loft, we all shuffled bedrooms, trying to figure out exactly how we fit into this space. It felt strange for any one of us to claim Blaze's room as our own—like doing so would be admitting defeat—so we moved his things from my careful stack in the living room back into his bedroom, where they wait for him, gathering dust.

Neon and Indah naturally shared a room, having spent the majority of their time at one another's apartments, and I finally ask Neon about it one day while we're hauling unpaid-for groceries up the metal steps of the former warehouse where the loft is situated.

"What do you mean, what am I going to do about it?" she huffs, a few steps above me, carrying far more bags than me, my weak and flabby arms unable to lift as much as hers.

"I mean," I pant, "you guys seem happy. And now you live together . . . why not just make it official?"

Neon doesn't seem to have an answer for that, just continues to trudge up the stairs, a thoughtful look on her face. She's seemed happy about the move, even though it involved moving in with someone whom she doesn't seem to want to commit to, but Indah still has the moments of reluctance she had on the first day. She never seemed to be close to her roommates or care all that much for her old apartment, so I have to assume her dissatisfaction is about what everything is always about: Neon.

I want Indah to be happy—want them *both* to be happy, even if there's a little river of jealousy that runs through me every time Neon pays more attention to Indah than me—and I think this is the fastest way to accomplish that. They'll be together and they'll smile more and I will have done something correct and *good* for once. So I focus all my want on Neon's committing to Indah, try to want it more than anything I've ever wanted in my life, and, as is often the case, I eventually get my way.

As I cook us Denver omelets one morning at Indah's request, I look out over the butcher's block kitchen island and into the wide expanse of the living room, where the two of them are playfully arguing about where to put one of Indah's paintings. Until we moved in together, I didn't even know that Indah painted. In the two weeks we've occupied the same space, I've learned to associate the smell of turpentine with her. I've learned that the tattoos on her arm are ones of her own design and that she has several more that she'll never show me.

Neon is beaming with the big, gentle smile she reserves just for Indah, trying to convince her to place the painting—a beautiful green and blue seascape covering an enormous canvas stretched over a crude wooden frame—in a position of prominence in the living room. I see Indah blush as she laughs, and Neon kisses the spot where the pink creeping up her neck meets the pink blooming on her cheeks.

The smell of burning onions jolts me back to the task at hand. I take the pan off the heat and scrape at the burnt bits of vegetable, my stomach turning. It's not a bad smell—savory and sharp and a little mouth-watering—but there's still a roiling in my gut.

I look back up at Neon and Indah, their easy smiles and light laughter, and I want so badly for them to turn their focus toward *me*, for them to smile at *me*, laugh with *me*. They're too far away for that want to do anything at all, so I just stand there, stewing in the fumes of overcooked onions, tears stinging at my eyes. I don't know if they've lingered from chopping up the onions or if they're fresh from the jealousy battling contentment inside me, but I blink them away all the same.

"Fuck, *finally*," a voice hisses out in the hall as I hear the front door slam shut.

I was asleep a moment ago, I'm sure of it. Something woke me, some distant rattling. Someone fiddling with the lock of the front door.

The room I chose as my own—Twiggy's former room, I think— is nearest to the loft's entrance. Like my selection at the house in the Hills, this room is the darkest and most secluded. It has the added benefit of having the quickest escape route. I'm content here, with the Unusuals—happy even, maybe—but there's still a lizard-brain part of me that is always expecting to have to run away at the drop of a hat.

In this particular moment, however, I wish Marley had this room. Or, at the least, that Marley, with his big, burly body, was sharing it with me. I used to be unable to feel fear—always understanding that danger was something that could be tamed, just like everything else in the world—but the Tall Man set my sense of reality askew.

The hushed voice that just entered the loft didn't sound like Marley—I know the way he enters the apartment when he's coming home from a late night at the library and he's almost completely silent. Neon and Indah are asleep in their bed; I saw them go in together, heard their light giggles through the thin door as they settled in for the night, so whoever just closed our front door is not one of us.

I get out of bed as silently as possible, looking for anything in the room that might work as a traditional weapon if my typical, nonviolent methods fail. But I'm still in the habit of having as few possessions as humanly possible, so the room is as empty as every room I've had since leaving Nebraska. I guess I'll just have to hope whoever is out there is like the majority of people in the world and that I'll be able to politely ask them to leave and receive no pushback.

As I shuffle toward my bedroom door, I hear a thud and another muffled swear, and I nearly stop breathing completely. It's probably just one of Blaze's old roommates. My influence has probably worn off and they've broken back in to get something or try to reclaim the place. That's what I keep telling myself as I inch closer and closer to the door.

I turn the knob slowly, pulling the door open and peering into the hallway. It's dark—whoever it is hasn't turned on the lights, which doesn't make sense if it's one of the old occupants. Surely they'd know where the lights are if they lived here.

As I step gingerly into the hallway, I notice some of Neon's motorcycle tools scattered by the front door. I pick one of them up and tiptoe toward the living room, where the thud came from only moments ago.

There's definitely someone there—I hear shifting and shuffling, maybe even someone muttering to themselves. The sounds of a person moving around are starting to get drowned out by my rapidly beating heart, so loud I'm certain the intruder is going to hear it and come running.

As I turn the corner into the living room, my traitorous, deafening heart leaps to my throat. There's a shadow, skinny and compact, moving through the kitchen. They don't seem to have seen me yet, focused on whatever mission they have.

Their back to me, they open the fridge, illuminating their face. It's a man, about my age, I think, sallow cheeked and pale. I've never seen him before. His face disappears as he goes digging into the fridge. I stand stock-still, holding my breath, wondering what in the hell his aim could be. Is he robbing us for our produce? A few beats of my thunderous heart pass and his head remains in the refrigerator, his shoulders relaxing slightly as he hangs on the fridge door.

This is my moment. I can catch him by surprise, sneak up behind him, maybe even use the refrigerator door to incapacitate him in some sort of action-movie maneuver that I'm sure I couldn't actually pull off if I stopped to think about it for more than a second.

My feet padding silently across the floor, I move quickly and with more certainty than I feel. I'm three feet away from him, can see his shoulders pressing out of his thin T-shirt like twin blades, his skeletal body made even sharper by the glow of the fridge, and I'm lifting the wrench, preparing to bring it down on his head, when suddenly, he turns, and several things happen at once.

His eyes are wide, frightened, and red, but I only get a quick glimpse at them before the refrigerator door closes behind him and we're plunged into darkness. I've stumbled back in surprise, now out of reach of him but also too far to bring the wrench down on his head. As my spine collides with the island behind me, I hear him shout in shock as his back hits the fridge he just closed. And then, everything is light again and the man in front of me is very suddenly, and very completely, on fire.

The blaze is towering and terrible, and the roar of the flames threatens to drown out all other sounds until I hear a horrible screaming coming from inside the fire. And then I'm shouting, in confusion and fear, and there's more thudding and clattering and then a rush of footsteps and suddenly Neon, Indah, and Marley are behind me.

"What the fu—"

"Oh my god—"

"Is that—"

"Yes, I think it is!"

"Well, help him!"

"How?"

Everyone is shouting over each other, over the fire that's raging in front of us, that's making my face break out in sweat but that doesn't seem to be catching. I desperately want to run around the island and join my friends, hide behind the steadfast bulk of Marley, the warm comfort of Indah, the steel spine of Neon, but my feet are stuck to the ground in fear. The volume and pitch of the voices behind me rise and rise, then there's a surge of fire to match, and then a flash of bright blue light, and then no light at all.

Alex looks down at the unconscious boy splayed out on the couch in front of him and wonders if he had a fourth roommate that he's forgotten about.

Seeing his three most reliable friends in his apartment—along with that fresh-faced, terrified stranger—was about as much of a shock as his entire body lighting on fire was. He was almost grateful for the searing pain of Neon's electricity when it came, if for no other reason than to give him a moment of blissful unconsciousness.

"Is he gonna be okay?" Alex croaks, his throat feeling like a dried-out tinderbox.

"He'll be fine," Neon says, her face soft as she gazes down at the passed-out boy. "This isn't the first time he's gotten the Neon special."

"Who is he?" Alex asks.

"The more important question is if *you're* going to be okay," Indah says gently.

"Yeah, I'm fine." Alex shrugs one shoulder. "It's not exactly my first time getting the Neon special either."

"Sorry about that." Neon winces, settling on the arm of the couch. "It was the only thing I could think of to do with you on fire like that. Short-circuit you, short-circuit your ability. I didn't mean to get this one caught in the crosshairs though." She jerks her head toward the prone stranger.

"Robert'll be fine," Marley says. Alex has a name finally: Robert. As to who—or what—Robert is, that remains to be seen. Alex doesn't know when Neon found the time to take in another stray, but if they're all living together, Alex has to assume this Robert is an Unusual. And, based on the concerned but simultaneously fearful looks on his three friends' faces, Alex assumes that Robert is as dangerous as him.

"And you don't have any idea where you were?"

There's a soft surface beneath me and quiet voices murmuring above me.

"Somewhere in the desert, I think. It was hot. And I got a glimpse when they brought me in . . . it was empty. And *so* quiet."

My eyes flicker open slowly, the lids tacky and stiff. Every single muscle in my body is sore and tense, like my limbs have been filled with lead. I'm lying on our couch, my blurry eyes picking up three sets of familiar legs—Neon's arms leaned on her dark knees, the fuzzy flannel legs of Indah's pajamas standing in front of the coffee table, Marley's pale legs stretched out from the chair to my right—and a fourth person, a young Asian man curled in a blanket on the armchair on my left.

"And they just let you go?" Neon asks, not noticing that I'm beginning to rouse, her eyes completely focused on the young man. I want her to pay attention to me, to ask if I'm all right, turn her worried gaze toward *me*, but she feels distant and unreachable and every inch of my body screams in protest at the thought of moving.

"I guess so." I see a skinny shoulder shrug from underneath the blanket. "I woke up a few hours ago in some flophouse a coupla miles from here." His speech—a raspy but melodic voice—becomes slurred, and he bursts into a fit of coughing.

"Here," Indah says, taking a few surefooted steps toward the armchair, "drink some more water."

"Thanks, Indah," he coughs before taking the glass from Indah's outstretched hand and gulping the entire thing down.

A tense silence settles over the group and I use the opportunity to moan in pain, drawing everyone's attention away from the newcomer and back to me.

"There he is," Marley says, his soft, light voice a balm to the ringing still reverberating in my ears.

"What the hell happened?" I groan, trying my best to get my stiff muscles to push myself up to a sitting position. I feel the strong hand of Marley grab my arm and pull me up, and I come face-to-face with the intruder who was completely on fire what feels like mere minutes ago.

"Hey, man," he rasps. "I'm Alex."

"Robert," I say automatically before correcting myself. "Damien. I'm Damien."

"Gotcha," he says, and nods like something is clicking into place. "You can call me Blaze."

"Right," I say, like I'm totally okay with the fact that this guy has barged in without so much as a by-your-leave and gotten all my friends to coo after him like he's just returned from war.

And then the penny drops, embarrassingly late. I forgot why we were here, in this space, this dirty and defunct old factory that's been converted to a wannabe-artsy-hip loft. It's all because of him: because of Blaze. Or, at least, that's how I framed it. That's what I told them, the excuse I gave to get them all in the same place, to live with me, look after me, devote more and more time to me. And now here he is, and I'm wishing I just made them want to move into the house in the Hills.

For the first time, I have a real chance to actually look at him, in light not caused by an enormous fire in front of my eyes. Like I thought, he seems to be around my age, but there's a weariness to him. He looks gaunt—not in the way that Marley does, not like he's been carved out of marble, but like something has been drained from him. The sharpness in Marley's cheekbones is intentional, by design; in Alex's, there's a feeling of absence, like he's been starved. He's unnaturally pale, with dark circles under his eyes, sagging on his face, giving him an almost melted look. His hair is dark and greasy, and I can see his skinny fingers poking out from underneath the blanket, skeletal and long.

"So you're the guy that kicked my skeezy roommates out?" he rasps, his eyebrows lifting slightly in a challenge.

"Uh, yeah," I say. "Guess these guys caught you up?"

"Mm-hm."

He nods and I wait for him to say more—for him to flinch or fawn. But he simply purses his lips, his eyes narrowing slightly in my direction. I want to know what he's thinking, if he's scared of me, angry that we've moved into his space; if he feels bad about nearly burning me alive or if he's wishing he finished the job.

"Someone wanna catch *me* up?" I ask, exasperated.

"Blaze got kidnapped," Neon tells me. "He only just escaped."

"Technically he didn't escape," Marley says, correcting her. "They just let him go."

"Always the lawyer," Alex teases, smiling warmly at Marley.

"Kidnapped by who?" I ask, the simplest question rising out of the maelstrom of questions in my head.

"The Tall Man," Marley says.

"Yeah, I figured that." I roll my eyes. "But who *is* he?"

"Told me his name was Isaiah," Alex says, "but I assume that's a fake. I met him at a party a while back—I thought he was hitting on me at first but turned out he'd pegged me as a user from across the room."

"User?" I ask, my mind still feeling sluggish and dull from Neon's shock.

"Drugs," Alex says blankly. "I do drugs."

"Oh. Right," I say, and Alex's eyes narrow again, like he's trying to puzzle me out.

"They helped," he explains, "with the whole, you know, pyrotechnic show. Isaiah spotted me from across the party and started to sell me something. Said he had a new drug that's stronger than anything you can get on the street. Said it would take the edge off and round all the sharp corners. And he was right. I didn't have a flare-up for two weeks."

"A flare-up?"

"What you just saw," he says.

"It's never been *that* bad, Alex," Indah says. "When your ability got out of control before it'd be your finger, maybe the whole hand, never your *entire body*."

"Yeah, okay, so it's gotten worse." He shrugs. "But for two whole blissful weeks, the only time any part of me was on fire was when *I* wanted it. And then it wasn't enough."

He pauses, swallowing and looking down at his hands, the flippancy gone. His face crumples and his voice is noticeably quieter when he speaks again.

"It was never enough. No matter what I do, the fire always comes back. Letting it out a little every day helps—heroin helps even more—but it always comes back, worse than ever. Isaiah found out about me, said he'd met other people like me, other Unusuals who wanted their ability *gone*. He said there was a way. A way for me to just be . . . normal. No fire, no flare-ups, no more drugs. Just Alex. So we made a time to meet, some shady back alley where he said we were going to meet his supplier, but he never showed. The next thing I know, I'm waking up in some dark room, my whole body on fire."

Alex pauses, his words hanging in the air like knives over our heads. My eyes dart from person to person, not landing on anyone;

I'm too afraid to make eye contact and see my own panic reflected in my friends' expressions.

"I think they did something to me," he continues, his voice thick with unshed tears. "It's worse than ever before. What you saw, everything up in flames . . . that happens a lot now. Whatever they were trying to fix, they just broke it further."

As he finishes, Indah starts rubbing her hand up and down his back as if he isn't a dangerous explosion waiting to happen. I see a tear roll down Alex's cheek and am surprised that it doesn't heat into steam from contact with his skin. I'm terrified, sick to my stomach at the idea that there are people out there looking to hurt us, so I do what I always do—deflect the feeling with an ill-timed question.

"How does it work?" I ask.

"For fuck's sake, Damien," Marley hisses, "the guy just told you that he was kidnapped and experimented on and you want to know how he lights up?"

"It's just a question," I say defensively.

"It's okay, Marley," Alex says, wiping the tear from his face. "I'd be curious too. In fact, I *am* curious."

He peers at me again, a silent challenge. I rise to it.

"They didn't already tell you?" I lift my chin a bit, looking across at him with hooded eyes. I see his mouth twitch once before he responds.

"They gave me the gist," he says. "And that Neon knocks you out."

"Only temporarily," I sneer.

"So when you haven't just been hit with several thousand volts . . ."

"I can make people do what I want." I grin. "Like your skeezy roommates."

"Well, that's not *exactly* how it works," Marley says, ever the pedant.

"Whatever," I say, rolling my eyes. "I make people want what *I* want. So the result is essentially the same. I wanted your room-mates—well, former roommates—to leave and never come back, so they did."

A lump forms in my throat as I finish talking. *Will* they come back? They'd be easy to deal with, to get rid of again, but I don't think I could stand being reminded that my ability has an expiration date. That the people I make leave me are eventually in control of that choice again. And that They chose not to return.

"Pretty impressive," Alex says, snapping me back to the present. "Sounds dangerous though."

"It can be," I preen. "But so can setting yourself on fire."

"True," he concedes. "Sorry about that, by the way. I hope I didn't get you."

I still feel warm, almost like I've got a sunburn, but that is just as likely a result of Neon as it is of being so close to Alex when he was on fire.

"I'm all right. You don't seem any worse for wear though."

It's not strictly true—Alex looks terrible, malnourished and strung out. But his hair isn't singed, his skin isn't blistered. If anything, he looks . . . cold.

"Yeah, it doesn't really have an effect on me," Alex says, shrugging one shoulder. Indah's hand stops rubbing his back, giving him a little push instead as she glares at him. He rolls his eyes and keeps talking.

"Okay, it has a *huge* effect on me. It's super painful and I can't control it well in the best of circumstances, so when I'm in a ton of pain it just gets worse and worse. But it doesn't *burn* me," he finishes.

I nod like I understand and shift uncomfortably on the couch, my muscles wincing in protest.

"Wait," I say, the thought occurring, "Neon was able to knock you out and she rewires my ability for a couple hours. Can't she just . . . make it stop?"

Neon sighs wearily, leaning back in her seat.

"We've tried," she says. "So many times. It doesn't do shit."

"I don't get it, why not?"

"We think it has something to do with the fact that both Neon's and Blaze's abilities are physical," Indah says. "You and Marley have powers that don't manifest physically—"

"Tell that to the very vivid audiovisual hallucinations," Marley quips.

"Okay, yes, yours has an element outside of you, but it's not like electricity or fire. You're not creating something physical that can potentially harm other people. Neon can knock anyone out if she uses enough electricity—"

"Thanks, babe."

"And she—you're welcome—can rewire a mental ability by messing with the electrical impulses in your brains, but a physical ability involves too many different elements for her to be able to rewire it."

"How do you know this?" I ask.

"It's just a theory," Indah says. "I mean, it's not like we have a huge sample of people to pull from. But I do think there's a difference. You all . . . feel different to me."

"What do I feel like to you now?" Alex asks.

It takes me a moment to understand what Indah is talking about. And then I remember—she can sense us. Unusuals. She didn't know I was one right away when we first met because I wanted to fly under the radar. I've never asked about how her non-ability ability works, and now seems like an inappropriate time.

"You feel like Alex," Indah says soothingly, and if I wasn't still thrumming with electricity, I'd be able to find out if she's lying or not.

A heaviness is starting to weigh my eyelids down and I feel myself sink a fraction farther into the couch. The silence in the living room isn't the tense quiet that appeared like air bubbles throughout this conversation but the weary hush of exhaustion. Indah starts to murmur softly in Alex's ear, and the low tones of her voice pull my eyes completely closed and usher me into sleep.

Looking down at Alex sleeping fitfully in her lap, Indah is having a difficult time finding the feelings of relief and happiness she was expecting to feel when they found him. Of course she's relieved, of course she's happy that he's back, but it's drowned out by the screaming fear in her head. Alex doesn't feel like Alex. Indah hates lying but she couldn't bear to tell Alex that something is wrong, not after everything he had just told them.

It's not just the way he looks—the fact that his hair has thinned, that *he's* thinned, lost an unhealthy amount of weight, his skin hanging loosely off his bones. It's not just that his voice is quieter and raspier than it ever has been. There's something else, something intangible, that Indah knows only she can feel. She can help the other things—feed him, soothe his throat—but the way he feels, the way his ability feels to her, isn't something she knows how to fix.

The light buzzing, that frothiness that she feels on the surface of her skin when she's near an Unusual, is still there. But it's *sharp*. It pokes and fits wrong and it doesn't feel like Alex at all. It feels like something unknown, something dangerous.

Alex has always been dangerous, always prone to explode. But it's a danger she knew how to handle. Indah has encountered too many dangers in the past few months, has been pulled out of her comfort zone too far. She wonders if she'll ever feel safe again.

I wake up to the kind of chaos I've become accustomed to in the past few weeks. After Blaze settled in and recovered, he became the life of the party. The Unusuals have been adamant about his staying clean—Neon gives him cigarettes to curb the craving, Indah mixes him mocktails and talks him through his darker moments, and Marley reads him health reports about what heroin does to your body—but Blaze still goes out partying most nights. When he's home, he's boisterous and endlessly energetic. I'm glad that my friends have their friend back, but Christ, it's exhausting.

There's loud talking coming from the kitchen, and as I shuffle softly down the hall and into the shared space, I see the source: Indah, Marley, and Blaze are gathered around the kitchen island as Blaze flambés various food items.

"Robert!" Indah beams at me as I approach the trio, her smile bigger now that Blaze is back. "Good morning, sleepyhead."

"What the hell are you all doing?" I grumble, scratching my head.

"Making lunch," says Marley, grinning, also happier and more carefree than I've ever seen him. My stomach curdles with jealousy.

"Lunch?" I croak.

"It's after noon, dude," Blaze teases lightly, emphasizing his point by lighting an entire watermelon on fire.

"What's your point?" I say, rubbing my eyes, annoyed by Blaze's charming smile and easy rapport with my two friends. I know that they were *his* friends first, but I still resent his barging back into our lives and becoming the center of attention.

I open my eyes again to find three earnest stares pointed in my direction.

"Do you want some pancakes?" Marley asks, turning to the stove behind him. "The batter's gone a bit clumpy but they should still be good."

"I could cook something up for you," Blaze says. "We're making fruit skewers but I could go out and get anything you want."

"That's really okay . . . ," I say awkwardly.

"How about some coffee?" Indah offers, turning to the cabinet behind her to pull a mug down.

"Yeah, coffee would be good . . ."

The three of them bustle around the kitchen like busy worker bees trying to appease their queen. I'm a little surprised at how quickly and effectively my desire for them to pay attention to me took hold, especially given the fact that there are three of them and I've been conscious for about two minutes.

Blaze continues to sear fruit, which smells amazing and looks completely inedible. The small stream of fire coming from his right hand lights up the grin that's plastered across his face. Despite our first meeting and his descriptions of the horrors of the past few months, Blaze seems remarkably in control.

"It's easier to manage when I get to use it," he explains suddenly, answering the question I didn't have time to ask. "There's never been a good place to do it before—other than Neon's place—but now that we've got this huge kitchen all to ourselves . . ."

There's a strong surge of flame as he laughs manically at the pineapple in his left hand that is now completely ablaze.

"Watch where you're pointing that thing!" Marley yelps, taking a step back.

"It's all right," Blaze shouts back, the sound of the joint fires from the pineapple and his hand drowning him out. "I've got it totally under control."

Except it rapidly becomes clear that he doesn't. I want him to stop, to put out the fire on the fruit and close his hand, draw the flame back into himself, but nothing happens. Marley and Indah are practically out of the kitchen entirely now, moving toward me, and the three of us watch in terror as the fire licking Blaze's fingers starts to crawl up his arm.

"Alex," Indah says calmly, though I can hear a slight tremble in her voice. "Please put the fire out."

"I can't," he gasps, and the fire climbs higher on his arm, starting to nip at his shoulder. The flames are reflected in his wide, terrified eyes.

"Yes you can, bud," Marley pleads. "Just like we talked about, okay? Breathe deep, close your eyes, and imagine the fire just . . . going away."

Marley's voice sounds certain, like it always does, but I'm skeptical about the idea that meditation is going to solve this problem. Blaze seems skeptical too, because he doesn't follow Marley's instructions, instead looking at him with big eyes.

"No, I can't do it." He shakes his head and the fear starts to drain, leaving disappointment behind. "I've just got to let it run its course."

He sighs, resigned, and stares at the flames engulfing his entire right arm. The three of us stand several feet away, the island between us and him, but I can still feel the warmth of the fire on my face. Blaze holds his arm out, careful not to light anything on the countertop on fire. The crackle of the flames fills the quiet between the four of us and I watch the light play on Blaze's defeated face.

We stand still and silent for several minutes until, finally, the flames start to die. When they've crept back down to his wrist level, Blaze picks up a dish towel from the island and hits his hand a couple of times, precise and unflinching. With a few whacks of the towel, the flame goes out completely, and he flexes his unlit right hand a few times before putting down his arm and looking back at us.

"Sorry about that."

"It's okay, Alex," Indah coos, her focus completely on Blaze again. "Are you okay?"

He just shrugs.

"Singed another fucking shirt," he says, indicating the edge of his T-shirt sleeve, which is, in fact, lightly burnt.

"You can borrow one of mine," Marley offers, voice shaky, his shoulders still up around his ears, his face white as a sheet.

"At least it didn't hurt," I say, looking between ghostly Marley and Blaze's blank, unfeeling face and trying to contribute to the cheer-up.

"It did hurt," he says flatly, turning on his heel and walking toward his room. I almost don't hear what he says before he disappears into his room, but it makes me flinch even before the slam of the door.

"I've just gotten used to it."

It keeps happening—Blaze going up in flames. The fire disrupts the natural rhythm of our days, makes everything about Blaze, his power, his problems. The spacious loft starts to feel claustrophobic, so I get back into the daily runs that kept me occupied when I was living in the Hills. *At least now I don't have to run alone*, I think at first, coercing Marley into joining me, now that we don't have looking for Blaze to bond us. But after exactly one run with Marley, watching him barely break a sweat as I'm panting alongside him, I decide that, actually, going alone is probably best.

I'm in a park, running a loop, when I decide to find a place I can do some push-ups, Marley's arms and broad chest at the top of my mind. Even though she's in domestic bliss with Indah, I still sometimes catch Neon looking at Marley's bulky form and think maybe if I beefed up a little bit, she might look at *me* that way.

As I step off the path and onto the grass, I see a group of a dozen people, sitting on yoga mats, eyes closed. A woman is sitting facing the group, her mouth moving. I'm too far to hear what she's saying, but I'm captivated by the stillness of her shoulders, the serene look on her face. The whole scene is mesmerizing. I've never seen so many people stay so still, making it seem like time has stopped in their corner of the park.

I don't know how much time actually does pass but suddenly the group is moving, everyone's eyes opening as they stand up and start to roll up their mats. Before I have a chance to think about it, I'm walking over to the group and right up to the woman in the front, who is packing up as she smiles and waves to the various members of the group walking off.

"Um, excuse me," I start, feeling clumsy. I can't remember the last time I approached a stranger without a specific goal in mind. "What . . . what is this?"

The woman swivels to look at me and laughs softly, swinging her yoga mat over her shoulder.

"Meditation," she says warmly, taking a step toward me. "We're here every Monday and Friday morning."

"Right." I nod, pushing down the desire to roll my eyes. Marley has been trying to get Blaze to meditate, focus on staying calm— why is it that everything in my entire life right now seems to come back around to Blaze?

"You're welcome to join us next time," she continues. "It's free."

"Not really my thing," I say as politely as possible, taking a small step back. I don't really know what I was expecting, but I'm somehow disappointed all the same.

"What *is* your thing?" she asks gently, stopping me from walking away.

I look at the woman, her face open and patient, and try to figure out if she's hitting on me. I would guess she's about fifteen years older than me and I notice a wedding ring on the hand that's wrapped around the shoulder strap of her mat. So why exactly is she talking to me? It must be me, wanting her attention, though I can't think of why.

"I see a lot of people like you," she explains, answering my unexpressed confusion. "Young people who are a bit lost."

"I'm not lost," I say automatically.

"Why did you come over here?" she asks.

"Curiosity." A simple answer. A lie. A lie I tell myself when I don't know what the truth is.

"Do you do a lot of things out of 'curiosity'?"

Her face is still open. There's no heat of judgment in the question, though it does sound like she sees through the lie.

"Would you like to go for a walk?" she asks after I don't answer.

So that's how I find myself walking through a park with Francine. She's not the hippie guru that I thought. She's a doctor, a therapist, who runs meditation as a hobby, trying to bring a degree of mental health practice to people who can't pay for it. She seems to be one of those nauseatingly altruistic people who sees the good in everyone, so once I've got the basics of who she is, we don't talk about her anymore. I'm not sure if it's because I don't want to—I don't have the patience to hear all about her good deeds and kind heart—or if it's because she's a therapist and talking about other people is what she does. But either way, we end up talking about my new roommate situation.

"He's just hard to live with," I sigh. "I know it's not his fault, but he's . . . destructive."

"Hm," Francine hums. Every other sound out of her mouth is a hum. It's irritating, but I still find her less annoying than Dr. Crane. "Why do you say it's not his fault?"

"It just isn't," I say, willing her to take my word for it so I don't have to try to explain Unusuals.

"How do your other roommates deal with the destruction?" she asks, the difficult question successfully evaded.

"They don't seem to mind it. They just feel bad for Blaze and, like, coo over him."

"You sound bitter," she says.

"Yeah, well I *am* bitter," I say, realizing it's true. "Blaze gets a free pass because his ability hurts him, but it doesn't matter that I also can't control what I do—I don't have a choice—but I still get chewed out for using it sometimes. It isn't fair."

"Ability?" she asks. Whoops. So much for avoiding the explanation.

"Just . . . Blaze and I are both special, okay? We all are. And that's great, it's amazing that they all understand what it's like, except they only understand halfway. They know what it's like to be different but . . . but . . ."

"No one understands what it's like to be you," she says, nodding her head.

"Yeah . . ." I'm surprised. Surprised by her insight, by this whole conversation. I didn't realize how much Blaze's being around was bothering me, how replaceable I've felt since he's come back. I tell Francine as much.

"Have you told your friends that you feel this way?" she asks.

"God no," I snort.

"Why not?" she asks, like the suggestion isn't ludicrous.

"I don't want to be proven right," I mumble, looking down at my feet. Talking like this to a woman I know I never have to see again, whom I could make forget this conversation ever happened, makes it easier to admit the things I have a hard time even admitting to myself.

"You think they'll reject you if you need something?"

"I think they'd reject me if I let go."

"What do you mean 'let go'?"

I don't know how to explain it to her. How to explain the deep-seated fear that if I stopped using my ability for even a moment, the Unusuals would wake up to the person I really am and realize that they don't actually want to include me in their little family after all. They would stop wanting to take care of me, spend time with me, learn about me.

"It's easy to feel like a burden to our loved ones when we have emotional needs that aren't being fulfilled," she tries.

"It's not that . . . my needs are being met." It's an automatic response, but I'm not sure it's true. I'm not sure it's *ever* been true. "I have—I have *everything*," I continue, an echo of talking to Dr. Crane. "I know I'm not a burden because I don't want to be, but I don't understand how—"

I groan in frustration.

"He's a mess! Blaze is a mess and out of control and they still love him and want to take care of him and—and—they *searched* for him. He left and they never stopped looking. But if I slip for a *millisecond*, that's the end of it. They leave and they don't come back. They forgive him for disappearing, for the drugs, for setting their lives on fire, but I got left behind and I—I—"

"Do you forgive yourself?"

"What?"

"Do you forgive yourself?" Francine asks again, voice blank. I stop walking and look into her eyes. Her expression is as flavorless as her voice. She's not asking the question. *I'm* asking the question *through* her, and suddenly we're not talking about Blaze or the Unusuals anymore.

I don't answer her. We stand in silence, my heart beating against my rib cage as the desire to run away and hide rises up in me. Her face stays blank as she turns her back on me and walks away, back to her real life, already forgetting all about the strange boy she tried to talk to in the park. I watch her go, wondering if there's anything good that stays good once I've touched it.

When I get home, there are new scorch marks on the ceiling. Marks that can be scrubbed away, painted over. I wonder if there's a way to do that to my past. To Them. Cover Them in white paint until I forget the black mark was there to begin with.

Marley is worried.

It's something that Marley is extremely good at—he's had plenty of practice. He worried when his grandmother, the person who had taken care of him for so many years, got sick. He worried about having enough money to pay for school. He worried about closing his eyes and seeing other people's ghosts behind his eyelids.

Marley is *good* at worrying. And he's especially good at worrying about his friends. And that's what's keeping him up now, staring at the ceiling of the bedroom he's only been in for a few months, in an apartment he can't quite remember why he moved into.

Blaze hasn't told them the whole story. Marley knows this because Marley has seen it. When his friend's arm went up in flames, Marley started seeing double. On one side, Blaze in the present, calmly looking at the fire expand from his hand. On the other side, Blaze from another time strapped down, entirely ablaze, screaming, screaming, *screaming*. Screaming in a way that Marley had never heard from another human being. Screaming in pain. Screaming in fear. And behind this past Blaze, this version of the young man being tortured, was a tall man. The Tall Man. Isaiah.

Marley is very, *very* worried.

"We still need to find him."

Marley's voice is hushed and uncharacteristically sharp as I click the front door shut.

"I know," Neon hisses, "but how do we go about doing that exactly? This isn't some shady dealer that Blaze got in too deep with— this guy is *dangerous*."

"I know, Nee," Marley whispers. "That's exactly why we have to find him."

I'm tiptoeing from the front door to the living room, where the voices are coming from. It's dark and quiet in the loft. Marley and Neon are standing by the window, leaned toward each other, the glow of a streetlamp illuminating their tense faces.

A plank of wood creaks below me as I take another step and their heads snap in my direction. I see both of their shoulders drop as they realize who it is.

"Oh," Neon breathes. "Hey, Damien. Where've you been?"

"Out," I say vaguely, hoping to build some intriguing mystique around myself, desperate to find new ways to keep the Unusuals interested in me. In reality, I was sitting at the bar at Indah's new workplace, drinking free drinks and making sure that the more sauced patrons didn't bother her. "Where's Blaze?" I ask, deflecting.

"Sleeping," Marley says. I flop on the couch and look up at them expectantly, waiting for my desire to be part of their conversation to do its work.

There's a beat where they both stare expectantly back at me and then I feel a little click in my brain—a rope latching on to a dock—and they sit down, Marley in an armchair, Neon on the couch next to me.

"We need to find the Tall Man," Neon tells me.

"Isaiah," Marley says, correcting her.

"Right, Isaiah."

"Why?" I ask. "Blaze is safe. We know what Isaiah looks like, we can protect him."

"Can we?" Neon asks. "You said it yourself: both times you met him, you didn't think your ability was working on him. What if that's true for all of us?"

"What, you think he's like . . . immune to Unusuals or something?"

"Maybe," Marley says calmly, nodding like he's talking about torts or whatever dumb law thing it is that he's always going on about. "We know there are people out there who aren't Unusual but relate to them somehow—maybe he's like Indah, but the exact reverse. Not overly sensitive to Unusuals, but resistant to them."

"And that's the point," Neon continues. "If he is immune to everyone, not just you, then we might all be in danger. Sure, Marley is strong—"

I see the tiniest smile twitch at the corner of Marley's mouth and a blush bloom on his cheeks.

"—and I know my way around a fight, but if I can't use my electricity, we're fucked."

"You really think he's going to come after us?" I ask incredulously. "He asked about Blaze *once* and hasn't come back around. He's probably moved on."

"Or he's lying low. Waiting for his moment," Marley suggests darkly.

"Plus," Neon sighs, "what if he still has the others?"

"What others?"

"I've seen some stuff," Marley says quietly. "In Blaze's past. He was being experimented on. Tortured. And he wasn't the only one. I wasn't sure at first but . . . I think . . . I think it's a pretty big operation."

Hearing Marley sound uncertain is always like having cold water dumped on my head. And now he's sounding *scared* and it's like that cold water is filled with spiders.

"So what do we do?" I croak.

"Blaze and I are going to go back to the warehouse he woke up in tomorrow," Neon says. "Start there. And then maybe . . . maybe we'll have to go out to the desert. He thinks that's where he was being held."

"The desert is pretty big," I scoff. "Trust me, I've driven through it."

"Then I guess we better get going," Neon snaps, and I see blue flash through her eyes. Neon may not have my ability, but as always, she has her own special magic that convinces anyone of anything, even me. *Especially* me. If Neon says "jump" and I say "how high," maybe she'll want to stick around and watch me leap into the sky and pull down the moon, just for her.

"So you haven't been around very much, huh?" I ask.

Indah and I are in the kitchen, cooking dinner for the rest of the group. No one's home at the moment. It's the first time we've spent more than a few seconds in the same room in the past week or so and I want to know why she's ignoring me.

"What do you mean?" Indah asks, looking at the vegetables in front of her instead of at me.

"I mean," I sigh, "that we haven't done anything fun lately."

"Do we normally do fun things?"

"Yeah, of course. That time in the park, all the times we've drunk together, *this*." I gesture to the veritable feast around me.

"We don't drink together," she says.

"You know what I mean."

"I've just been busy, that's all." She shrugs, flipping her hair—the ends now blue instead of pink—off of her shoulder, revealing the tattoos underneath. I find myself staring at them, drinking in her figure like a thirsty man who's come across water. There are the vines, delicate and intricate, that climb up her arms, like she's a tree, a home for other blooming things. The vines fan out when they reach her shoulder, ending in gossamer pink flowers that look like they're swaying in some invisible wind.

"Did you get a new one?" I ask, noticing a bright pink flower on her back, blooming over the place where her spine meets her neck.

"Mm-hm," she says noncommittally.

I haven't used my ability much on Indah recently. We're friends, we have a rapport, and most of the time I don't need to. But I can feel myself getting frustrated with her vague answers, can feel the want pushing out of me and on to her. I know my friends don't like it when I use my ability on them—and I don't like it when they use theirs on me—but they usually don't even notice. A little push to get Indah to talk to me won't hurt.

I let the want out.

"It's a *Mirabilis jalapa*," she tells me. "A flower from Indonesia—from the province my family is from. I haven't been there but I've been saving up money to go."

"You have?" I ask, surprised I haven't heard about this until now.

"Mm-hm." She nods. "I probably shouldn't have spent some of that money to get the tattoo but . . . I don't know, I wanted to do something just for me. Living here with everyone, it's nice, but it wasn't my choice."

My stomach starts to sink and Indah just keeps talking.

"I keep thinking that I'm gonna say something, *do* something, call my old roommates and tell them I'm moving back in, but then I come back to the loft every night and suddenly I want to be here again. And I wonder if it's just that I forget how nice it is to be around everyone—to see Alex safe and getting better—or if it's be-cause you want me here. And then I leave to go to work and things start to clear up, but I can never fully get out of the fog."

"Why don't you ever call him Blaze?" I ask abruptly, desperately wanting to get out of this conversation before I have to examine what she's saying too closely.

"Because it's not his name," she says, easily going along with the subject change. I exhale in relief before continuing, keeping the engine of the new subject moving, pulling us away from a topic that could tear us apart. Indah said herself that it's nice to live here with everyone. She just gets muddled sometimes; I'm sure that's just a natural side effect of being around my ability all the time. Everything's fine.

"Well, Neon and Marley aren't real names either," I point out, voice forcefully light. "And you use those."

"Those are self-selected," Indah explains. "When they first met, Neon and Marley were bonded by what made them different. They went from being alone—from being dangerous freaks—to being a unit. I think they wanted to separate those two parts of their lives. The time before they met, when they were still Sarah and Jason, and the time after they met, when they could finally be who they really are: the electric girl and the boy who sees ghosts."

"I can understand that." I nod absentmindedly, reeling from hearing Neon's and Marley's "real" names, which suit them so much less than their chosen ones. "I don't like to think about my life before I met all of you."

Indah hums maddeningly vaguely and I realize something.

"You don't really ever call me Damien," I say. "Is it just because Neon gave me the name, like she did with Blaze?"

"Not exactly. With Alex . . . he hates his ability. He always has. I think there's a real chance that he always will. And as much as I would like him to accept who he is, love himself without any qualifications, I'm never going to force someone to grapple with a quality about themselves that scares them. Sometimes I worry that the name 'Blaze' is just a torturous reminder of everything Alex can't control. I don't want to rub it in."

I think about the look on Blaze's face when he was flambéing fruit the other day and think that maybe Indah isn't entirely right. He seems to enjoy his ability, when he can control it. But then I remember his expression as the fire grew out of his control—the fear mixed with a quiet resignation, a look of abject disappointment as his worst feelings about himself became manifest.

"Is that what you think about me?"

"I don't know, Rob," Indah says, and the want for her to be honest is so raw and desperate I know she's telling the truth. "I think your ability scares you like Alex's scares him, but you're not hurt by your power. It isn't trying to destroy you. It makes things easier for you, makes things better. But you're still scared of it."

"I just don't know the limits of it, that's all," I say, deflecting.

"And doesn't that scare you?" Indah asks. "Do you want to be someone who tames the world around you?"

"My ability is nothing like Blaze's," I say defensively. "It can't destroy buildings, it can't *kill* people."

"That you know of."

"I've always hated the name Robert," I spit, avoiding Indah's unspoken question. "I like the name Damien. It doesn't matter that someone else gave it to me. It fits."

"But, Robert," Indah says, my name pointed like an arrow, "if that were really true, then you'd want me to call you Damien. But I don't. So what does that tell you?"

I'm having a good dream, for once, when I feel someone violently shaking me awake.

"Damien," someone whispers. "Damien, wake up!"

I open my eyes to see Neon right above me and think for a second I'm still dreaming, but then I clock her freaked-out face and I scramble to sit up in bed.

"What the hell?" I croak, rubbing at my eyes.

"You need to get up," another voice says, and I look around Neon to see Marley standing in the middle of my room.

"Why?" I moan.

"Blaze," Neon breathes, and the terror in her voice is enough to launch me out of bed.

As I hastily pull on pants and a T-shirt, feeling self-conscious all the while about Neon and Marley's seeing me in my boxers (eerily similar to my dream in all the wrong ways—and thank *god* Indah is closing tonight, I couldn't handle all three of them), they catch me up.

"We got a call from the LAPD," Neon tells me. "Blaze has been arrested."

"Again," Marley adds.

"What?" I ask, my head still fuzzy. "Why?"

"Why do you think?" Neon says. "Arson."

When we get to the police station, the officer on duty gives us the full story.

"Your pal in there caused quite a lot of damage," he says around a piece of gum in his mouth. "We think he must have had a bomb— he blew out the windows of a bar. No casualties, thankfully, just some burns, but the Feds are on their way."

"The Feds?" Marley gulps.

"Alex Chen is already in the system for multiple counts of arson," he tells us. "This was an escalation—an act of terror. That's above our pay grade."

"Oh my god . . ." Neon leans her hands on the counter separating us and the officer and puts her head between her arms, her hair hanging down and hiding her face.

"You're gonna let him go," I say to the officer, and I feel Neon's head snap up to look at me. "You're gonna let him go and call whoever you need to call to make sure that Alex Chen is never arrested again."

"Why would I . . . ," the officer starts to chuckle, and then, the familiar smoothing over, the well-known blank face of someone who's starting to comply with what I want.

"Damien . . . ," Marley warns.

"It's okay."

"This isn't a free drink or someone else's car," he says through gritted teeth. "This is the *law*."

Despite what he describes as his "morally dubious" ability, Marley is the consummate law student, often seeing things in stark black and white. I ignore him, looking to Neon instead for support. She's peering at me, her expression unreadable, before she says:

"Do it."

Marley starts to protest, but Neon lays a placating hand on his arm and I get to work. Moments later, Blaze is coming out from the back, careening directly into Neon's and Marley's arms in a tight group hug that no one bothers to include me in.

"Thank you, man," he says to me when he's extricated himself from his worried friends' grasp.

I want to tell him I didn't do it for him—that I don't actually really care if he goes to jail or not, if he lives or dies. Trying to track down Blaze with the Unusuals was a lot more fun than actually finding him. Now that he's back in our lives, he's a nuisance, pulling focus onto himself and leaving me out in the cold, taking my spot in my friends' warm embrace. I did this for *us*, because we already have a dangerous armed man on our tails and we don't need the cops on our backs either.

But I don't tell him that. I just nod.

"You guys should go," I tell them. "I need to stay here for a little bit, just to make sure everything's clear."

Marley nods, his arm around Blaze as he starts to steer him to the door.

"I'll wait with you," Neon says, giving the go-ahead to leave to Marley and Blaze with a nod of her head, and my heart surges. She's choosing me over Blaze, choosing to sit in a police station for a few hours—the last place I think she'd want to be—so that I don't have to be alone. Neon and I haven't had one-on-one time in a few weeks, and sitting side by side with her under the grim fluorescent lights makes me feel more special than manipulating a police officer to wipe a slate clean ever could.

Blaze might be a thorn in my side, but tonight, he actually proved himself pretty useful.

Alex and Marley go to the warehouse, and it's just like Alex barely remembers—damp and too cold for LA, a slightly burnt metal smell barely covering the stench of human waste. Alex sees Marley flinch.

He may look tough and imposing, but Alex knows Marley wouldn't be able to stomach half the stuff that Alex has seen. Just the other night, Marley got a glimpse of something in Alex's past—something from the past that Alex can't remember—and promptly went to the bathroom to throw up.

They wander through the run-down building, stepping over discarded needles and the occasional junkie. Alex's heart bleeds for these people, with vacant eyes that he's so familiar with. He wants to take them all home, care for them, pull them out of the hole that he himself is still trapped in, but he knows that he's in no position to be anyone's savior. He's barely scraping through each day himself.

"Anything look familiar?" Marley asks softly.

"This whole place looks familiar," Alex says. "It looks like every other shithole I've ever had the misfortune of waking up in."

Marley doesn't laugh at that, his mouth a thin, tense line.

"I don't think there's anything here," Marley admits.

"I told you," Alex says. "If it hadn't been for all the stuff you've seen, I'd be half-convinced that the whole thing was a drug-induced fever dream."

"One that lasted for months?"

"Weirder things have happened." Alex shrugs casually.

"No they haven't." Marley is clenching his jaw as he stomps past Alex and toward the hole in the building that used to be a door. Alex watches him go, his back like a bucket of ropes, and wonders what he did to get friends so fiercely protective of him, even when it seems like all he's capable of is fucking up.

Blaze is noticeably grateful to me over the next few weeks, going out of his way to smile at me or pay me a compliment. I still haven't warmed to him, but the effort to include me makes his near-constant presence at the apartment more bearable. *Everyone* is at the apartment more, per my unvoiced request. Even though I'm confident that I was able to erase Blaze's record entirely, I still think it's important for us to lie low for a little while. With the investigation of the Tall Man stalled—Marley and Blaze having found nothing at the warehouse or on their trips to the desert—I'd rather just pretend that he and the LAPD don't exist.

I also do my best to put the conversation with Indah as far out of my mind as I possibly can. I don't think she meant it—that she didn't want to live here. Because every single night for the past week, she's taken shifts with later starts so that she can be home to make dinner with me. She teaches me some Indonesian dishes that her mom taught her, and when we're not doing that, we're trying strange recipes we find in Blaze's former roommates' old cookbooks that they left behind.

We have all our meals together in the living room, everyone bright and laughing. Blaze eats like he's a starving man and each meal is his last. Color starts to come back to his cheeks, the circles under his eyes lightening each day. He even stops spontaneously combusting, using his ability only occasionally to light candles or Neon's cigarettes.

"Don't you remember that?" Marley laughs, his smile broader than I've ever seen. This whole time I assumed that Marley's natural state was buttoned-up and judgmental, but the past few weeks of lightness have made me reevaluate that assumption.

"I swear I don't!" Blaze is almost crying with laughter on the couch, Indah and Neon curled into each other next to him, giggling. I didn't know that Neon *giggled*.

"I swear to god," Marley chuckles, "everyone thought you were part of the show. They just assumed it was pyrotechnics."

"Why would anyone think that an All-American Rejects show would have *pyrotechnics*?" I ask incredulously.

"I still can't believe that you guys went to see All-American Rejects in person," Neon teases. "You're such dweebs."

"Whatever." Marley rolls his eyes. "*You* like Fall Out Boy."

"You do?" I gasp, faux-scandalized.

"I like the way Patrick Stump sings!" Neon shouts, hitting Marley on the arm.

"Can you even call it singing?" Blaze says. "It's, like, incoherent screeching."

"Says the guy that went through an entire screamo phase," Indah quips.

"At least I don't own *every single* Black Eyed Peas album," Blaze teases, pointing a finger accusingly at Marley.

"Now, wait just a minute—" Marley starts, and the group explodes into laughter and shouting.

I lean back in my chair—one that Marley brought home randomly one day, saying that we didn't have enough seats for everyone and making my heart feel warm in a way I didn't think was possible—and just watch, basking in the glow of the evening.

There's nothing I want in this moment; no influence is being exerted over these people. All I want is for it to be like this always: the five of us together, in this loft, eating a dinner that Indah and I almost burned down the kitchen making, teasing each other for our music tastes. The conversation with Francine, the fear that none of this is real, washes away. That's all it was: fear, lingering in Their stead. But my Unusuals aren't like Them—they *do* understand. They laugh with me. They *accept* me.

I've been to so many different places in this country, seen all kinds of cities, met all kinds of people, and nothing compares to this ratty downtown Los Angeles apartment. Forget the Grand Canyon: *this* is the most beautiful sight I've seen. This is home.

I really didn't think that I'd be coming back to the desert.

I've got the window on the Plymouth rolled down, the hot air sweeping in and swirling my floppy hair around. I should get it cut. I never think much about my appearance—only ever getting new clothes when mine get worn, only cutting my hair when it gets long enough to be annoying—but my dark bangs have started to hang over my eyes and I'm constantly swatting them out of the way. Maybe I could get Indah to cut them—I know she dyes her own hair, so maybe the skill translates.

"What're you thinking about?"

I turn my head to Marley, folded into the passenger seat. Only Marley could make the Plymouth seem like a toy car. His hair isn't at all bothered by the wind—I don't know how often he has to shave it to keep it at such a close buzz.

"Hair," I say, turning my eyes back to the road.

"Huh?"

"I need to cut mine."

"I don't know," he says, "you kinda rock the shaggy look."

"I do?" I turn to him again, involuntarily grinning at him. He grins back and it just makes me smile bigger.

"Yeah," he laughs. "Fits with the name too. Damien, the emo boy."

"Shut up," I groan, and he laughs harder. Marley has been laughing a lot more recently and it always feels like winning something.

"What about you?" I ask. "Why the perpetual buzz?"

"Just got used to it, I guess," he says, and I see him rub his head out of the corner of my eye. "Used to have really long hair—down to my shoulders—and they made me shave it all off in basic."

"Basic what?"

"Training."

"What?" As is often the case with Marley, I feel like I've missed several steps. His steady, reliable personality is a comfort at times, but the reticence that comes with it can be maddening.

"I was in the army," he says.

"*What?*" I repeat, now feeling like I've missed an entire mile of steps. "How the hell did I not know that?"

I look briefly away from the road in front of us to see him shrug.

"Dunno," he says. "You never asked."

"When were you in the army?"

"I enlisted when I turned eighteen," he tells me.

"*Why?*" This boggles my mind. Marley is very law-and-order, I guess, given his aspirations, but he's very much not a rah-rah patriotic type. When he does talk about school, he spends most of his time complaining to all of us about the flaws in the American justice system. I have a very hard time picturing him in the military.

"Didn't have anything else to do. My grandma died my senior year of high school and she was the one who took care of me."

"What about your parents?"

"I'm like you," he says, and doesn't elaborate. I know he's being kind to me—or else answering my constant, latent desire to never talk about my parents—but I'm certain in that moment that he's gotten the gist of my situation by looking into my past. That would bother me, except Marley isn't judging me for it—he's saying he understands, and I didn't even have to go through the awkward trouble of saying anything out loud.

"Right," I say, wanting him to continue but afraid to ask. The want must be strong, because Marley proceeds to tell me everything I would have asked about, and plenty of things I wouldn't have.

"Yeah, so, I needed money and a job and a place to live after graduation. My grades were good enough to get into lots of colleges but no one was gonna pay for it. It was just after 9/11, and there was a recruiter at my gym, so . . . I joined up. I even liked it for a while. It was nice, you know? Having three square meals a day, people telling me what to do, a built-in community. I didn't think my thing would be a problem—it didn't happen that much, and I'd mostly gotten used to it, enough that I didn't wig out when it happened.

"But then the war started and I got my orders. Iraq. I'd been hoping to climb up the officer ranks, avoid seeing any actual fighting. I'm smart, I think I would have been good at it, but it doesn't matter how smart I am looking the way I do. People always think I'm gunning for a fight—they see me, see my size, and assume that I'm a bruiser. But I'm not. I've never liked fighting. So when I got over there . . . it was *bad*. Really bad. I—"

Marley stops himself and swallows. I can't tell if he's stopping himself from sharing something he doesn't want to share or if I really don't want to hear about whatever gruesome things he saw or did over there. I have such a clear image of who Marley is in my head and I'm not sure I want to have that shattered.

"Well . . . eventually things got so rough that I had to get out," he continues. "Things were bad enough for me, but then I started seeing everyone's past, and, well . . . I saw a lot of death. A lot of really horrible violence. Things that were happening to my unit, things they were doing, things the army was doing to itself . . . you know the expression FUBAR?"

I shake my head.

"'Fucked up beyond all recognition,'" he explains, jaw clenching. "The army has a specific shorthand, just for that phrase. Because everything always is. Everything is FUBAR, *especially* inside the army, and when I think about what we did—"

He swallows.

"Then I started seeing things that weren't even there," he continues quietly, "things that weren't an echo of someone's past. I was hallucinating, for real, haunted by everything that we were—"

He stops himself again and I'm relieved.

"It just got to be a lot," he finishes simply. "Luckily, I got shot—"

"You got *shot*?" My head whips to look at him. "*Luckily?*"

"Everyone I knew was getting stop-lossed—some guys still are. This isn't an easy war to get out of, Damien." He gives me the Marley Serious Eyes—a look we're all very familiar with that tells us we need to pay close attention to whatever Marley is saying.

"I know that," I say petulantly.

"So, yeah, it was lucky," he says. "I don't know that I would have gotten out of it. And it all turned out okay—the military is paying for college and will hopefully help me get financial aid for law school. But I . . ." He trails off for a moment, before swallowing and whispering: "I still have nightmares. The things I saw . . . the things I *did*. That never really leaves you."

"Jeez," I say, turning back to the road.

"Yeah."

"How long were you in combat?" I ask after a moment, not wanting to linger in the silence.

"Two years."

"Jeez," I repeat.

"Mm-hm."

It seems that's all there is to his story—or, at least, all he's willing to share. I keep staring at the road, turning over the new information in my head. It explains a lot, I think, about the way that Marley is—stern and serious so much of the time. He's been relaxing over the past few weeks, seems to loosen when he's with people he knows, but there are still times when he goes blank and tough. Today is one of those times. He's barely cracked a smile all day, at least until he started teasing me about my hair. And it's not like this impromptu errand has been a barrel of laughs—we've gone driving a few hours out of LA in search of more clues about where Blaze was held. But the desert is big and it's like looking for a tan-colored rock in, well, the desert.

Marley and Blaze have been going on these trips for the past few weeks, routinely knocking off every major road out of LA that leads into places barren and hot. I gifted them with a car—just a basic Camaro—for the purpose, but it backfired on me a little. They haven't gotten closer to finding Isaiah, who becomes less scary in my head the farther I get from the encounter at Lubitsch. After all, in both of our weird encounters, he never actually did anything to me. The result of this effort has been that Marley is spending a lot more time with Blaze than he is with me. So I volunteered for this particular drive.

It reminds me of Marley and I looking for Blaze, playing detective, which now feels like another lifetime. We have a nice rhythm, the two of us, and I missed it. I know that Blaze was technically there first, but I staked my claim in his absence and I'm not going to give it up without a fight.

We drive along in a contented silence and my mind begins to wander to what Indah and I might make for dinner tonight. We got a new tablecloth for our big table, blue like Indah's ocean painting on the wall. The dining area is quickly becoming my favorite place in the world; I'm not even bothered by the fact that I stare at a painting of the ocean instead of the real thing. Months and months in Los Angeles, and I keep moving farther and farther away from the Pacific but closer to something I never thought to want.

"I don't talk about that stuff, Rob," Marley says suddenly and sharply, washing the ocean from my mind. My head whips around and I see him scowling, jaw clenched, as he stares through the windshield.

"Okay . . . ," I drawl, uncertain how to respond.

"I don't bring up your past," he continues, "so don't go digging up mine."

"I was just curious," I say.

"I know." He sighs heavily, sounding irritated. "You're always curious. I get it. I was curious too once—still am sometimes—but that's not an excuse."

"I'm your friend, Marley," I say, the words feeling strange but right as they exit my mouth. "We're supposed to talk about this kind of stuff."

"I barely talk to Neon about it and we've known each other for years," he spits. "What makes you think that I'd want to talk about it with you?"

It feels like a punch to the gut, so I go punching back.

"You want to if I want you to," I sneer, knowing immediately that it's the wrong thing to say.

"So just because you can, it means you should? So I can talk about your past with you, look as much as I want?"

"Go right ahead," I say. "There's nothing there I'm ashamed of. Not like you and your army days."

"Fuck you," he growls. "I might not be able to read your emotions or get you to spill your guts about things, but I know you're ashamed of what you did to your parents. Anyone would be."

That shocks me into silence. I keep staring at the road, long and flat and empty, and can't even muster up the genuine desire to hear Marley apologize. After all, he's right.

Do you forgive yourself?

"Honey, I'm home," I call out to the loft with false cheer, tossing my keys onto the entryway table. I love the clink they make in the ceramic bowl that Indah brought from her apartment. It's the sound of owning something, of having something stable and permanent.

It's the only sound in the apartment right now. My hollow sitcom cry of return has fallen flat in an empty and quiet apartment. I walk toward the living room, silently relieved for once to be alone, still fuming and hurting from my fight with Marley. I dropped him off at the library without either of us saying a word, and I'm not sure I want to say anything to anyone right now.

Then out of the darkness comes a hand, lit up with blue sparks, from the direction of the couch.

"Is Blaze with you?" I hear Neon say.

"Nope." I walk over to the couch to see her lying there, staring at the ceiling, electricity dancing around her hands.

"What's up with you?" I ask, starting to move toward my arm-chair, the one that Marley brought home, specifically for me, before my stomach swoops painfully. What if Marley never does any kind thing for me, ever again? I reroute to the couch, flopping down in the limited empty space, Neon's feet brushing against my leg.

"Indah and I had a fight," she says, moping. "And she had to leave for work and Marley is, I'm assuming, at the library—"

"Yeah, he is—"

"And Blaze is out god knows where, hopefully not setting anything on fire or shooting up, and I'm just . . ."

"Yeah," I say, like I understand what she's feeling.

"But you're here," she says, nudging my legs with her feet and looking up at me. Her eyes are electric, piercing, like they're trying to see through my skull and into my brain. "You're always here when I need you, Damien."

"I am?" I ask, genuinely surprised but warmed by the sentiment.

"You're reliable." She shrugs and smirks a bit at me.

"Can't say that's ever been said about me before," I scoff.

"Have you ever given anyone the chance to?" she asks, cocking her head to one side like getting a different angle on me will reveal my secrets.

"You don't strike me as the type that needs reliability." I'm deflecting, happy to sink into Neon's problems for a little while. "Doesn't that make life infinitely less interesting?"

"Not at all," she says. "Reliability isn't the same thing as being boring. Trust me, I say this as someone who is neither."

"You're definitely not boring." I grin.

"According to Indah, I'm not very reliable either." She pouts, swinging her legs down until she's sitting beside me.

"Is that what your fight was about?" I ask, confused. Neon has seemed plenty reliable to me since we all moved in together and she made it official with Indah.

"She wants me to commit," Neon says with a nod. "Fully commit. It's one thing for us to share a bed, a home, call each other girlfriend, but she wants . . ."

"You already *are* committed, aren't you?" I ask, wondering if my wanting them to be together and happy has worn off. "What, does she want to get married or something?"

"Well, no, obviously," she snaps. "We're not allowed to do that."

"Oh. Right." I blush, embarrassed at my small-town ignorance. Not that I didn't know women couldn't get married to each other, but it never occurred to me to think about it until this moment. The idea of spending my life with another person is so foreign I can't imagine its being appealing to *anyone*.

"She just wants something *more*, though, than what we have," Neon continues. "A declaration of lifelong devotion or something. And it's not that I don't want to—I *am* committed to her. I love her and I think I show it, but . . . I can't get her to believe me.

"She scares me, you know?" she continues softly. "She's so warm and beautiful and fucking *good*. And I know that she gets me—gets us"—she waves her hand between us—"the Unusuals, what we are—but she'll never really understand, and that . . . that scares me. I'm worried that she's going to wake up one morning and look at me and realize that she wants someone normal. So it's just easier to keep her at arm's length, easier to just call her my girlfriend and not ever talk about it, because if I don't talk about it, I never get hurt. But she can tell. She can tell that I'm distant, that I've always got one foot out the door. And I don't know how to fix it."

Neon says all of this without looking directly at me or taking a breath—it pours out of her, her fingers crackling occasionally as she talks. She finishes with a heavy exhale, there's a moment of silence, and then she turns to me and says:

"You did that, didn't you?"

"What do you mean?" I ask, playing dumb.

"You made me say all those things. You know I don't like it when you use your ability on me, *Damien*."

"I wasn't trying to," I tell her. "It just . . . happens."

"How long is that excuse going to work?"

"It's not an excuse—"

"You're an adult, you're responsible for what your power does."

"What, you've never had your ability go rogue on you?"

"Of course I have," she concedes, rolling her eyes. "But not really badly. Not in years."

"So it eventually just . . . calms down?" I ask. "Like Unusuals puberty or something?"

"Ha, can you imagine?" She snorts. "What a nightmare that'd be. But no—I worked at it. Like most things in life, you can't just wait for it to be handed to you."

She pauses for a moment before tossing her hands up and rolling her eyes again.

"Well, I mean, for those of us that aren't *you*," she moans. "I get that you're used to literally having everything handed to you, but most people have to work to get better."

"I know that," I spit. "I'm not some spoiled child."

I can't win. Marley knows I'm not spoiled—knows that I've had to deal with difficult things in my life—but he only knows that because he knows about the monstrous things I've done in my past. Neon can't know any of that, and so she assumes I am what I appear: a boy who gets everything he wants.

"I'm sorry," Neon says softly.

Neon *never* apologizes to me.

"Fuck, would you stop that!" she shouts.

"How do you even know it's me doing it?" I retort. "Maybe you just realized that you should actually apologize once in a while."

"I don't need this from you too, Damien," she snaps.

"Guess I'm not so reliable after all, huh?"

We sit there in the darkness, avoiding each other's eyes. I'm coiled tightly into the warmest corner of the couch, feeling prickly and sad and incapable of not hurting every person I know. It's happening, I can feel it. The only people I've ever met in my life who could maybe understand and accept me are starting to grow tired of the way I am. They'll run like all the rest. A heavy, sour weight starts to sink in my gut as I think about all the ways I'm breaking what I have, unsure if my wanting it to heal itself will be enough.

"Do you *want* me to feel good?" Neon's voice comes up from the darkness like a wisp of smoke.

"What?"

"Is that something you can do?" she asks, voice quiet as she leans toward me. "If you wanted it bad enough, could you . . . fix people?"

"I don't know," I say, shaking my head. "I don't see how."

"You get whatever you want, right? So just want for me to figure it all out. Want me to be happy." Her eyes are bright and wanting and *I* want. I want so badly.

"Trust me, Neon, if wanting to be happy was something I had control over, I think I'd be a pretty different person."

"I'm not sure it'd be real happiness anyway," I murmur after a moment, afraid to admit it.

She cocks her head at that, the sparks on her hands pausing and dissipating. After a moment, she digs into her pockets for cigarettes and a lighter and I wonder if it's just that she always has to be doing something with her hands.

"It keeps me from shocking myself and everyone else into oblivion," she explains, answering the unvoiced question.

"You can shock yourself?"

"I do it all the time by mistake. Sometimes on purpose, if I need to stay awake or . . . well, there are other applications."

"Is this one of those things that I don't want to know about?" I ask, half-serious.

"Probably." She snorts around her cigarette.

"I never thought about if you could use your ability against yourself. I guess because it's physical . . ."

"You mean you can't?"

"How would that work exactly? The whole deal is that I want

stuff and then other people do too. I can't want what I already want . . . *more.*"

"Good point," she says, flicking the lighter and lighting the cigarette between her lips.

The weighty silence descends again as the air between us fills with smoke and the light sound of Neon's breath.

"What *do* you want?" she asks after a moment.

I don't answer her. I turn the question over and over in my brain, trying to look at all sides of it, tear it apart, rearrange it until all the different bits of the question form a new shape and reveal an answer.

I want so much, but I have no idea what it is that I want. I look at the woman across from me—her curious brown eyes that spark with blue, her soft, dark skin that looks so warm and touchable but that I know could kill me with a single surge of electricity. Neon is the most interesting person I've ever met, and here she is, looking at me like *I'm* the most interesting thing she's ever seen, and I want so badly for that undivided attention to be real, to be genuinely hers, that my ability starts to go round and round, like a snake eating its own tail.

I'm collapsing in on myself, burrowing deeper into my mind, trying to bury the desire to have Neon love me that's rising up my throat. It isn't working—the desire too strong despite the fact that I know it's wrong, the darkness inviting more darkness—when I suddenly find myself jumping out of my skin with a shout.

"Jesus, calm down," I hear as every hair on my body stands on end.

"What the hell, Neon?" I pant, settling back into the couch. "Did you just shock me?"

"Just a little." She smiles, flopping back to lie down again. "I could feel you starting to want something when I remembered that my ability can shut down yours."

I rub my arm where she shocked me, smoothing out the hairs, trying to feel her touch lingering there. I'm so worn down, so hollowed out from my fight with Marley, that any touch, even in the form of electrocution, makes my heart ache with need. But mostly

I'm relieved that Neon lit up the darkness before it enveloped me completely.

"You can really feel it?" I ask, blinking away tears that I think I can pass off as a reaction to the shock. "When I'm using my ability?"

"Kinda." She shrugs. "I couldn't at first, of course, but I'm assuming no one can."

I nod.

"Right," she continues. "And I'm guessing most people never really figure out what you can do?"

"People sometimes get suspicious, but . . ."

"It's easy for you to make them *not* suspicious?"

I shrug. "People never really know what to be suspicious *about*," I tell her. "They can feel that there's something different about me—they realize they're doing things that maybe they wouldn't normally—but no one's ever guessed it. How could they?"

"What about your parents?" she asks, and my blood turns cold.

"What about them?"

"Are they like you?"

"What, thoroughly Midwestern looking?" I quip. "Yeah, yeah, they are."

"You know what I mean," Neon says. "Are they Unusual?"

"I don't know," I answer after a moment, choosing my words carefully to avoid repeating the argument I had with Marley. "I don't think so. They never—they never said anything to me. They never did anything out of the ordinary. They were just . . . they were really standard parents, you know? Always telling me to eat my vegetables and get my elbows off the table, shuck the corn . . . all that boring stuff."

"'Shuck the corn'?" Neon laughs. "I mean, I know you said you had cornfields, but damn, you really are from the middle of nowhere, huh?"

"You have no idea," I groan. "Nothing but cornfields for miles and miles. At least, that's what it felt like. I haven't been back there in years."

"Why'd you leave?"

"Why does anyone leave their hometown?"

"Fair point."

Neon is smiling softly at me now, relaxed and vulnerable. I don't know that I've ever talked to anybody this way. My ability doesn't seem to be doing anything to her and here I am, willingly talking about Them. The topic feels less dangerous than it did in the car with Marley. I'm fully in control this time; I only have to reveal as much as I want to.

"Where are they now?"

"Huh?"

"Your parents," Neon clarifies. "They still in whatever nowheres-ville you come from?"

"Nope," I say, shaking my head. "I've got no clue where they are."

"Oh," she breathes. "Gotcha."

"What about yours? They know about you?"

"Nah." She grimaces. "They're back in Arizona. I call them once a week—"

"Once a week?"

"Yeah, dude." She smiles. "Why, is that weird?"

"I have no fucking clue what's weird," I say, and Neon laughs that big, sharp laugh she has. It makes me smile, loosening the tight knot in my chest that Marley and talking about my parents put there.

"Yeah, okay, fair enough." She nods.

"So, they're cool with you?"

"Like I said, they don't know about me," she says. "They know I repair motorcycles in LA and that I date women sometimes—"

"And they're cool with that?"

"Yeah, they don't care." She shrugs. "They don't like that I smoke, but . . . do you think your parents wouldn't have been okay with it?"

"My dad smoked, he couldn't exactly tell me not to."

"I don't mean that, you barely smoke as it is," she tells me, sitting up, and I roll my eyes. "No, I mean the not-being-straight bit."

I blink at this, surprised by the turn this conversation has taken. I watch Neon squish what's left of her cigarette into the ashtray in front of her, before she flops back into the couch with a sigh.

"I'm not . . ." I flounder. "I'm not gay."

"Okay," she says simply.

"Why do you think I'm not straight?" I ask, my heart beating faster.

"Indah said you kissed some guy—"

"I kissed a bartender when I was wasted and sad." I snort. "I'm not sure that qualifies."

"Gotcha." She nods sagely. "Did you like it?"

"Eh." I shrug one shoulder.

"So you *are* straight," she says.

"I'm—" I start before realizing I have no answer to that question that I can give confidently. "I told the bartender that I hadn't thought about it much when he asked."

"Because your parents were homophobic?"

"What?"

"Have you not thought about it because your parents would have had a problem with it?" she clarifies, and I try not to be offended by the cloying pity in her eyes.

"I don't know that they had a problem with it," I say truthfully. "You and Indah are the first not-straight people I've ever really met."

"That you know of," she points out.

"Right, yeah, I guess," I agree, even though I've never thought of that.

"So it never really occurred to you, huh?" she probes. "Having options?"

"Do I have options?" I ask, my face heating. "I've never thought about *any* of it because my first kiss was when I was thirteen and I liked the way that Anna Slauson's hair looked in a ponytail and then the next thing I know she's kissing me and it's warm and soft but then all of a sudden she's pulling away and she looks *terrified* and starts crying because I guess *she* didn't want to kiss *me* but she did anyway because I'm a *freak of nature* who puts people in situations they don't want to be in, so, no, I don't feel like I have options."

A breath is punched out of me as I collapse back into the arm-chair and try to pretend that I didn't just say all that. I want Neon to forget, but there's still a faint buzzing underneath my skin that tells me it won't work. Does Neon's power make me want to speak? Does the electricity somehow loosen up my lips?

I hear the flick of Neon's lighter and tear my eyes from my lap to look at her. She's lighting another cigarette and peering at me over the flame, silent and unreadable. I swallow and stare back, waiting for her to talk so that I don't have to.

"Fuck, dude," she says simply, pocketing the lighter. "That is some gnarly stuff."

I just nod my head, pursing my lips and resisting the urge to run away. This is what friends do, isn't it? That's what I said to Marley. Friends talk, they share, they accept each other. If anyone can accept me, it's Neon.

"I'm sorry," she sighs.

"Sorry for what?" I ask.

"I'm sorry that that happened to you," she explains. "That sounds like some traumatizing bullshit."

"Yeah," I breathe. I squint at Neon through the smoke curling out of her mouth. She doesn't have the sad, pitying eyes that people who say they're sorry to me usually do. I'm not making her sympathize with me, she's just . . . doing it. I didn't know that was possible and I'm filled with a sense of warmth I've never experienced before.

"But, I mean," I continue, feeling brave, "I didn't *mean* to traumatize her. I just, I wanted to be close to her, to touch her—"

"I meant traumatizing for *you*, dumbass." She snorts.

"What?"

"I mean, yeah, what happened to her was super shitty, but that doesn't mean it didn't suck for you too. Kissing someone for the first time and having them cry over you is kinda messed up. Like, I know that a lot of people have crappy first kisses but . . . Christ," she finishes, taking another drag of her cigarette.

"Oh," I say dumbly. "I hadn't thought of it that way."

"Really?"

"Well, yeah," I answer. "It was my fault—I'm the one who made her kiss me—"

"But you didn't mean to."

"Well, no, but you literally *just* gave me shit for using my ability on you without meaning to," I point out, my voice developing an edge.

"Yeah, that's because we're both adults and you should know better," she says, like it's as easy as that. "You were a kid. I'm sure your power did a lot of things back then that you regret. So did mine. It doesn't mean we're bad."

"So what, once you turn eighteen you have to take responsibility for everything you do?" I ask.

"Kinda." She shrugs. "It's not a cut-and-dried thing, I guess. Kids mess up, of course, and there *are* certain things you can't ever take back"—I think of my dad stepping off the roof, my parents getting into their car and driving away without looking back—"but for the smaller stuff, that's how you learn. And I still mess up all the time, but it's not like I'm fifteen and barely in control anymore. At a certain point, you just have to own up to what you can do and figure out how you're going to use it. No one else can figure that out for you."

"I didn't ask for this," I snap. "And I can't just . . . turn it off."

"I know that," she says calmly, sitting up and crossing her legs in the space between us so she can face me head-on. "But that doesn't mean it gets to control you. That doesn't mean it's a catchall for treating people badly."

"Do I treat people badly?" I ask quietly after a moment, terrified of the answer.

"I don't know, Damien," she says, and the name sends a chill up my spine that *isn't* the thrill of excitement. "Do you feel like you do?"

The warm feeling of a few moments ago has turned toxic and roiling as I think about the people I've tricked, stolen from, accidentally hurt. I think about Them.

"My parents left," I say, breaking the heavy silence and surprising myself.

"Did they find out about you?" Neon asks, her voice a smooth balm, free of judgment or probing curiosity. Is that what Neon means about control? Not only controlling your ability but controlling every single part of you and how you interact with people? Controlling your voice, your manner, the things you say? Neon is *always* in control in a way I wouldn't even know how to begin to get to.

"Sort of," I say, voice quiet and breaking. I want to stop speaking, want to get up and go to bed, but there's a power greater than even the one I assert over people driving me. All these years of being alone, of keeping everything tightly held to my chest, and now it's desperate to come pouring out on *my* terms, not because someone has peered into my past.

Neon takes another drag, exhaling smoke into the space between us, clouding my face from hers for a moment. I take the few seconds of cover to speak again.

"I think they knew," I continue softly. "I lived with them, you know? Every moment of me discovering what I could do, having it run wild without me . . . they were there for all of it. I couldn't stop it. I couldn't stop my dad from stepping off the roof to hand me back my Frisbee, I couldn't stop my mom from making me cake for dinner every single night for a week. I couldn't stop them from leaving."

Neon just sits there, listening. I can tell she wants to ask questions—wants to respond with a witty remark or a creative swear—but she stays silent.

"I wanted them to leave me alone," I whisper. "I was mad about something . . . I don't even remember what. Honestly, it could have been about Anna Slauson." I laugh softly for a moment at the thought. Was I really crying over a botched kiss? It all seems so unbelievably long ago, the cornfields of Nebraska and the dusty house like someone else's memory.

"Anyway," I say, "whatever it was, I was upset. And my parents were trying to comfort me, and for once, I just wanted to be left alone. So I told them to leave. And they did."

"Fuck," Neon whispers.

"They got into their car and they drove away and they never came back," I say.

I can tell Neon is about to jump into whatever reaction she's been having, but before she can, something leaps unbidden from my throat.

"They could have," I whisper, eyes prickling. "They could have come back. My ability wears off. It couldn't make someone stay away—I have to be near a person for it to work. But they didn't come back. My want for them to leave wore off and they stayed away. They chose to stay gone."

"Fuck," she says again, even quieter than before.

"I haven't seen them since," I finish, though I'm sure that much is obvious.

We sit in silence for a few moments and I start to retreat inside myself again, worrying that I shared too much, wondering if I can get Neon to forget. I can do that from time to time—can make people forget they met me or talked to me—but it always comes from a place of survival. Making the hotel clerk forget I ever stayed, the grocer forget that I come in every day and never pay. If I'm being honest with myself, I don't think it would work on Neon in this moment. I finally told someone the full truth of my existence—my sad little orphan Annie past—and they haven't run away. As much as my stomach is roiling in fear, there's also a lightness in my chest, a sense of deep relief. I don't *want* Neon to forget. I just want her to help me.

"Dude, you need to go to therapy," Neon says finally, exhaling a large plume of smoke.

"Therapy won't bring my parents back," I snap, thinking of Dr. Crane, of Francine, of destroying chances at vulnerability in even the safest of environments. If your parents don't love you, if a therapist gives up on you and walks away, what hope is there?

"Is that what you really want?" she asks.

"I don't know," I say again quietly, the irony of it all hitting home. The boy whose wants infect everyone else can't even articulate what he wants, even though it's as simple as wanting to be wrapped up in someone's arms. To feel loved. To feel safe, for just one goddamned second.

Suddenly I feel a hand on my arm and cigarette smoke curls up my nose.

"What are you doing?" I ask, looking at Neon's face, now just a few inches from mine. She's shifted closer to me on the couch, her knees touching my leg, her warm hand traveling up my forearm and gripping my bicep. Her eyes are big and so close that I can see the smudged blue eyeliner curling at the ends of her lids.

She doesn't answer me, just leans to the side to smash her cigarette—only half smoked—into the ashtray on the coffee table. When she leans back in, she's impossibly closer to me and I can smell the smoke on her breath, mixed with the sweet scent of a perfume I recognize as Indah's. My head is swarming with confused emotions—I shouldn't be this close to Neon, not when she smells like Indah, but her hand is so warm on my arm and I just want to *matter* to someone for once.

"Neon . . . ," I breathe, uncertain what I'm going to say, and the next thing I know, she's leaning in, closer, closer, and her lips are pressed to mine.

For a second I think she's shocking me. I immediately tense, waiting for the pain that follows the brief moment of pleasure when the electricity hits, but it never comes. Instead, there's simply a sweet buzzing on my lips, a surge of tingling through my body as she presses harder into me.

I think about pushing her away, demanding to know what exactly she's thinking, following the script that Indah laid out for me when I surprised her with a kiss, but then Neon moves her lips, bringing her other hand to my shoulder, surrounding me, and I'm convinced I'm going to black out. But she's still not using her ability on me. The electricity I'm feeling isn't supernatural, isn't painful. It's like nothing I've ever felt, like warmth and starlight, and I think about leaping into the sky to bring her the moon.

I kiss Neon back.

The stars above me are bright and shining. I've snuck out of the house again. My dad says I'm not allowed to go into the fields at night until I'm at least in double digits, but I'm braver than he thinks I am. I know there's nothing out here that can hurt me. I'm surrounded by tall corn stalks all around me, protected and safe in their shadows, and nothing in the entire world can hurt me.

"What are you doing?"

I feel the sentence on my lips before the words make their way
to my ears. All my senses have been dulled, my mind in a trance,
focused entirely on Neon's mouth on mine, her arms around me,
the way my hands feel on her waist. But her voice starts to bring
me back to my body and I feel her hands digging sharply into my
shoulders, and then a surge of electricity that pushes me away from
her, setting my hair on end.

We flop back on opposite ends of the couch, both gasping for
breath.

"Robert, what the—" she pants. "What the *hell*."

"I—" I start, discombobulated, my head still somewhere high
in the clouds, my lips still tingling, my shoulders buzzing with her
shock. "What do you mean what the hell? *You* kissed *me*."

"Yeah, well, did you *want* me to?" she snaps, her eyes staring a
hole through me, a freezing black worse than the coldest lake.

My stomach drops.

"No, I—" I stutter, "I—I just wanted to—to—"

"Oh my god." She swings her feet to the floor, standing up and
moving away from the couch. "Look, I get that you—that you have
a little thing for me—"

"I don't have a *thing* for you," I scoff, standing up to follow her.

"Then how do you explain this?" she shouts, sweeping her arms
wide.

"You kissed me!" I repeat, jabbing a finger at her. "You shocked
me earlier, I don't have any control over you—"

"Are you absolutely *sure*, Damien?" she asks, bringing her voice
down and narrowing her eyes at me. She crosses her arms and I see
a little spark fly off, prompting me to take a step back.

"I . . ."

I'm not sure. I'm not sure at all. Yes, she shocked me, stopped
me from influencing her too much, but it was a little spark, a
brief jolt. Was it enough to keep my ability suppressed this whole
time?

"You promised us that you wouldn't use your ability on us," she spits.

"No I didn't. When did I promise that?"

"It's what we *do*, Damien. We only use our abilities when we have to and we don't ever use them on each other without *explicit* permission."

"Bullshit," I snap. "You've used your ability on me plenty of times. You used it on Blaze when he first got here—"

"Yeah, to save him from himself!" she shouts, and I'm relieved that we're alone in the apartment. Suddenly I think of Indah, think of how I might smell like her perfume now too, and that makes me feel just as cold as the look on Neon's face. What if Indah finds out? What if Neon finds out I tried to kiss Indah all those months ago? What if Marley looks into my past and sees the whole ugly truth about how I don't know anything about connecting to people and they all just give up trying with me for good?

"Damien, are you listening to me?"

Neon's razor tone snaps me back.

"I don't get what you're so mad about, Neon," I groan, trying to sound casual. "It was one kiss."

"Yeah, to start! But I don't trust you, Robert," she says, her voice low and cutting into me like a knife. "I don't trust that you wouldn't take it further if I wasn't here to shock you."

If I thought my stomach couldn't drop further, I was wrong. The slice of Neon's words hit an artery and I want her to stop, want her to wrap me in her arms again and tell me she loves me, despite what I am. But it doesn't matter what I want. The most recent shock is still running through my body, putting Neon and me on an even playing field, at least for now. And I know myself and I know Neon—all things being equal, her will is much stronger than mine and she'll shock me again if she has to. That in and of itself is a kind of relief, but I'm hurt that she assumes she'd have to. So I fight. I fight dirty.

"What, you think I want you that badly?" I scoff. "You're not as amazing and magnetic as you think you are, Neon."

"Oh, bullshit," she cries again. "I see the way you look at me—I always have—but I thought you understood. We're *friends*. Hell, I just spent twenty minutes crying to you about how much I love Indah—"

"Yeah, and how you don't want to fully commit to her—"

"Because I'm scared!" she shouts. "That wasn't an open invitation!"

"What do you want me to do? Say I'm sorry? Then fine: I'm sorry."

"That's not—" She grinds her teeth, pacing in frustration. "I can't tell you what to do. An apology means nothing if you don't actually *believe* what you're saying."

"Well *sorry*," I singsong sarcastically. "I guess nothing I do is good enough for you—"

"God, Damien," Neon exclaims, "you shouldn't need someone to teach you how to respect other people. You're an adult."

"Barely!" I shout back, teeth clenching. "I'm nineteen, give me a break!"

"Haven't you been listening?" she shouts. "You're old enough to take responsibility for your own actions. When I was nineteen, I was fighting to survive—trying to figure out how to live with this ability that was constantly trying to tear me apart—"

"And you think I'm any different?" I snap, hurt. "I'm fighting, just like you—"

"No, you're not!" she laughs, eyes to the heavens. "You couldn't possibly understand what it's like to really claw your way through existence. You're a white man in America who has the *literal* power of persuasion! You've always gotten everything you ever wanted. Your ability has made things *easy* for you, not made it impossible for you to carve out your place in the world."

She finally stops pacing, the air pushed out of her as she finishes, huffing and puffing and staring daggers at me.

"Is that really what you think?" I ask softly, wondering how we got to this place. "After everything I just told you—everything about my parents, about what my life has been like . . . you think just because the world falls at my feet now without me asking, I should be . . . what, grateful?"

She shrugs and flips a stray loc over her shoulder with her hand—a gesture that is so familiar to me that it stops me in my tracks for a moment. I know Neon. Like, *know her* know her. Over the past eight months she's become closer to me than anyone ever has. I know her expressions, her habits, her pet peeves. I thought, like she said, that I understood her. I thought she understood me.

"I thought you understood me," I say aloud, echoing her, my voice more fragile than I want it to be. "That's why . . ."

I stop myself, but Neon grabs on to the unfinished sentence.

"Why what?" she insists.

"I just wanted it to mean something. For once." I look down at my feet, too terrified to look at Neon in the eyes. "It seems to mean so much to other people and I—I just want to matter. I thought you understood me. I thought it would matter."

"I don't know that anyone's ever understood you, Robert," she says, and something inside of me breaks. "How could they? With you always wanting to keep everyone and everything at arm's length . . ."

"What if I wanted you to understand," I say quietly, looking up at her, the hope caught in my throat. "If I wanted you to understand, then you would, right?"

"You tell me," she says, cocking her head like she's looking at me for the first time. "Is that really how it works? You need to actually *want* it, right? Like you said."

I nod, scared of where she's going with this.

"So . . . *do* you really want people to understand you?" she asks, her face crumpling in sympathy. "Or is it just that you want people to see you how *you* see you?"

"What's the difference?"

That makes her pause and straighten her head, her expression slackening, her posture collapsing. It's like the wind has been let out of her sails and when she speaks, it's as if I'm talking to a completely different person than the Neon who was yelling at me a few minutes ago.

"Oh, kid," she breathes, and the diminutive endearment is so laced with genuine pity it doesn't even sting. "There's a huge difference."

Completely unbidden, I feel tears gathering at the corners of my eyes. I've never heard Neon use this tone of voice before, not even when talking to Indah.

"Understanding is like love," she continues. "You can't tell someone else how to do it."

"Why not?" I plead, feeling like a little boy asking his mom why he can't have ice cream for dinner. "Why can't someone tell *me* how to do it? No one ever told me how to do it."

I blink my eyes rapidly, trying to dispel the moisture that's gathered there, but all I succeed in doing is sending tears down my cheeks. I want to wipe them away but am loath to draw attention to the fact that I'm crying in front of Neon, the strongest person I know. I've never cried in front of anyone before and it feels like having my rib cage cracked open for everyone to see inside.

When the water has cleared from my eyes, leaving tracks of salt on my face, I see my expression reflected in Neon's. She looks lost and sad and all I want is to feel her touch again, to have her comfort me without needing to exchange words, but I know there's nothing I can do—ability or no—to make her reach for me.

It's just occurring to me that maybe *I* can do something—take a step forward, reach out, pull her in close to me, let her either come into my arms or push me away, put the choice on her—when the front door handle rattles and turns and two laughing people pile into the loft.

Neon and I both turn reluctantly toward the door to see Indah and Blaze, red faced and giggling, hanging over each other.

"Oh, hey, you two!" Indah gasps for breath, spotting us. "What are you guys doing up so late?" Her eyes settle on me and guilt rises up in my throat like bile. Her soft, open expression—loving and trusting and far more than I deserve—is the same expression I saw on my dad's face before he stepped off the roof to give me the Frisbee I wanted.

"Uh, we . . ." Neon starts, but quickly gives up. I see her swallow, see her eyes shining before she turns her back and moves toward the kitchen. "Do you want some tea, babe?" she calls without looking over her shoulder at Indah, going to the stove, far away from me.

"No, that's all right," Indah sighs. "I'm gonna go crash. Maybe you can join me before I fall asleep?" she adds flirtatiously, and my gut twists further. Indah so rarely flirts with Neon in front of us, always the more serious of the two, but whatever she and Blaze got up to seems to have put her in good spirits.

Neon fiddles with the kettle and gives a noncommittal grunt in response, which just causes an affectionate smile to bloom across Indah's face.

"Me too." Blaze yawns, stretching his arms tall above his head. His shirt lifts as he bends left and right and I see that he's starting to put on weight, his skin no longer stretched over his bones like a taut canvas. For a moment, I hate him and his smile and his improving health and his easy way with the Unusuals so much that everything else fades away.

Both Indah and Blaze walk toward their respective bedrooms, murmuring and laughing to each other as they go. I stand, unmoving, in between the kitchen and the living room, in a strange no man's land both literally and metaphorically, and listen to the clicks of their doors shutting. I can feel Neon moving around the kitchen behind me, hear her fill the kettle and pull down a mug, like she's the one who likes tea, even though she only ever makes it for Indah.

"At least she seems to have forgotten about your fight," I say, wincing immediately at how flippant my voice sounds.

"Shut the fuck up, Damien," she snaps, making me wince further.

She walks past me, toward the front hall, and turns on her heel, somehow looming menacingly over me despite her tiny stature.

"Not a word to Indah, you hear me?" she hisses. "She doesn't know anything about this."

"Okay." I nod. "She won't know anything."

That, of course, doesn't last.

The next morning, I'm sitting in the living room, having been too scared to leave the apartment. I want to keep everyone in one place. Marley came back late last night and rose sometime around noon before retreating back into his bedroom to study, seemingly oblivious to what happened between me and Neon but still clearly miffed about our fight, resolutely ignoring me as I sat still and silent in the chair he gave me.

I'm just thinking about maybe seeing what's in the fridge and figuring out if I can rustle up some dinner for everyone as an unspoken apology, when I hear a bedroom door slam and angry footsteps marching toward me.

"You know, Robert," Indah starts abruptly, voice trembling in anger, "you *can* be friends with someone without trying to get with them."

"That's not—"

"That's *exactly* what it is, Rob," she snaps. She's wild-eyed and fuming—I've never seen her look so angry. "You clearly have lots of wires crossed in your head—you don't know how to love, how to *be* loved, so you just go for the most obvious choice."

"It wasn't just me that did it, you know," I bark, defensive even though I know I'm wrong. "Neon was there too."

"Neon is committed to *me*," Indah spits. "I know that she's waffled until now and that she—she has her doubts from time to time, but she would *never* cheat on me. That's not the kind of person she is. Once she gives her word about something, she *means* it."

"Clearly not, because she said she wasn't going to tell you about last night, and yet here we are!" I stand, throwing up my arms in frustration.

"What are you talking about?" Indah asks, eyes narrowing.

"She told me not to tell you anything," I say. "Which was fine with me—after all, I didn't tell her about *our* kiss—"

"Oh please." She snorts. "You drunkenly lunged at me, that hardly counts as a kiss."

"See?" I shout. "What happened with Neon was different. I wasn't doing the same dumb thing I did with you and you know that."

"No," she says, shaking her head, "no, Nee said that you wanted it, that that's why she kissed you back."

"Kissed *me* back? Is that what she said? She's the one who kissed *me.*" I'm feeling like a broken record, unable to stop spinning, breaking into shards that will fly across the room and cut anyone in the vicinity.

"Because you wanted it, not because she—"

"No, she *shocked* me and then kissed me and then I kissed her back, and you know what?" I'm digging the knife in further and I'm not sure why. "We kept kissing! She seemed pretty into it."

"Don't delude yourself, Robert," she snarls, taking a step toward me. "I know Neon a hell of a lot better than you. She *loves* me. She would never, ever do anything to hurt me."

"Yeah, except keep one foot out the door," I mumble.

"Excuse me?" Indah demands. "Just because you don't know what a real relationship looks like, it doesn't mean there isn't one staring you in the face."

"Oh, *trust me*," I shout, laughing manically, "I know what a real relationship looks like. After all, I'm the one that put you in a real relationship!"

"What are you talking about?" she demands, like I'm speaking a different language.

"Why do you think she finally committed?" I ask quietly, my voice like smooth venom. "And why do you think she hasn't been fully in it since?"

"You didn't . . ." Indah shakes her head. "No, you didn't do anything. That's not . . . no."

She's started pacing again, shaking her head all the while, avoiding eye contact with me. I can see that she's nervous, see that she doesn't want to believe what I'm saying but that something in her gut is telling her the truth.

"You're welcome," I sneer.

"That's not . . . ," she says again. "Okay, but even if that were true—which it's *not*—then why would you try to take her away from me?"

"I didn't! It was . . ." I search for a word. "Borrowing."

"Borrowing?" she echoes incredulously, and I wince. "She's not a library book—"

"She didn't do anything she didn't want to—"

"How can you know that, Robert?" she spits. "How can you *really* know that?"

"I *know*, okay?" I lie.

We stare at each other in a tense silence, the air between us crackling with unease. I should be wanting Indah to be calm, to be forgiving me, but for some reason, I can't muster up the desire.

"I don't . . ." Indah is shaking her head again. "I don't understand you, Robert."

"What's *that* supposed to mean?" I snap back, my heart beating fast.

"How could you want her to commit to me and then turn around and do *that*?"

"A person can want two things, Indah." Her face flinches at my condescension. "Neon loves you, she does. And just once, I wanted someone to love me like that. Is that so wrong?"

Indah sighs deeply and I want to shake her—grab her by the shoulders and rattle her until she tells me what's going on in her head.

"You really don't get it, do you?" she exhales, her arms crossed in front of her like armor.

"I clearly don't," I snap back, trying to use the truth as a weapon.

"We would have accepted you," she says, and her verb tense sends a shiver down my spine. "I think we all understand—it's not that long ago that we were where you are now. Not a kid anymore, not really an adult, trying to figure it all out. Alex is *still* in that stage."

"Don't pretend like you know what it's like," I say, getting up from the couch and stalking toward her. "You're not one of us, however much you try to be."

She reels back at that, and I can tell that I've stunned her into momentary silence.

"You're right." She nods, her voice soft and broken. "I'm not. But I've lived with enough Unusuals to understand that it can be difficult, to get your ability under control."

"*Exactly*. I don't see you giving Blaze lectures about how to behave and he nearly burned down the apartment the other week."

"She does give me lectures, dude."

We both turn to see Alex standing at the edge of the living room, his arms crossed and his brow furrowed.

"Thanks, man, but I think we've got this handled," I say, trying to wave him off.

"I'd like him to stay," Indah says, taking a step back from me. At that moment, more footsteps shuffle into the living room and Neon and Marley join the party.

"What's going on?" Marley asks, bleary-eyed.

"Damien and I kissed," Neon says, and I see both her and Indah wince.

"Oh . . . kay . . . ," Marley says, looking between the three of us. "Hey, Blaze, wanna go get a bite to eat?"

Marley takes a step toward the front door, but Neon grabs one of his meaty arms and holds him in place.

"No," she tells him. "We should really all talk."

"Oh, is this just the 'gang up on Robert' hour then?" I scoff, taking a few steps deeper into the living room in an effort to get away from the four-headed attack dog.

"We're not ganging up on you, Damien," Neon says, following in my footsteps, slowly, cautiously, like she's afraid I'm going to lunge and bite her. Doesn't she understand that *she's* the one with the teeth?

"Neon . . . ?" Indah asks in a small voice. "Could you . . ."

Without answering, Neon lifts up her hands, sending a strong bolt of electricity through me, making me double over in pain.

"Ow!" I cry. "Goddamn it, *why*?"

"Because we need to be able to be honest with you," Indah tells me, a pleading edge to her voice.

"Honest?" I parrot. "What the hell are you talking about?"

I look at the four faces in front of me—Neon and Indah have that twin look like they're my worried parents and I've just gotten caught putting my hand in the cookie jar. Marley is characteristically hard to read, his jaw clenched, his statuesque frame unmoving. Blaze stands the farthest away, still in the liminal space between the living room and the entryway, looking strangely uncomfortable for the person who has lived in this loft the longest.

"What is this, some kind of intervention?" I scoff, and there is a noticeable lack of smiles in the group. "Oh," I breathe. "I guess it is."

"We've all had a lot on our minds recently," Indah starts, and everyone's eyes flit around as they all give each other significant looks. "And we haven't been able to talk to you about it because, well . . ."

"You don't exactly ever *welcome* criticism, kid," Neon finishes, and the glint in her eye tells me that the use of the hated diminutive is purposeful. She wants me to know that she's in charge again, even though she *always* is.

"So this *is* 'gang up on Robert' hour?" I snap.

"No." Marley speaks up finally, his light voice the only comforting thing. "But you have to understand that you're a hard person to be honest with sometimes. You don't often want us to be, especially when it's something that concerns you."

"And you've been abusing your ability, Robert," Indah says, her voice so much kinder than it was a few minutes ago and far more so than I deserve.

"What? How have I been abusing my power?"

"Look at all of us," Neon says, her arms sweeping out to the rest of the group. "A month ago we never would have even considered living together—four Unusuals in one place is a recipe for disaster, *especially* with Isaiah on our tails—"

"Don't pretend like you haven't been loving this," I say. "You all didn't seem to have any problem with me getting us an apartment or free dinners or backstage passes, or getting you out of *jail*," I spit at Blaze, "or any of the hundreds of ways that you guys have been mooching off of me—"

"Mooching?" Neon scoffs. "Have you noticed that none of us have quit our day jobs? We're not relying on you to take care of us, Damien."

"But you don't seem to mind," I retort.

"Yeah, when it's dumb shit like furniture and rent and all the other trappings of civilized society that we're forced to participate in—"

"I really don't need a lecture about capitalism right now, Neon."

"But we're not things, Damien," she spits. "And you can't treat us like we are. It's *different*. It's different when you use your ability on us and I know you know that."

"Yeah, I *do* know that," I say, wanting desperately to believe it. "And I haven't been using my ability on you guys—"

I don't even get through the sentence before both Neon and Indah are shooting daggers at me.

"I don't *mean* to," I correct. "I'm bound to slip up every now and then, I'm not perfect—"

"No one's asking you to be," Marley says. "But you *are* influencing us, like . . . a *lot*."

"What are you talking about?" My voice is shaking in fear. I don't understand why the only three people I've ever trusted are looking at me like I'm a wild, untamed animal. I haven't made anyone step off a roof or drive away never to return. Sure, sometimes they tell me things more easily than they otherwise would, spend a little bit more time with me than they intend to, but what's the problem with that? Other than making them a little late for work or knowing their secrets—which I would never tell anyone, who else do I even talk to—I don't see how I'm doing any harm.

"I never wanted to live here," Indah says. "I loved my apartment, loved my job at Lubitsch. I haven't seen my old roommates in *weeks*—I just up and left without saying goodbye and now they won't take any of my calls. They were my friends. You're not the only people on the planet I care about."

"I'm not stopping you from seeing them," I say. "You could move back in any time you want to."

"Except I can't," she tells me. "Every time I come back to the loft, all I want to do is be here. So I don't go anywhere except work. And sometimes the fog lifts when I'm there, but sometimes you're at work too and I never get back to normal."

"You're keeping us here, Damien," Marley says calmly. "Haven't you noticed how much time we're all spending here? None of us are exactly homebodies—"

"And yet things have been distinctly domestic around here," Neon finishes. Unlike Indah, I normally find the way Neon and

Marley complete each other's sentences charming—the sign of a bond between them that I'm inching closer to having myself—but right now it feels like nails on a chalkboard.

"I'm not—" I sputter. "You don't have to stay here! You could all move out if you wanted."

"Except we *don't* want to," Indah says. "Because you don't want us to."

"What about Blaze?" I say, pivoting. "I don't want him here— not that—I like you, Blaze—"

I'm floundering, looking apologetically at Blaze, but he stares back blank faced.

"I'm not your biggest fan either," he says. "But this is my home. I actually *want* to live here. Why do you think I put up with those shitty roommates for so long? And this is definitely an improvement, as is the free rent—"

"See? *He* gets it," I say. "He knows how lucky he is—"

"But, as nice as it is to live with my friends," he interrupts curtly, "I don't want them living here unless *they* want to live here. Not to mention, you've been fucking with me too."

"What the hell are you talking about?"

"I haven't gone up in flames at all," he says. "When you're around, I guess you don't want me to, so I don't. I don't know how your ability is overriding mine, when nothing else has, but it *is*."

"You're welcome then," I snap. Blaze uncrosses his arms and starts to stalk toward me, fire in his eyes.

"Yeah, except it all just builds up," he continues sharply, "so when you're *not* here, it's worse than ever. Why do you think I blew up that bar? I didn't *mean* to but because I hadn't used my ability in a few days, it just . . . boiled over. This thing has already ruined so much of my life and now it's even *less* in my control. Do you have any idea what that feels like?"

"Oh boo-hoo," I moan. "I'm so sorry that I'm preventing you from *bursting into flames*."

"Listen to what he's saying, Robert," Indah says. "He's telling you you're hurting him. That's what we're *all* telling you. You've been influencing all of us, keeping us here, making us neglect other parts of our life in order to put more attention to-ward *you*—"

"I'm sorry I've been such a burden to you!" I shout, my throat clogged with emotion. "But I'm doing my best—"

"No you're not!" Marley shouts back, something he almost never does. "We've told you time and time again to get your ability under control and you don't think you're doing anything wrong, you don't ever apologize, it's like you don't even see that what you're doing is wrong—"

"This is the way I am! I'm not going to apologize for being my-self. If you don't want that person, then fuck you guys. Figure out how to pay rent yourself, stop being carefree and happy—that's all I was trying to do. I was just trying to make you *happy*."

"Remember what you told me last night? That's not real happi-ness, kid."

I look at Neon pleadingly but her expression is stern. She thinks she's right. They think they're all right.

"Fine," I say, my energy to fight gone. "Fine, I'll just . . . I'll leave you alone. I'll leave you all alone."

I stomp past the four of them, shove my shoes on, and grab my keys from the bowl. No one tries to stop me as I walk out the door, even though I want them to. I don't think I've ever wanted anything more in my entire life, and for once, it doesn't matter.

The cabin is dark and cold. I don't know what I was thinking, driv-ing north in February. I've never been anywhere else in my life except Nebraska, didn't think about how much colder things could get. But Montana is desolate and freezing, and a month into life out on my own, I just want to go home.

But I don't have any home to go to. The skeleton of my child-hood home still stands among the cornfields, but there's nothing there for me. I think about going back every single day, won-dering if maybe now that I'm done haunting it, They'll return. Could I make things better if They did? Could I make Them forget about what happened, make Them love me, make me a son again?

The possibility that I'd return only to find an empty, crumbling house is enough to keep me away. All I can do is keep marching forward, leave Montana, maybe go south, try to find a warmer, more welcoming environment. But the idea of moving—of doing anything ever again—exhausts me.

I think of the lake on the edge of this lodge community, iced over and smooth. When I passed it the other day, it was pockmarked with fishing holes—black and bottomless and strangely enticing.

I wonder what would happen if I jumped into one of those crudely cut holes in the ice. I wonder if anyone would notice.

I'm going to march in there and I'm going to apologize. I've taken a couple of days to cool off—crashed at the Ace Hotel in the nicer part of downtown—and I'm ready to take them all back. I've been playing the last few months in my head over and over—the conversations I've had with Indah, the things that tight-lipped Neon and Marley have shared with me, Blaze's lack of pyrokinesis around me—and yes, maybe I got a bit carried away.

But maybe I can pay closer attention now, can make sure that I stop influencing everyone. I'm pretty sure that I'm not going to stop wanting all of us to live together, but I can work on the other stuff. I'm definitely certain that I can give a convincing apology, even more convincing than the first time I left and came back. I'll let Neon shock me a little bit before I do it, so that they all really believe me. I was too close—I was too close to having a family again and I won't let myself mess it up. They haven't left yet, I haven't completely driven them away, and I won't let it get to that point. I won't.

By the time I trudge up the echoey metal stairs and come to the door of the loft, I feel more determined than ever before. So much of my life has been passively wanting things and then having them dropped in my lap. For the first time, I feel like I'm an active participant in my life.

I take out my keys—my most prized possession, the only thing I ever keep on me at all times—and breathe deeply, arming myself for what I'm expecting to be a fight.

They've changed the locks.

The stretch of road before me is endless and empty. There's still a chill in my bones, settled in deep from standing at a lake's edge for hours, but chasing the sun westward is starting to thaw me out. When I left home and started driving, it was cornfields for miles and then rambling prairies and then the tall pines and mountains of Montana, and now I've come to a part of America that feels like an unfinished painting. The lake in Montana is behind me, Nebraska even farther, my parents god knows where, and a plain of untold possibilities stretches before me.

I've lost track of exactly which state I'm in. They all blur together, indistinct and yet each completely unique. It would take me a while to see each of them. To explore the far reaches of this country. And that's what I'm going to try to do. I'll see as much as I can, drive as far as I can, and I'll do it all alone. I don't need anyone or anything. With what I can do, what I am, I can go anywhere I want.

PART FOUR

THE WEST SIDE

I go to Venice.

As I sit on the porch of my bungalow, looking out on the canals, I wonder if I went far enough. Maybe I should have gone to Italy after all—to the *real* Venice. Instead, I kept driving west.

It's been a few weeks since the intervention–slash–character assassination and I've done my best to put the Unusuals out of my mind. After throwing my useless keys against the door of the loft, hearing the metal clatter to the floor, I got into the Plymouth and pulled onto Venice Boulevard and just drove, trying my best to focus on the road through the tears clouding my eyes. Eventually, the road stopped and in front of me was Venice itself: a neighborhood of colorful bungalows on straight-edged canals connected by fairy-tale bridges. One of the bungalows had a "For Sale" sign out front, so I broke in. It took five days for anyone to come by, and when they did, I just told them I'd bought it, took the sign down, and that was that.

I think I'm only a few blocks from the beach, but I haven't ventured outside much. There's a pay phone at the end of the street that I've been using to call for food delivery, and the house was already furnished—for sale by the owner, I guess—so there are plenty of books for me to read.

This is the first time in three weeks that I've sat outside. The porch is only a few feet from the canal and the little sidewalk that separates me and the water is constantly trafficked by people—neighbors and tourists alike. Occasionally, someone paddles by in a boat. It's tranquil and a little weird and I don't know if I'll ever be happy here, but I'm not sure I have a better understanding of what happiness is than when I arrived in LA.

I start to explore the neighborhood, little by little, avoiding the beach for reasons I can't fully explain to myself. Maybe I'm worried the water will be too cold, the waves too tempting, but all I know is that I'm not ready to finally see the Pacific Ocean, the thing I feel like I've been driving toward for the past two years.

But there's a busy main street, Abbot Kinney Boulevard, that keeps me occupied for a week or two. There are restaurants and local markets, and I keep up the tradition of cooking elaborate meals, even though the activity feels hollow without Indah by my side. One Friday, I stumble upon some kind of street fair, and instead of avoiding it like I did my first night in Los Angeles, I wander around, taking in the sights and the smells. There are hundreds of people, all smiling at me whenever I want them to, trying to make me feel welcome, but my heart isn't in it.

In a sea of faces, there isn't a single one I care to look at. I float along, an unmoored boat on the water, and think about sinking.

A banging wakes me up, which is odd for a couple of reasons.

The canals—for all their quirks—are actually extremely quiet. I've discovered that this is the kind of place where everyone who lives here knows each other and expects a certain kind of conduct from fellow residents. Fine by me. It's not like I have anyone knocking down my door.

Which is another reason why the incessant banging is odd. A month plus and I haven't made an effort to get to know anyone. I did finally get cable and a phone line, and the guy who installed them and I had a nice chat about the LA traffic, but other than that and the bartender at a local bar called the Brig—un-tattooed and without a crinkle in his brow—I can't say I've made friends.

I pad quickly from the bedroom to the front door, wondering if I should arm myself with something. Whatever. I don't really want to get in a fight right now—not that I *ever* do—so I won't.

I pull open the door in one quick gesture and the banging immediately stops, doing wonders for my head. But nothing could have prepared me for what's on the other side of it.

"You gotta help me, man."

Blaze is bent over, one arm leaned against my door frame, the other—presumably the culprit of the noise—hanging limply at his side. He looks better than when I last saw him—even more weight on him, color in his cheeks—but right now he's sweating profusely, his thin T-shirt clinging to his shoulders.

"What the hell," I croak.

Blaze is the *last* person I would have expected to show up on my doorstep. As much as I wanted them to, I didn't expect *any* of the Unusuals to show up. But if any of them had (not that I've dedicated a lot of time to thinking about it, of course I haven't) I would have thought it'd be Indah. Definitely not the guy I barely knew and didn't like very much, who didn't like *me* very much.

"Can I come in?" he pants, looking nervously over his shoulder.

"Uh, sure."

I take a step back to let him in, closing the door more softly than I opened it. He stumbles past me, collapsing on the couch, getting what looks like ash all over the seat cushions. I liked those seat cushions. And I hate shopping. Maybe I could try ordering them online, though I'd need to get a computer and Internet hooked up and that seems like a hassle—

"Damien?"

I focus on Blaze, who's folded over his knees, his face looking up at me wearily.

"Sorry." I shake my head a bit to clear it. "I was, uh . . . I was asleep and I'm . . ."

"Yeah, I figured," he says, the ghost of a smirk on his face. "I wouldn't have barged in like this if it wasn't an emergency."

"How did you find me?" I ask, slowly sitting down on the other couch, opposite him.

"Indah," he says, throwing the second major surprise of the evening at me.

"What?"

"She's been keeping tabs on you," he explains. "Not in a creepy way, just . . . she worries, you know?"

"How did she . . ."

"Bartender's network," he answers before I can articulate the question. "After everything went down and we all had a moment to cool off, she felt bad—"

"You mean—"

"No, everyone's still pissed," he says flatly. I can't tell if he's answering my want to know what everyone's thinking about me or if I'm just that easy to read. "But you know Indah—she's never met a stray puppy she didn't want to take home."

"I think she'd probably resent that," I point out. "*I* resent that."

"Probably." He shrugs. "But she would know that I'm right."

"The Brig," I breathe.

"Huh?"

"Neighborhood bar," I explain. "I've gotten fairly chatty with the bartender—that must be how Indah found out." I don't know what to do with this information that's been laid at my feet—my heart starting to fill with stupid, useless hope—but Blaze distracts me before I can examine it too closely.

"Guess so. Listen," he says quickly, "we can't stay here. I think there's a good chance that he's followed me."

"Who?"

"Isaiah."

Blaze's face is crumpled in fear, his hands trembling.

"Okay, catch me up here," I demand, my skin prickling. There aren't many people I'm afraid of, but Isaiah . . . it was one thing to go hunting for him with Marley, knowing that we'd probably never catch him, but having him know where I live, maybe even show up on my doorstep—

"He found me again," Blaze pants. "I was out with some friends in Santa Monica—"

"*Why?*" I ask, distracted by the fact that I've never known any of the Unusuals to come west of the 405, which is partly why I moved out here.

"To follow a cute boy, what else." Blaze grimaces. "And every-thing was going totally fine—good even. I actually think this guy likes me, though it's always hard to tell, you know? I mean, I met him through another gay friend, so I think the chances of him being—"

"*Blaze.*"

"Right, right, sorry," he chatters, his excess of nervous energy feeling like it's sinking into me. "Not the point. The point is: Isaiah was there."

"He tracked you down?"

"No, I don't think so. I think he was doing his whole routine—going to bars, looking for users or burnouts and offering them something new."

"So, what, this is all about drugs?"

"Yes and no," he says, starting to calm a bit but still twisting his hands in his lap. "I've been letting Marley look—really get the de-tails of what happened to me—and they were definitely, you know, experimenting on me."

He swallows, looking pale, before he continues.

"But I don't think that they were giving me drugs to calm my ability down, like Isaiah promised. I think they were trying to make it stronger."

"'They'?"

"Marley's seen a couple of other people in my past," he explains. "It looks like it's a whole, like, operation. And I think Isaiah is look-ing for more test subjects—that's why he was at the bar tonight, to try and lure people in like me, or at least find some, and then he spotted me and I ran out of there like a bat out of hell."

"Did he try to come after you?"

"I don't know," he says. "I don't think so, but if he did, I figured I'd be safer here than anywhere else."

"My ability doesn't really work on him," I tell Blaze. "It's not like I hit a wall or anything, it's just that . . . it doesn't seem to have any kind of effect."

"Maybe you just haven't tried hard enough," he says hopefully.

"Maybe you just haven't tried hard enough to stop blowing up," I snap back.

"Okay, yeah, I see your point," he concedes, flopping back onto the couch cushions, his body finally relaxing.

"Want a beer?" I offer, for lack of anything else to say.

He shrugs and sighs and I take that as a maybe at worst, so I get up and grab two beers from the fridge, handing him one. He flinches at the cold bottle as he takes it, but then sighs again and presses it to his red and sweaty face. I crack mine open, leaning back on the opposite couch, feeling muddled and useless. There's never been anything I want from Blaze—other than for him *not* to explode, and given how he's holding the icy glass to his chest like it's anchoring him to the world I think I'm probably doing that now. Good. I like these couches.

"Oh damn," he says, peering at the bottle. "This is that fancy craft shit."

"Only the best." I give him a mock cheers from across the living room.

"How much did you pay for it?" he teases.

"I'm very beloved at the local grocery store." I smile, surprised at how pleased I am to be playing along with Blaze like we have an inside joke.

"It's so fucking cool."

"What is?"

"What you can do," he says, and I reel back a little bit in surprise. "Like, yeah, it's a double-edged sword, and I think everyone was right to be pissed, but that's why I came here. I know that you might not be able to protect me from Isaiah, but I really didn't want to burn the West Side down and you . . . you keep me calm."

"I like this house," I say dumbly.

"Yeah, exactly." He smiles. "So I'm not gonna freak out and

burn it down. And yeah, it'll hurt like hell later, but, lesser of two evils and all that. You know, if you just lived down the block from all of us, I think we'd be fine."

"And, what, just let everyone decide when they want to actually be friends with me?"

"Um, yeah," he says, narrowing his eyes at me. "That's sort of how friendship works."

"One-sided?" I snap.

"Mutual. You can't be the only one dictating the relationship. Friends don't actually usually live together and spend all their time together." He takes a swig of the beer, smacking his lips and then cocking his head at me. "You didn't know that, did you?"

"Well, excuse me for never having friends before," I snap.

"That explains a lot." He nods.

"If I always left it up to everyone else, no one would make the choice to hang out with me," I mumble, picking at the label on my bottle. I don't know why I'm talking to Blaze about this, but the fact that I don't really care about being his friend is making it easier to be vulnerable.

"Are you sure?" he asks. "Have you ever tried?"

I shrug.

"Listen," he sighs, "if someone doesn't want to be with you without you influencing them, you probably don't want to be friends with them either."

"Who does that leave?"

"There's millions of people in this country, Damien—billions in the world." He laughs. "I'm sure there're people out there who would like you without all the extra stuff. Hell, I think you've found a couple of them already. Indah genuinely cares about you and Neon is mad as hell at you right now, but she only gets that way about people she considers family. And Marley—well, I can never really get a read on Marley, but I've seen you make him laugh, and that's a pretty big accomplishment."

"That's because I like making him laugh," I admit. "I don't know if any of it was genuine. I *never* know if it's genuine . . ."

The penny drops. I want something from Blaze after all. I want him to reassure me, but not about the way he feels—about the way *they* feel.

"You think if I came back, they'd forgive me?" I ask, something slotting into place. I've never been in this position before—wanting something emotional from someone I'm not emotionally invested in—and it's causing gears to click together inside of me, creating a sense of calm focus that I've never felt before.

"I think they've already forgiven you," he says, the words giving me a rush. "They want you back."

"You should call them," I say, wheels turning. "You'll need a ride back to the loft—tell them to come pick you up."

He does it immediately, hopping up from the couch like he's not completely worn out. He picks up the phone, dials, and I can hear the ringing on the other end.

"Hey," he says. "Yeah, I know, I'm sorry it's so late . . . Is everyone around? . . . Yeah, please check . . . Okay, then just tell him to meet us . . . Yeah, I'm with Damien—no, no, it's cool . . . He helped me out tonight. I had a run-in with Isaiah—everything's fine, I'm fine. We're at Damien's place—Indah knows where—yeah, the canals . . . Okay . . . Yep . . . See you soon."

He places the phone back in its cradle and turns to me, grinning.

"They're on their way," he says. "And they're gonna call Marley at the library and tell him to meet us here."

"Cool." I nod slowly, trying to process the last minute. For the first time ever, I felt every inch of my ability working. Once I recognized the thread connecting me and Blaze—recognized what I wanted from him, what I was getting from him—it was easy to pull on it. And then I felt a bunch of strings and suddenly, it was like making a marionette dance. I couldn't have scripted that phone conversation better. Every time I heard the topic turning, doubt creeping in from the other side—I couldn't even *hear* the other side—I was able to steer it back, keep Blaze happy and compliant, singing the gospel of helpful Saint Damien.

Blaze sighs contentedly as he sinks back into the couch, picking up the beer and taking a big gulp from it. I feel as satisfied as

he looks. That was . . . intoxicating. How c of the Unusuals
have an issue with this? Think about how hap uld keep them.
They could be happy and easygoing forever if I

Happy and easygoing is *not* the mood that they d it.
when they arrive. Neon and Indah rumble up on N with them
cle, and Marley must be right behind them at 's motorcy-
the street, walking up to the house as they're dismountin arked on
e bike.

"Welcome." I smile, hanging on to the front door and eling
the tendrils of my ability go out to greet them. It's like some ing
clicked in my brain and now I can't help but know what I'm do ng.
Is this what Neon meant when she talked about learning control? If
I could have imagined this, I would have listened to her ages ago.

"What the hell is going on, Damien," Neon growls as she races
up my front steps. Indah and Marley are close behind and soon
we're all standing in my living room, Blaze smiling up at everyone
from his place on the couch.

"Blaze came over for a drink," I say sarcastically.

"Where's Isaiah?" Indah demands.

"We don't have to worry about that now," I say, ushering them
into the living room. Beer sits on the coffee table and they all automatically grab one, piling onto the couches and uncapping the
bottles.

"We don't?" Indah asks, taking a sip of the beer. Oh god. I probably should have put out something non-alcoholic for her. I want to
say something, point it out without making it my fault, but I think
we probably have bigger issues at hand. Like getting everyone to
stop worrying about Isaiah and settle in to wanting to be here.

"We're safe here, I promise," I say, and that's all it takes. Everyone relaxes into their seats and starts talking over each other, telling
me what they've been up to for the last few weeks. Marley is almost
done with his semester, Neon's got a vintage bike at the shop that
she's fixing up, Indah has a new job at a bar a little farther away
where she has to throw out patrons a lot less. We sit and have beers
and laugh and it's like the old times. But I want to go home.

"Here." Indah puts her hand on my arm, warm and familiar,
and smiles at me. "Come home."

With her o....nd, she holds out a set of keys, shiny and newly
pressed. I do...w if they're hers or if she had a set made for me
just in case... I don't want her to tell me the truth. I take them,
leaning fo...d to kiss her on the cheek, and I can feel her smile
grow as r...ps press to her face.

"Let...o," I whisper, and seconds later everyone else is standing.
I'm go... home. I can feel the threads connecting me to everyone
and now they won't stop me from going home. I have keys now. I
hol... open the door for everyone, mentally going through the stan-
dad checklist I go through when I leave a place and confirming
that there's nothing I'm leaving behind here.

Neon is laughing, her head thrown back to share the joke with
me as I step out onto the porch. Alex is already bounding down the
steps, so much more carefree than when he arrived, with Marley
and Indah trailing behind us, solid as ever.

Everything that happens next happens very quickly. Neon's
laugh dies abruptly as a tall figure steps out of the shadows. There's
a click and a buzz and then Blaze, at the foot of the front steps,
is twitching on the ground, two wires stuck to his T-shirt. Marley
shouts and Indah runs toward him, but half a second later, Isaiah,
in his long black coat, picks up the unconscious Blaze and throws
him over his shoulder like a sack of potatoes, before disappearing
into the dark of the alleyway next to the house.

"Blaze!" Neon yells, and we go rushing after Isaiah, his pale
head easy to follow in the darkness. But he's moving unnaturally
fast, getting to the street in record time and screeching away with
Blaze in a car.

"*Fuck*," Marley says, and I look at the others for a clue as to what
to do. Neon is gone and for a heart-stopping moment I think she's
been taken too. But then her motorcycle screams around the corner
and takes off after Isaiah.

"Come on," I shout to Marley and Indah, gesturing to the Plymouth, parked halfway down the block. The three of us run toward it,
piling in and giving chase. I catch up with Neon quickly, her body
tense and bent over the bike. We rumble through the quiet streets

of the neighborhood before the road opens up and we catch a clear sight of the other car before he makes a sharp turn.

Following, we pull onto a narrow, two-lane highway, cliffs on one side and blackness on the other. I don't have time to look or think about where we are, because Isaiah is driving at a breakneck speed and I have to push the Plymouth to match. He's driving without headlights, and I keep losing him in the twists and turns of the road.

We drive and drive, the road becoming more narrow and curved with each mile, the dark night sky above us oppressive and claustrophobic. I'm so focused on not killing Neon that I barely notice when I can't see the other car at all anymore.

Suddenly Neon's bike, which has pulled ahead of me, turns and skids, wobbling for a millisecond, and my hands tighten around the steering wheel. I slam on the brakes, realizing just in time that she's pulled into some sort of turnoff. There's dirt and dust in her wake as she spins to a stop, and I turn the wheel sharply.

"Fuck," Marley yelps next to me, and I hear the slap of leather as Indah tries to get a grip on the seat.

The Plymouth rumbles onto the dirt, kicking even more of it up, creating a cloud that I can barely see Neon through. We hurtle to a stop, our bodies slamming against the doors and one another as the car finally stills.

The dust is swirling around the car and through the haze I see Neon, her leg swinging over her bike as she reaches up to take off her helmet, and, distantly, another car, long and black like mine and yet somehow more hearselike.

"Stay here," I snap to Marley and Indah, pushing the driver's-side door open and stepping out onto the dirt.

I'm met with a rush of dust into my lungs and I cough. When the fit stops, I realize that, wherever we are, it's *loud*. There's a deep rumbling coming from the direction of the other car but it doesn't seem to be turned on. I squint through the darkness and dust and see a tall figure emerge through the cloud.

"The Pacific Ocean," Isaiah croons, gliding toward me. "It's quite noisy, isn't it? Then again, it *is* right beneath us. It would be so terribly easy to tumble in."

The dust that the three vehicles kicked up is starting to settle and I get a better look at our surroundings. It's not just a highway turnoff, it's an overlook. There's expansive, yawning black stretched out above us and across from us. It must be a moonless night, because there's nothing reflecting on where I assume the water must be. Just inky black.

"However, the racket will be useful in a moment, I should think." Isaiah drifts past me, unconcerned with the fact that we tailed him here. I swivel my head around to look for Neon and see the blue ends of her hair first. She's crouched slightly, moving toward the car, which seems to be moving amorphously.

No, it's not the car. There's another dark figure, squirming on the ground next to it.

"No," the figure gasps, "you have to stay back."

Neon halts, her boots skidding on the uneven ground.

"Blaze—"

"Neon, get *back*!"

Just as Blaze shouts, there's an enormous explosion and fire fills my entire field of vision. The blast is so strong that it blows me off my feet, my back colliding with the Plymouth.

There's a horrible screaming, inhuman and piercing, and I clamber to my feet to see Blaze, his entire body consumed in twenty-foot flames, the tendrils of the fire snaking out onto the ground.

"Very unfortunate, that," Isaiah shouts over the flame. "Thank goodness we pulled over in time."

He looks toward Neon and me, grinning, his teeth glinting in the firelight. With the light coming off of Blaze, Isaiah is like something out of a horror movie, like a skeleton come alive, his eyes wide and unblinking and lifeless. He looks so pleased with himself, so unconcerned that the man he kidnapped has gone off like a bomb. It feels like the fire is inside me, rising up my throat, choking me with anger and disgust.

"It will be over in a moment," he sighs calmly. I want to walk toward Neon, who is panting, her hands on her knees, looking worriedly at Blaze, tears rolling down her cheeks.

As much as I hate to admit it, Isaiah is right. A minute later, the fire is starting to come back down, soon just in a small radius around his body, and then Blaze isn't on fire at all anymore and it's as if the flames were holding him up—he collapses to the ground like a puppet whose strings have been cut.

I hear the crunch of Neon's boots as she takes a step toward him.

"I wouldn't do that, my dear," Isaiah croons, pointing something at her. Neon straightens and stares Isaiah down.

"That can't hurt me," she scoffs. "I'm a living Taser, that won't do anything to me."

"This isn't a Taser," he says, and there's the distinct click of a gun being cocked. Neon's face drops and she shuffles back a few steps.

"You can't take him!" Indah shouts, and I look behind me to see her and Marley clambering out of the car.

"I'm fairly certain I can," he says, grinning.

"I'd think again," I growl, reaching my ability out, out, trying to grab hold of him.

"You're not strong enough to go up against me, Robert," he says, moving the gun in my direction. I feel like I'm grasping at air, trying to catch hold of a cobweb. I thought I wanted more excitement, wanted to go on adventures with the Unusuals, but I don't want to be shot by the side of a road, leaving my friends defenseless.

Except, they're not defenseless. Our bomb might be passed out, but we still have a very potent weapon—I know firsthand how debilitating Neon's ability can be.

There's the snap of lightning, a bright flash of blue, and Isaiah falls to the ground.

"Neon—" Indah gasps from behind me.

"I didn't—" I hear Neon gasp as she stops the stream of electricity. "He's alive, right?"

I'm too focused on the gun skittering out of Isaiah's hand to check on the man himself, but before I can take two steps toward it, I see Isaiah is struggling to sit up, his arm reaching toward his weapon. I move faster, unencumbered while he still regains his faculties, and grab the gun just as his fingers stretch to touch it.

"Stay down," I say, pointing the gun at him like I know what I'm doing.

"Damien, put the gun down," Marley says, and I hear him take a few slow steps toward me.

"Happily," I say, hurling the gun with all my strength over the edge of the cliff, watching it disappear into the darkness. The ocean is so loud, I don't even hear it hit the ground.

"I don't need a gun to grapple with you children," Isaiah pants, struggling to his feet. When he's upright, I'm reminded of how tall he really is—we're only a few feet away from each other now and he looms over me like a tree.

"Neon . . . ," I say, urging her to shock him again.

"I—I'm not—" she stutters, sounding genuinely scared for the first time in her life.

I can feel Marley behind me, equally as imposing as Isaiah, but I watch Isaiah reach into his pocket, maybe for the Taser, maybe for something worse, and I act fast. I reroute my focus away from Isaiah, all the while maintaining eye contact with him, keeping his attention on me, while I click into Neon instead.

There's another blast of blue, this time longer and more potent, and Isaiah is suddenly back on the ground, squirming like an ant under a magnifying glass, screaming in pain.

Neon is shouting too, in surprise, as she watches the arc of electricity between her hands and the man convulsing in the dirt.

"Neon, that's enough—" Marley shouts when she doesn't stop, and out of the corner of my eye I see Indah inching cautiously toward her girlfriend, her arms outstretched.

"Nee, please stop," she says soothingly, fear shaking her voice.

"I'm not—" Neon gasps, and her terrified eyes are lit up by another surge of her electricity. Indah and Marley instinctively stumble backward, the glow of the electricity brighter than it's ever been.

Isaiah screams louder.

"I can't stop," she shouts. "I don't know what's happening, I can't stop!"

Tears track down Neon's cheeks, her hands trembling even as powerful streams of lightning shoot out from them. Indah and Marley are shouting as Neon sobs, the surge of power growing stronger and stronger. I watch Neon try to pull back her hands, make the electricity stop, but it comes pouring out of her, pushing violently into Isaiah's body.

Isaiah's clothes are starting to smoke, but he's still twitching, still shrieking. I don't know how or why he hasn't passed out yet but I know we can't leave him conscious.

"It's okay, Neon," I shout over all the noise. "You're almost there."

"You . . ." Indah's head whips toward me, a new kind of horror dawning in her face. There are tears in her eyes too, making the fear in them shine in the darkness. "Robert, are *you* doing this? Making her do this?"

"We can't leave him conscious, he'll come after us," I explain.

"*Please*—" Neon whimpers, spurring Marley into action.

"Then let's just get in the car and *go*," Marley says, groaning in effort as he picks Blaze up into his arms, cradling him like a swooned damsel. "He won't be able to drive in that state—"

We all look down to Isaiah, whose long black coat is singed on the edges, his short cropped hair standing on end. The screaming stops.

As my horrified friends stare at the man, now gone quiet, but still wide-eyed and convulsing, I look back up at Blaze, safe in the protective arms of Marley. He won't be safe as long as Isaiah is alive. And now that the Tall Man knows who we all are, has seen Neon's ability in action, he'll never leave us alone.

"He'll never leave us alone," I say aloud, my mind making a decision without my thinking too much about it.

"What are you—" Neon sobs as the lightning gets stronger, making Isaiah's body spasm particularly hard on the ground. "Damien, please stop," she howls, staring in horror at the body.

"Just—it'll be over soon," I shout, convinced this is the only way. The electricity keeps pulsing until—

Finally I see Isaiah's body go completely limp. It jerks a few more times unnaturally, the movement reminding me of popping corn, and then finally, the lightning abruptly stops and Neon collapses forward on her hands. Her hair falls around her face like a curtain and her body starts heaving with sobs.

"Is he . . . ?" Indah is crouched on the ground, her hand gentle on Neon's back, her gaze focused on the lifeless, open-eyed Isaiah.

I take a few tentative steps toward the body, the smell of burnt flesh rising to meet me. Blaze's skin isn't affected by his ability, so it can't be him. Looking down at Isaiah's blank, pale face and his wide, unblinking eyes, the full weight of what just happened starts to settle on my shoulders.

"He's dead."

Indah chokes back a sob and Neon gags, throwing up onto the dirt below her. I look across Isaiah's body to see Marley, still with Blaze in his arms, looking at me like he's never seen me before.

"What did you do," he whispers.

"I . . ." I swallow around the lump in my throat, my eyes darting from petrified face to petrified face. I'm exhausted, in shock, the tethers connecting me to my friends gossamer and breakable.

"Blaze," I say to Marley, changing focus, "put him in the Plymouth."

Marley complies; whether it's because his arms are getting tired or he's listening to me or I'm influencing him is unclear, but I don't think it matters. He lays Blaze in the backseat so gently, like a father putting his child to sleep.

Marley's spine straightens, his shoulders as tense as two slabs of marble, and he turns to me in one smooth motion on his heel, expressionless as he peers down at me. Suddenly I can picture him in the army very easily.

"We need to get rid of the body," he says, and Neon dry-heaves.

"What . . ." Sweat breaks out on my brow. "No, we have to *go*. We have to get out of here—"

I want nothing more than to leave, for all of us to pile into the Plymouth and drive off and never look back. But that desire doesn't seem to be compelling anyone—the three of them stay still, looking at me expectantly, like maybe they need to get rid of my body too.

"He's evidence," Marley explains. "This isn't some back highway—it's the PCH. Someone will find him and then, eventually, find us."

I walk over to the edge of the bluff, the adrenaline and heat starting to drain from my body, and look out over the edge. Cold wind rushes up from below, hitting my face as I stare into the freezing black of the Pacific, what feels like worlds away from the neon darkness of Los Angeles.

"Can't we just, I don't know, throw his body in the ocean?" I say, the surreality of the words keeping me in a state of disbelief.

"Not without a boat," Marley says practically, like he's talking about the best way to clean the loft after a night of drinking. "We wouldn't be able to get him far enough out. He'd just end up washing back up to shore."

"Okay." I swallow, my throat increasingly dry. "So we find a boat—"

"And how are we supposed to do that?" he snaps, glaring at me.

"I don't know, Marley, but we can't just bury him on the side of the road—"

"There's a spot I know, up in the canyon."

The two of us turn to Indah, her quiet voice steadier than I would have expected, steadier than all of us. Her arms are around Neon now—who is curled tightly into her, like she's trying to melt into Indah and disappear—but her face is angled up to stare daggers at me.

"What do you mean, 'there's a spot'?" I whisper.

"I do actually have a life outside of you, Robert," she snaps. "Or, I used to. I like to go hiking."

Marley nods sharply, like he's been given his orders, and moves toward Isaiah's body, whacking my shoulder as he walks past me.

"C'mon," he grumbles, and I follow him automatically, only realizing seconds later that he means for me to help him pick up the body and put it in my trunk.

The next half hour moves in a strange, gruesome haze. Marley picks up Isaiah from underneath his arms, silently telling me to grab the feet with a jerk of his head, and I'm shocked by how heavy the body is. I've never dealt with a dead body before. Based on the way that Marley and Indah are looking at me, I'm not sure they'd believe me if I told them that.

As we shuffle the body over to the Plymouth, I have an absurd and inappropriate thought: How did they move my body from the floor to the couch when Neon shocked me unconscious in the loft? Am I really that much lighter than Isaiah? He's tall and older, yeah, but thin as a rail. If the dead weight of my chunky body is anything like his—

The next thing I know, I'm sitting in the passenger seat of my own car, feeling like there should be blood on my hands and not just the smell of burnt leather from Isaiah's shoes. Indah is in the driver's seat next to me, driving iron jawed through the darkness, her eyes unblinking as they track the winding road in front of her. I turn around to look in the backseat, where Blaze still lies unconscious, now with Neon spooning him, holding on to him like he's a security blanket.

"Where's Marley?" I croak, my voice feeling like sandpaper. Did I yell more than I thought? Was I screaming at one point?

"On Neon's bike," Indah says.

"Oh."

I didn't know Marley knew how to drive a motorcycle.

Seconds—or maybe hours—later, Indah pulls the Plymouth to a slow and steady stop. We sit in the silent car for a moment, the claustrophobia of the space both crushing and comforting. If we get out of the car, we're going to have to get the body out too, and then perform the ghoulish task of *burying* it, and as much as I want to stay in the cocoon of the car, I find myself opening up the car door and leaning out of it to throw up.

"Finally, he reacts," Neon croaks, deadpan, when I'm done. I pull myself back into the car and look into the backseat to see her sitting upright, Blaze's head in her lap. "Wasn't sure if you realized that you just *murdered* someone," she sneers.

Instead of responding, I kick the door open fully and launch myself out of it, my feet landing on the ground just as the rumble of Neon's motorcycle greets me. Marley isn't wearing a helmet—Neon's was probably too small for him—so his pale, bony face makes him look like Ghost Rider. All he needs is the leather jacket, not just the thin Alkaline Trio T-shirt hanging off his broad shoulders.

"Give me a hand?" he pants, walking toward the trunk of the car. The gulp my throat performs is audible in the quiet clearing we've found ourselves in.

Indah must have off-roaded it a bit, because we seem to be miles from any kind of civilization. We're in the woods; the rustling of trees and occasional scurry of what I hope are small, harmless woodland creatures are the only noises that surround us. The sky seems brighter here somehow, the light of the stars not being sucked into the endless deep black of the ocean.

The creak of the trunk brings me back to the task at hand and we proceed to slog through the grimmest two hours of my life. And large portions of my life have been very grim. By the time Isaiah is in the ground—accomplished solely through a crowbar that happened to be in the trunk and our collective hands—I'm covered in dirt, sediment pushed so far under my fingernails I fear they'll never be clean.

"All right," Indah wheezes, pushing herself to her feet. "That's done. We don't ever speak of this, ever again, not even to Blaze."

"Fine by me," I breathe. As grotesque as this outing has been, we're bonded now. We have a secret that we all share. "It stays between us," I continue. "Just between those we trust."

"No."

We all turn to look at Neon, who is shaking her head.

"Neon, we can't tell Blaze, he's better off not knowing—"

"*You*," she spits, rounding on me, "are not someone we trust."

"What—"

"You're a virus." She stalks slowly toward me, blue electricity starting to play around her fingertips, making us all flinch. "You infected all of us, made us do things we never would have, and we just went along with it. We had no choice."

"You locked me out, remember?"

"After you'd been holding us hostage—"

"Do you all still live at the loft?" I ask, receiving no response, just furtive glances between the three of them. "Yeah, that's what I thought."

"You just made me *murder* someone, Damien," Neon shouts. "You can't brush this off—"

"You have full control of your ability, remember?" I snap back. "That's what you told me. If you didn't want to kill him, you wouldn't have."

"Come on, you're not that willfully naïve," she sobs. "You took my ability, my *hands*, and you made them do the worst thing imaginable. How could you do that? How could you *want* something so horrible?"

She's fully crying now, face crumpled, tears rolling down her cheeks in great quantity. I've never seen her like this. Strong, confident, take-no-prisoners Neon, completely broken. The kind of power she's been holding over me—the power that can't be manufactured, can't be gained through my ability, the power that hypnotized me, seduced me, made me jealous and enticed in equal measure—has snapped with this one act. A small part of me feels hope—hope that maybe now we can *truly* connect. She doesn't have to hide behind her tough exterior anymore, and I don't have to hide behind indifference. But the bigger piece of me sees the hate in her eyes—sees the tears streaming down her face, sees all her raw vulnerability—and gets the sinking feeling that I've been right all along. Letting people in is a mistake. Show someone your soft underbelly and they're going to stab you in it.

In the end, the Unusuals are just like everyone else: weak. Too weak to stand up to me, too weak to stop me.

"You were supposed to stop me," I snarl, and all three of them are looking at me like *I'm* the weak, pathetic thing. "You're the only one who ever has. I can't stop myself from using people but *you* could have."

"How am I supposed to stop you from that when I'm one of the people you're using?" she half laughs, half cries. "My god, Damien, it's not my job to make you a person. The only person who can do that is *you* and you just—you *refuse* to."

"It's hard—"

"Tough shit," she snaps. "Life is hard. Get over it. I just *killed* a man, against my will, and I still helped bury the body. I'm still *here*. And I swear on the grave I'm standing on that if you *ever* come near me again, I'll kill you too."

She whips around so fast that her hair slaps me in the chest and I get a brief whiff of Indah's perfume, making my heart ache. I know she means it. This is what she meant about things you can never take back.

Without a word, Neon climbs onto her bike, violently kicks back the kickstand, and takes off into the night. Marley and Indah's eyes trail after her but they don't make any move to follow. Am I keeping them here? Please say that it still works. I'm so tired, nearly dead on my feet, but I *need* them to stay with me.

Just as I think it, Marley starts to walk toward me, the disgust still plastered across his face.

"Don't go getting any ideas," he says, and I don't have time to think about what he means before I see him pulling his arm back, crowbar in hand, and then speeding toward me.

I start to cry out in protest but then the crowbar comes down on my head and everything goes black.

EPILOGUE

THE WATER

So this is the Pacific Ocean.

Morning is dawning behind me, beautiful and warm, completely at odds with the way I feel. I look out over the stretch of water, just endless blue, as endless and empty as the roads I drove to get here, and I think that most things people call extraordinary are really just too big to comprehend. Why do people like that? I want to understand, want to be able to fit everything in my head; why would I think an infinite body of water is extraordinary?

It was a long walk to get here. I woke up a few feet from Isaiah's grave, the Plymouth gone, my head bleeding. With no idea where to go next, no idea what to *do* next, I just started walking. I followed the slope of the mountain down until I hit sand, and now, here I am.

The sun is already too warm for my liking, but it's at least drying my clothes. Diving directly into the water was another unwise choice in an evening of unwise choices—I don't really know how to swim and it was, to say the least, fucking freezing, bringing up too many dark memories that choked me as much as the cold did—but at least it got most of the dirt off and cleared my head.

I killed someone. Sort of. That thought has been running

through my head over and over and over and I'm starting to come to terms with it. Sort of. I don't regret Isaiah's being dead and buried in the woods—he was dangerous, a sick predator of Unusuals, and it was either him or us.

An easy choice.

I do regret the role Neon played in it. The role she says I made her play. I wonder if she'll always feel that way. If maybe someday she'll realize that she probably wanted to kill him as much as I did. I'm not solely responsible. I can't be. Because if I am—if I actually took ownership over the things I've done—I'm not sure I could live with the person I am. But I *have* to live with him. So it has to be everybody else's fault.

Over the crash of the waves, I hear a soft crunching as someone approaches me across the sand. I look over cautiously, not wanting to seem suspicious, and am surprised by the person who stops at my side.

"What the hell are you doing here, Marley?"

"I wanted to return your car," he says, dropping the keys into my lap before settling down in the sand next to me, placing his shoes at his side.

"Why?" I ask, confused. "*How?* I didn't compel—"

"No, you didn't," he confirms. "It seemed like the right thing to do. Besides, I don't want to be caught with what I'm assuming is a stolen car."

"You have a stolen car already," I point out. I never told Marley exactly where I got his car, but he also never asked, so I feel like that's on him.

"Fair enough."

"How'd you find me?" I ask, too afraid to ask anything else.

"Well, this is the third beach I've tried. But I figured . . ." He sighs. "I figured you'd want to see the ocean. After all this time."

I don't say anything in response, too annoyed that Marley knows me, that I was ever vulnerable with him, so we sit there, not talking, the push and pull of the waves a soothing rhythm that breaks any tension between us.

"Aren't you afraid I'm gonna hurt you?" I ask quietly after a few minutes.

"Not so much."

"Why? Because you can just punch my lights out?"

"That," he says, grimacing, "but also, I've seen your past, remember? I know how much regret you have about what you made your father do."

"Oh, so you can read minds now too?" I say, ignoring the stinging at the fact that he knows about my dad.

"Regret can be a really tangible thing," he says solemnly. "I know that you're not going to hurt me. I don't think you want to. You don't get any joy out of it."

"Of course I don't," I grumble.

"But you *do* get joy out of controlling people," he says. "Don't you?"

"No," I reply automatically.

"Liar," he says, but there's little heat to it. "I saw the look on your face tonight. The perverse pleasure you got out of having Neon in the palm of your hand—"

He stops abruptly and I feel that tether pull taut. I don't want to fully control him, want to give that rope some slack, but I can't take more verbal abuse right now.

"I don't know what to do," I mumble, pushing my feet farther into the sand.

I can feel Marley breathe deep next to me, but he doesn't say anything. I want him to speak, want him to comfort me, tell me everything is going to be okay.

"She'll forgive you eventually, I think," he says, and there's a rush of satisfaction through me at his words. "We all will."

"How could you?" I ask, needing more.

"It's what we do. We're family. We forgive each other."

Family. That's what we are. We're family.

But something in the way Marley says it sounds hollow. Even if they did forgive me, is this how I want it? Does it count if the family I have is coerced into being there? Does it count as abandonment if the family I had was coerced into leaving? Does it matter who forgives me as long as I'm forgiven?

"Are you just saying that because I want you to?" I ask, uncertain if I actually want the truth.

"Yes," he says, and I can feel the thread between us snap.

I swallow around the lump in my throat, doing everything I can to hold in the tears I can feel gathering at the corners of my eyes. I just nod, making a sound of agreement, too scared to actually open my mouth in case nothing but a sob comes out.

"There are limits," he says harshly. "Everyone has to have their limits."

"What are yours?" I choke out, afraid of the answer, but the burning need to hear the truth is driving everything.

"I don't know," he says, and once again I'm amazed at how often "I don't know" is the truthful answer from people. I thought growing up meant figuring it out. I thought it meant never having to admit that you don't know something. I thought it meant that that wouldn't even apply. But, as far as I can tell, no one knows much of anything about being a person, no matter their age. I take cold comfort in the fact that I'm not the only one who has to playact at being a person sometimes.

"What about you?" Marley asks.

I roll my eyes. I can feel several other threads between us, but they don't seem to be doing anything. Marley is deflecting again, somehow overriding my ability.

"Why do you always do that?" I ask.

"Do what?"

"Turn the question back on me."

"Oh." He pauses and looks out over the ocean. "That."

"Yeah, 'that,'" I echo. "It doesn't actually distract my ability from getting more information, you know that, right? Or, at least, it won't for long."

"Yeah, of course," he says, turning his face back to me. "Is that what you think I was doing?"

His brow is furrowed and I feel like I missed a step.

"Aren't you? You feel the need to tell me things about yourself but you're aware that it's just my power doing that to you, so you try to fight against it by making it about me." His brow furrows impossibly more. "Isn't that what you're doing?"

"No, Rob," he says, sounding surprised. "That's something *you're* doing."

"What?"

"When I ask about you," he says, "it's because *you* want me to."

His eyes have widened now, like he's pleading with me to understand. Like he's explaining to a child that their dog died.

"Not that I wouldn't ask," he rushes to explain. "I would, I totally would, but . . . you always beat me to it. I thought you knew that."

"No," I say, eyes stinging. "I didn't know that."

"You're still doing it, you know," he says, looking at his feet as they burrow deeper into the sand. "I've gotten better at recognizing it and . . . I think you have too."

"What do you mean?"

"You can control it more now, can't you?" he asks, swiveling his head toward me, his brow quirked nonconfrontationally. He should be screaming at me, punching me again, pushing me into the ocean—*something*—but instead, he's talking to me like we're on one of our little adventures. Like he's just curious about me.

"Yeah," I say. "I can."

"Mm," he hums. "Yeah, I can feel it. It's more . . . intentional now."

The thought of Marley—or anyone—being able to feel those threads, feel the way in which my wants slither underneath people's skins, sends chills through my body.

"It scares you, doesn't it?" he asks. "You keep pulling it back; it feels like a tide going in and out."

"I might be getting better, but I wouldn't say I have control," I snap. "Don't act like it's as simple as just . . . pulling back."

"But you *can* feel it, can't you? When you're making someone want something?"

"Sometimes," I say, sifting sand through my fingertips absentmindedly. "But it's not that simple . . . it's not like I just make up my mind and people do exactly what I say. Sometimes . . . I just want stuff without really realizing it and stuff happens and it's too late for me to stop it."

"That's bullshit," he snaps.

"I can't stop wanting what I want—"

"But you *willfully* got Neon to—to—to—*kill* Isaiah—"

"She did that all on her own—"

"You *know* that's not true," Marley says, more stern than I've ever heard him. "You made her do that, Damien, and you can either own up to it or not, but there's not a third option. There's no middle ground."

"God, Marley, that is so like you," I groan. "Everything always a binary choice, black or white, when you *constantly* complain about how our justice system is fucked up and gray—"

"It *is* fucked up and gray but there're some things that just *are* fucking black and white!" he yells. "Committing murder? Bad. Committing murder by accident in self-defense? Complicated. *Forcing* someone to commit murder on your behalf—even if it's in self-defense? Very, very, *very* bad. And I think you know that, Damien. If you don't, you're not the man I thought you were."

That hurts me more than anything else in a speech that mentioned murder three times. The idea that I've somehow disappointed Marley—that he had enough of an idea of who I was to be disappointed—cuts me to my core.

"So what would you have me do?" I sniff. "You were lying when you said they'd forgive me eventually. If they won't ever forgive me, then why do I care?"

"Do you only care about us if we're in your life, doing what you want?"

"I mean . . . yeah," I answer. "What do you mean? Of course I care about you because you're in my life. I'm not saying you have to do what I want but—"

"Okay, answer me this: If you knew you were never going to see us again, would you want us to be happy?"

I sit there, staring out across the water, trying to absorb what Marley is suggesting. I've never been in this position before. The only people I know who are no longer in my life are my parents, and I resent them too much to want good things for them.

"That idea has never even occurred to you, has it?" Marley says, echoing my thoughts.

"I don't . . . what's the point?"

"Why do you care about us, Damien? Why do you even want to be in our lives?"

"Because you care about me," I answer truthfully. "And because you make life . . . *mean* something. That's all—that's the only thing I ever want. Life is *so long*. So long and empty, just like every fucking road that brought me here to this big and empty ocean."

"You can't demand meaning from other people," Marley mutters, and I look over to watch him watching the waves. He's squinting into the sun, his Cro-Magnon brow hanging over his eyes like a cliff face. He hasn't gotten up and left yet, the tenuous strings still between us, keeping him here but accomplishing nothing else.

"What can I do?" I plead. "What can I do to make it better?"

"You can learn from it," he tells me. "Don't be the Damien that we allowed you to be—encouraged you to be. Let go of your ability. Use it just when you need to, when it's not causing harm to other people. Be Robert Gorham again."

"I hated being Robert Gorham," I grumble.

"But Robert is a person. He's someone that I actually kind of liked." Marley is smiling sadly at me now, and tears start to gather at the corners of my eyes.

"But Damien is a guy that made me knock him out with a crowbar," he continues, the frown overtaking his face again. "And that's not the person *I* want to be. I'm not the bully people assume but I'm also going to do what I have to to protect the people I love."

"That's all I want to do too." I sniffle, wiping away the tears as surreptitiously as I can. "I just want to protect you. I don't want to have to let that feeling go."

"Yeah, well, I don't see a world in which we get over this," he sighs. "I'm honestly not even sure that the four of us will be able to stay friends, with or without you. We buried a body together. Maybe the best thing we can do is to all go our separate ways."

"I never wanted that," I say. "I never wanted any of this."

"I know. But it's what we have. I think maybe the best thing you can do is to put it all behind you—that's what's best for all of us. Start over. Find people who understand you. Try to remember the good times."

Marley says it like it's easy. Like I'm going to be able to walk into a new bar tomorrow and find people who get me the way that the Unusuals got me. People who could love me, who I don't have to hide from. I refuse to accept that resignation and running away are the only options in front of me.

"I think I have a better idea," I say, and I feel Marley tense beside me.

"I don't think—"

"Call them," I cut him off. "Tell them to meet us. Here."

"Damien—"

"You've got a cell phone, right?" I ask, looking sharply at him. He nods. "Then call them."

The rope pulls taut again and I know that I have him.

"Thank you for meeting me."

Neon and Indah are standing ten feet away, digging their bare feet into the sand. Marley stands between us, like some kind of referee.

"We didn't have much choice, Robert," Indah growls. "We're all accessories to murder. Whether or not you'll use it—"

"Which I'm sure he would," Neon spits.

"—you have blackmail on us."

"That's not what I'm trying to do here," I say, bringing my hands up in surrender.

"Just say what you're gonna say," Neon says. "I hate the beach."

"I'd never seen it before," I admit. "Not until this morning. And I thought it'd be nice to meet here. Neutral territory and whatnot."

"No territory is neutral with you around," Neon says, her blue-lined eyes narrowed.

"How's Blaze doing?" I ask, feeling like I'm in a play, following a script.

"We don't really know yet," Indah says. "We need to . . . we need to find him help. *Real* help, from people who actually know about Unusuals. A regular hospital isn't going to be able to save him."

"Save him?" I repeat. "Is it really that bad?"

"He keeps going up in flames," Indah explains. "It stops pretty quickly, but it happened the whole way home, and the pain . . . he's been screaming a lot."

I spare a moment to try to feel something for Blaze but come up hollow. Blaze isn't my concern right now. It's inconvenient that he's not here, might create a loose end, but honestly, that presumes he'll wake up and remember anything that happened last night. As for the past few months . . . it could be a drug-induced hallucination for all he knows.

"I'm sorry," I say, following the next line in the script. "I never meant to hurt you, Neon."

"Yeah, well, you did," she says, her arms crossed, her power back. She's straight spined and steely eyed and suddenly my plan seems ill advised, uncalled for. I should be focusing on getting Neon and the others to forgive me, damn what Marley says, and bring me back into the fold. "You've taken something that I loved about myself—something that was just mine—and *ruined* it. I don't know that I'll ever be able to . . ."

She trails off, the confidence cracking, a single tear escaping down her cheek. I should soldier on, just get everything over with, but my curiosity—my need for them to love me—is too strong in that moment, overpowering any practical solution I had planned.

"Here's what I propose," I start, voice shaking. This is the last-ditch effort. If this doesn't work—doesn't convince her that we can get through this—then I'll have to go with the original, ill-advised plan, and I'm not even sure that will work. "We're stronger together. If we stay together, the secret stays with us, which is where it's safest."

I can see Neon wanting to jump in, cut me off and walk away, but either I'm holding her here with my wants or the threat of the secret hanging over all our heads is enough. Good. I can use that.

"We go back to the loft," I continue. "We go back to normal. And I'll let you shock me, whenever you want—*lightly*," I emphasize when I see a glint in Neon's eye, "and then you guys don't have to worry about me influencing you. You can keep me subdued, just enough."

"I just told you," she whispers. "I'm not sure I can ever—I don't know that I want to use my ability ever again. You've made it some-thing . . . something dirty. Dangerous."

"I'm sure with time, you'll bounce back," I tell her, and she snorts at that, wiping another tear away.

"Goddamn it, Robert," Indah scolds. "Could you be more in-sensitive?"

"I think this will work—"

"Even if it did—even if Neon chose to use her ability—what about when she's not around?"

"We can work out some sort of system," I suggest. "A rotation of sorts."

"Or you could just . . . try *not* influencing us," Indah counters, her voice dripping with disdain. "Did you ever think of that?"

"I don't think I can," I admit. "This is just the way I am, but *you* can fix it, Neon."

Her posture stiffens again, the hurt and pain in her eyes turning to cold anger. She clenches her jaw, her gaze piercing right into me, and a thrill of fear goes through my body.

"So, let me get this straight," she says, taking a menacing step to-ward me. "You want me to become like some sort of weird, electro-pathic caretaker for you? Following you around, keeping you from controlling people—"

"I don't control people—"

"Damn right," she spits. "You don't control *me*. You don't get to use my ability to kill a man and then turn around and ask me to use it to make *you* a better person."

"I'm not asking you to make me a better person!" I shout. "But you're the only one who makes me normal! Who makes me a per-son at all."

"That's not my job, Damien!" she yells back, throwing up her hands. "*I'm* a person. And you've never—you don't see that. You don't care. What you did—what you made me do. I can't *ever* forgive that. That doesn't make me unreasonable."

"But you can stop it," I plead. "You can stop *me*."

"Not if you don't want to be stopped," she says quietly. "That's the thing about you. No matter what, you always have the trump card. The house *always* wins, and I can't afford to lose anymore. None of us can."

"So that's what this is about, huh?" I growl. "Being friends with me means losing?"

"You tell me," she snaps. "You're the one who made us your friends."

My blood turns to ice.

"No." I take a few steps back, my feet sinking into the sand. "No, that's not true—you *cared* about me, genuinely cared about me. I didn't make you do that."

"Are you absolutely sure?" Neon asks. "Because I'm not. I thought I was—I thought I knew who you were—but you've made me second-guess everything I've done and thought since meeting you. *That's* your superpower. Doubt."

"Indah?" I peer over Neon's shoulder to look at Indah, who has her arms wrapped around herself, one hand rubbing the tattoo that climbs up her arm, tears rolling down her cheeks. Seeing that, the broken expression on her face, sets me crying in earnest too, for once unashamed of my tears. "You care about me, don't you? For real?"

"Of course I do, Robert," she says, weeping. "But that's not enough. Loving someone isn't enough."

"How?" I cry. "If that's not enough, what is?"

"Loving someone and having them love you back. You don't love us—"

"Yes, I *do*—"

"Control isn't the same thing as love, Robert," she cries. "I don't know, maybe you do love us—"

"I *do*," I sob, letting the tears fall freely.

"But that doesn't change the fact that you want to control us. Maybe . . . maybe things could have been different. But love needs trust and I'm not sure we can ever trust you again."

I sniff, pushing the tears off my cheeks with my palm, nodding resignedly. I look at my three friends—the only three people I've ever really, truly cared about—and see genuine regret in their faces. All four of us are crying—even Marley, slow steady tears cascading out of his eyes in perfect streams—and I know that I've broken things beyond repair. I can't erase what's been done, but I can wipe the slate clean.

"What if we could start over?" I whisper. "Do you think you could love me again?"

"Life doesn't work like that," Marley says. "We don't get fresh starts. Trust me."

"What if we could?"

The three of them trade confused looks.

"Here's the thing about that," I continue. "I can make people forget."

"What?" Indah gasps.

"I do it a lot. In small ways, like staff at a bar forgetting they didn't card me, or in bigger ways, like a real estate agent forgetting they didn't actually sell me that house. But if I want to stay under the radar, want to disappear from a place without a trace . . . I can make people forget that I ever existed. It's what I did with my hometown. As far as they know, Robert Gorham never lived there."

"How . . ." Marley's eyes are wide and shining. "How do you even do that?"

"I want it." I shrug.

"And you . . ." I see the moment it clicks in Indah's brain. "You want to do this to us. You want to make us forget and start over?"

"Just last night," I say. "It'd be so easy. None of you would have to remember what we did."

"No." Marley is shaking his head vehemently, his fists clenched at his sides. "You can't do that. It isn't right—the things that happen to people, our pasts, they make up who we are."

"They don't have to."

"No way." Neon vigorously shakes her head. "You can't just *erase* things. Not remembering is not the same as something never happening."

"It'll be the same to you," I promise.

"You're talking about messing with our heads," she snaps, then her eyes go wide. "Oh my god, you probably already have . . . what have you already done to us? What have you made us forget?"

"Nothing, I swear."

"How are we supposed to believe that?" Marley asks. "*This* is why we can't trust you—"

"I'm not asking you to trust me," I say. "I'm not asking anything."

"No, you're telling us," Neon snarls, lip curling. "Isn't that right? You've already made up your mind."

I don't answer her but the lack of response seems to be enough confirmation.

"Robert," Indah pleads, her voice quiet and breaking. "Robert, you don't have to do this."

My eyes move from Indah to Neon to Marley. Each of them is standing still, frozen, unable to leave until I release them. There's a mix of fear and loathing on their faces, a sheen of sadness over it. But mostly, they're staring at me in disgust. Like I'm a monster and they've only just seen my true face.

How dare they. Everything I've done these past few months has been for them, for their own good. And now I'm offering to take all the bad stuff away—stop the pain—and they don't want me to. They want to continue living as messy, untamed things and they want to do it without me.

"Please, Robert," she whimpers one last time, and I look back at her crying, terrified face.

"My name is Damien."

The Plymouth purrs as it turns onto Sunset Boulevard. Late afternoon brightness streams through the open roof, making the driver wince. His face, glowing orange from the sun, turns once more to get a glimpse of the Pacific before he permanently puts it to his back.

Driving past the rock clubs that freckle the strip is like strolling through a graveyard where every tombstone reads "Robert

Gorham." Los Angeles is where Robert Gorham died. He's six feet under now, in a crude, hand-dug grave in the woods, never to be heard from again.

Los Angeles is where Damien was born. He grew here, took his first steps, made his first mistakes. But Damien isn't someone who makes mistakes. He can't afford to make mistakes anymore. If no one can accept him, if everyone he meets wants to make him out to be a controlling monster, then fine, that's what he'll be. He takes what's his, just like this city taught him.

There should be a clear moment when the black convertible leaves the city—a marker of some kind, the sound of a door slamming shut, the road changing. But the urban sprawl never ends, it just keeps spreading out, morphing and shifting subtly and then starkly, until suddenly, there's desert again. The open, endless road. Infinite roads to go down, each and every one of them open. That's the beauty of being Damien. There isn't a single road in the world that he can't drive on.

Neon doesn't want to get back in the car and go home. Back to the loft. Is that home now? Still? Was it ever? Can it ever be? Can *Los Angeles* ever be home again?

"Nee?"

She looks around to see Indah—her beautiful, warm, soft, *good* Indah—sitting next to her, toes dug into the sand, her brow furrowed in that adorable way that has become so familiar to Neon. Neon wants to smile at her, assure her everything is okay, but can barely muster up the energy to keep her eyes focused on Indah's face.

"Yeah?" she says in response, turning her face back to look at the broad ocean.

"How are you feeling?" Indah asks, her arm reaching across the sand to rest near Neon's ankle. Neon's own arms are around her legs, hugging her knees to her chest, hoping she can become a ball of light and energy and not have to feel things anymore.

"How do you think?"

"You haven't forgotten yet, have you?" Marley asks from her other side. She glances over out of the corner of her eye to see him in the same position—arms wrapped around his legs, trying to make his enormous body as small as Neon's.

"No." Neon shakes her head. "Have you?"

They both respond the same, their voices tight and quiet. The three of them have been sitting here, silently on this beach, waiting for something to happen. Waiting for something to happen that they wouldn't even notice if it did.

"Guess he didn't want it enough," Marley adds, and Neon's throat tightens at that. Damien—*Robert*; he doesn't get to keep the name that Neon gave him, not in Neon's head at least—he wanted Neon to *kill* someone but couldn't muster up some genuine desire to have her forget about it. Not that she wants to. Well, she does, but she doesn't think she should. She knows she has to remember. She knows that's the right thing to do.

"At least he seemed to think it worked," Indah says softly. "Now he won't come back."

"He wanted to believe that he could be free of the guilt," Marley scoffs. "I bet he's halfway back to Vegas now, his stupid emo haircut blowing in the wind."

Neon can picture it perfectly. Robert with the window of his Plymouth rolled down, the desert breeze moving through his hair, the wide open road in front of him. It makes her stomach churn, a sob rise up in her throat, and before she knows it, she's crying again, her forehead resting on the tops of her knees, tears falling into her lap.

She feels two hands on her back as Marley and Indah move to comfort her, and that makes her sob harder. There's so much that she can do with these two—can *be* with them—that she never could with Robert. She can cry and scream and laugh and be the whole person she is, not just the person he wanted her to be. And she can still trust them, can still rely on them in a way that she's not sure anyone will ever be able to rely on her, especially not now. She's a murderer, a dangerous thing that can never be fixed.

But the harder she sobs, the closer Indah and Marley lean into her, the tighter they hold her. She softens into her friends' embrace, her hard edges rounding out in the way that they only ever could with these two people. She's not the monster. The monster is gone, carried away in a big black car, and Neon is still a person. And she has her people—people who met her when she was already broken, when she was different and strange and frightening, and they loved her anyway. They'll love her still. They'll love her because she'll try. With every day she'll try to repair things, try to trust other people again, try to trust *herself* again.

Neon's wanting never meant much, not like his, but that won't stop her from wanting all the same. It won't stop her from having. Having a good life, with good people, whom *she* chooses.

That's all she can do. She can't fix what Robert broke, could never fix Robert if he didn't want to fix himself. But she can try to be better. And, later, when the tears have dried and the love of her two friends has started to heal the broken places in her heart, she'll find the hope that Robert will someday choose to be better too.

ACKNOWLEDGMENTS

I had thought that the acknowledgments for my second book would be easier, but the beautiful thing about joining the publishing world is that my community has expanded beyond my wildest dreams. There are so many people who contributed to this book and who contribute daily to my continued existence.

First of all, I'd like to thank everyone at Tom Doherty Associates, Macmillan, and Tor Teen for believing in me and my stories and giving me a way to tell them: Devi Pillai, Fritz Foy, Eileen Lawrence, Sarah Reidy, Lucille Rettino, Melanie Sanders, Jim Kapp, Tom Mis, Dakota Cohen, and Tom Doherty. An enormous thanks to the incredible marketing and publicity team who come up with the most fun and inventive ways to connect with our audience and for keeping me company on tour: Saraciea Fennell, Anneliese Merz, Becky Yeager, Isa Caban, and Anthony Parisi. Thank you for being such bright spots in my world.

Most of all, I owe an enormous debt of gratitude to my editor, Ali Fisher, who makes me a better writer with every note. Thank you for your patience, for your gentle reminders that there are other punctuation choices beyond em dashes, and for helping me navigate such a tricky character who messes up so much. Knowing you were on the other side to help us gave both Robert and me the room to make the interesting mistakes.

To Matthew Elblonk, my north star in publishing and beyond. Thank you for being a sounding board, a stalwart advocate, and, most of all, a friend. Thank you for sharing in my love of Harrys, both Potter and Styles.

A deep thanks to my sensitivity readers, Dee Hudson and Sahrish Nadim; for your invaluable insights and wonderful words of encouragement.

As with anything I write, this book would not have been finished without the playlists that I put on repeat. So thank you to sixteen-year-old me, for having so much music from 2007 for me to pull from and for the bands that define that era for me: Motion City Soundtrack, Mute Math, Cold War Kids, Franz Ferdinand, Boy Kill Boy, The Starting Line, Gogol Bordello, Muse, Maroon 5, Keane, People in Planes, Sugarcult, Paramore, The Killers, Arctic Monkeys, Lovedrug, and, of course, Panic! At the Disco.

I am so lucky to be surrounded by my own ragtag group of weirdos with superpowers of their own. I would be nowhere without the original cast and crew of *The Bright Sessions*, especially Charlie Ian, whose voice I heard in my head throughout the writing of this book. My team at Atypical Artists—Jordan Cope, Briggon Snow, Evan Cunningham, and Lillian Holman—are the best support team and friends anyone could ask for.

Los Angeles has given me so many experiences and people that have shaped me and the stories I tell. From FTH to my Glow Up Crew to my Time Stories team, I wouldn't change my life here for anything. I'm so grateful to all of you and for Los Angeles for giving you to me. To Meghan Fitzmartin—thank you for showing me the beauty of this city we call home, for showing me the humanity in Robert and loving him as much as me. Thank you for being the first person to read this book and see the bits of me in it and being my best friend anyway.

Thank you to the people who have been with me since the beginning, through all the ups and downs. Mom, Dad, Betsy, Don, and my little OWL—I love you all so much.

To B—for always listening to me, for asking me questions, for challenging me and comforting me, and for feeding me endless mac and cheese. You are my favorite person.

And to all of you: Thank you for continuing this journey with me. Thank you for caring about Robert, for seeing something more in him, and for demanding that he be better than he is. That's something I want for all of us—for us always to show compassion and empathy, but never stop pushing each other to be better. We can all do better.

Stay strange.

[Notebook entry from Dr. Crane]

1/5/07

New patient: white male, late teens/early twenties, indicators of anxiety and depression. He left before giving his last name or insurance information, but I'm confident he'll return. Though he was reluctant to share the specifics of his life with me, I would wager that he's the child of a well-known industry figure, or on the way to enormous fame himself. Cagey and private, he seems terrified of emotional intimacy and expresses the kind of listlessness common in the privileged class of this city. Though it had been my first instinct to ask about his parents, the time never seemed appropriate. Despite his reluctance to share, he was surprisingly talkative and each time I thought about bringing it up, there was something else to discuss. At his next session, I plan to focus my efforts on learning more about his family life.

L. S. Crane

[Email from a doctor in St. Louis]

6-10-09
Dear Dr. Wu,

I hope this email finds you well. I'm writing in regards to a patient of mine, a young man who goes by Damien. He moved to St. Louis four weeks ago and has been seeing me three times a week the past two weeks. His next scheduled session is this coming Thursday at 2:00 p.m.—would you be available to sit in? Damien is a curious case—I think most of what he's told me is fabricated, but I find myself unable to push him to truth during his session. He seems to be extremely skilled at manipulation and evasion and I'm not too proud to admit that your assistance would be greatly appreciated.

Let me know.

Sincerely,
Dr. Sandra Black

[note to Damien from a NY therapist]

8 August '11
Damien—

My secretary called me yesterday to let me know that you've been stopping by the office every day for the past week. As I told you in our last session, I am at a family reunion upstate and will be returning to the city on Monday. As you've refused to give me your phone number or email, my assistant has been instructed to write out this note and give it to you next time you come by.

While I understand that you are eager to continue our work, you cannot show up unexpectedly. Max mentioned that you've been talking to the other patients who come to the office—I would appreciate that you not intrude on the other doctors and patients in the building. This was particularly disappointing to hear given how much we've discussed privacy and boundaries. You've continually said that respecting others' space is something you want to work on, but your actions suggest otherwise. I know that separation anxiety has been a significant issue for you in the past and I would like to keep working with you on it, but if you continue to cross the line like this, we'll need to discuss finding you a different psychiatrist.

Thank you,
Dr. Silverman

[Dr. Bright's personal handwritten notes]

January 24th, 2014

It's been a while since I've hand-written notes, but I can't simultaneously record myself <u>and</u> listen back to a session recording. And I <u>need</u> to listen back. To make sense of what's happened. Even though Damien only left twenty minutes ago, the memory of his visit is already hazy and confusing. I wonder if he would have let me record if he'd known that my recorder was still on. Something tells me no. He seems . . . secretive, even though he was clearly desperate to talk to someone.

He's a mind manipulator. I'd heard of them, vaguely, at The AM, but I never dreamed . . . it was so much more terrifying and thrilling than I ever could have imagined. Even with my most volatile patients—the pyrokinetics, the weather manipulators—I never feel unsafe. And working with Atypicals who have powers of the mind is always jarring, whether they're telepaths, psychics, or dream-walkers, but all my patients trust me: They respect me. And I trust and respect them in turn. I know there's always the possibility that I could get hurt, but it's a risk I've always been willing to take to help people. I don't know that I'm willing to take <u>this</u> risk.

Why did I invite him back? No—<u>insist</u> on him coming back? Does my curiosity really have that strong a hold? Was he influencing me, pushing his deep, unvoiced desire to be heard onto me? I don't know where to even begin with someone like him, how to help him, if he even needs or wants my help. But I know already that I'm going to keep seeing him. If he comes back.

He's going to come back. I can feel it in my bones.

J. Bright